RELATIVELY RISKY

THE BIG UNEASY BOOK ONE

PAULINE BAIRD JONES

PBJ

CONTENTS

RELATIVELY RISKY

RELATIVELY RISKY

When an aspiring illustrator attracts the attention of a New Orleans mob family, and secrets long hidden are unearthed from the past, a handsome homicide detective may be her only chance of surviving the Big Easy.

The oldest of thirteen, Alex Baker does two things: he solves murders and avoids children. Until the day Nell Whitby foils a carjacking, knocks Alex off his feet and turns his life upside down.

When the shots start flying and every rock he turns over reveals another wise guy, Alex decides he needs to stick close to the quirky yet captivating children's book author while he discovers who is behind a series of mob hits. But can he resist the urge to kiss the kid magnet now in the crosshairs?

A relative newcomer to New Orleans—with no family but her college friend—Nell spends her days in seeming obscurity, sketching tourists in the French Quarter and serving canapés for her friend's catering business. When a chance encounter makes Nell the target of a mob hit, the only silver lining is meeting the cute cop who is determined to protect her.

But when she finds herself at the head of a second line made up of goons and gangsters, and secrets start bubbling up out of her own past, Nell must figure out what she's made of so she can live long enough to kiss the cop again...

*This book is dedicated to
the City of New Orleans,
AKA the Big Easy,
both before and after Katrina.
You made this Wyoming girl love you.*

CHAPTER ONE

When Alex Baker felt the cold gun barrel press against the back of his neck he knew a bad night had just gotten worse. New Orleans at night was always a walk on the wild side, but when the moon was full, wild got super sized. The crazies came out, the bullets flew, and the emergency rooms filled up with the bloodied and the bowed.

When he already had the best view of the city's worst, working homicide for the New Orleans Police Department, it wasn't a good idea to piss off a mayoral aide, cause the view was worse at night.

Thank goodness it was his last night shift, at least until he pissed off someone else. It had felt like everyone was taking potshots at everyone else the whole damn night. The homicide rate had never been great, but it had gotten worse since Katrina.

If something didn't change, the city council really

would move to reclassify bullet holes as a natural cause of death, just to improve the stats for tourists. It was starting to feel like it didn't matter how many people lived in New Orleans, just how many died.

Nights like this, he wondered why he didn't find some quiet little town where only wildlife got shot at. But the Big Easy had moved into his head and his heart and worse, it set a good table. His stomach rumbled a reminder that it had been a long time since its last feeding.

No question the food wooed the taste buds, wined, dined, and entertained them. Lured a body like those sirens in the legends. Even when he hated the city, he loved it. If the devil had a home here and in hell, he'd live here, no question about it. Except in August, when hell was cooler.

In the quiet, semi-dark, with morning just starting to lighten the horizon, he'd turned onto the narrow street where home, breakfast and bed waited.

As usual, cars haphazardly crowded both sides of the street, fitting in where they could and where they shouldn't. Parking in New Orleans required patience, ingenuity, and a huge pile of luck. Sometimes he'd be driving along, spot a great parking place, and feel this over-whelming urge to grab it because it was there.

Alex had known he was running out of patience, was probably out of luck. This time of the morning no one was likely to clear as space just because he needed it. They were all sleeping something off in their beds. He should have taken the front fence down a long time ago so he could park on the lawn, but Zach insisted a white picket fence was a chick magnet.

A guy really didn't want his dad saying chick magnet, let alone having one in the yard.

He'd passed his house, wondering if he was going to be doomed to drive around until one of the college students across the street had to go to class, but as he passed a cross street, he'd spotted half a space just around the corner.

It was by a hydrant, but the parking Nazis weren't out this early, and he could get his dad to move his truck later. He pulled in, got most of his truck off the street, if he didn't mind blocking the sidewalk. He didn't. The dividing line between street and sidewalk was more imagined than real anyway.

He'd shut off the engine and thrust open the door, anxious to get unconscious as soon as possible. Should have known better. Should have kept an eye on his surroundings. Which was why the stinking little piece of crap got the drop on him, down shifting his night from bad to worse.

"Get out real slow with your hands where I can see 'em, mother—" The pressure of the gun against his neck eased some, as if the perp couldn't point and talk at the same time.

Alex rolled his eyes at the spate of unoriginal swearing. The education system was so screwed up, it was depressing. Kids couldn't even swear good and had nothing better to do than try to jack a detective who'd spent the night knee deep in bodies.

"Keep your cool," Alex said, more for himself than the

kid, as his temper tried to slip tired's leash. Making sure both hands were visible, he slid out and turned around.

The kid was as small as he sounded and looked like he was on the downside of a high. Probably looking to trade Alex's wheels for a trip back up. Man, the guys'd really roast him if he got jacked by a kid too young to shave.

"Shut up and give me your wallet and keys!" The kid practically foamed at the mouth as another round of filth poured out.

At his age, Alex hadn't known half that many cuss words. And when he got caught saying the ones he knew, his head had been down in the sink eating soap. If he shoved a bar down the kid's throat? Probably be called police brutality and get him a sit down with IAD.

"Life's not fair," his dad would say about now. "But it's always interesting, bubba."

And about to get more so, Alex realized. The swearing, while tiresome, had drowned out the unlikely figure on a bicycle bearing down on them both.

She was hunched over the handles, an intent scowl on a face that was ordinary, but not in a bad way. Her feet pumped hard on the pedals, as she steered around the numerous potholes and bumps that pockmarked the street. Her eyes were narrow slits and her hair stuck out around her head like a ragged, brown halo.

Alex sure hoped she didn't plan to ram the little crap while he had a gun pointed at him—oh yeah, she meant to. As if the kid sensed her incoming, he started to turn.

"Here, catch." Alex tossed his keys high in the air.

No surprise the kid followed the shiny object. Or that he stepped back to catch them.

The front wheel of the bike caught the kid in the butt and sent him running forward, right into Alex's waiting fist.

He crumpled into an untidy heap, though a final hand twitch fired the gun. Alex's driver's side window exploded into flying shards of glass.

And took his insurance rates with it.

Alex mentally deployed a few swear words. Didn't have time to say them as the bike and its rider skidded sideways.

No way she'd regain control. Alex jumped forward, tried to catch her. Instead, he got tangled in the bike. Gravity weighed in but not on his side.

Damn, he didn't remember the pavement being that hard. The front wheel spun against the side of his face through two rotations before he untangled a hand and stopped it.

He turned his head and found himself nearly nose to nose with the rider.

It was a nice nose. Short but straight and set neatly between her eyes. They were nice, too. He'd spent the night fielding angry looks. Didn't mind the nice change of gaze. They were a warm brown and...he tipped his head, trying to find the right description, and settled for nice. They were nice. She smelled better than all of his perps.

That wasn't a surprise. He noticed her lips were pursed, which sent his thoughts down a kissing side path.

If he hadn't been so tired, he wouldn't have thought about kissing her, of course—

As if on cue, she licked her lips, kick-starting something deep in his gut. Maybe he'd spent too long on the bench after his divorce. He blinked, a bit hazily, and realized she was engaged in a counter scrutiny.

Her curious, oddly innocent gaze intersected his and she blinked, lashes thick as a hairbrush sliding down, then up again. Despite the intrusion of the bike, they were as intimately entangled as lovers. Shouldn't have thought that. His breathing stuttered.

"Are you all right?" Voice matched the eyes.

"I'm fine." His voice was on the husky side, but she wouldn't know that. His gaze drifted to her mouth again. Wasn't a kiss a time honored thank you for a rescue? Did sharing her crash count as a rescue? His conscience kicked. "Are you okay?"

Her eyes widened. The mouth curved up. "Yes, thank you. Though..."

Apparently oblivious to his snarled thoughts, she untangled her legs from her bike and from him, wincing a bit in the process, and scrambled up.

He lifted the bike to the side. His nerve endings started sending an inventory of which parts hurt and how much. Gravity, as if sensing his desire to escape, tightened its grip.

When he turned forty earlier this year, he'd decided it was time to quit slamming his body against the ground, hard objects, and other people. It was getting embarrassing how long it took him to get up. Didn't remember it hurting that much when he was younger.

That's why he'd applied for a transfer to homicide. Life had a way of bringing you full circle—not to mention reemphasizing its most painful lessons. Lessons like, you can run, but you can't hide. And quit banging yourself against the ground, idiot brain.

He ignored the hand she held out to him and fought gravity until he got both legs under him.

He crouched and flipped the kid, cuffed him, then checked his pulse. He'd live to carjack again. Might even live long enough to be old enough to drive what he stole.

He secured the perp's weapon and then went to right the bike. He gave it a roll forward—seemed to be all right. Not too bent out of shape.

Something ironic in that thought, but he was too tired to figure it out. He deployed the stand, wondered what she was doing out so early, turned to ask, and found her staring at the handcuffs. Then she looked at him, her eyes a bit wide.

Some color scored his cheeks. "I'm a cop."

"Oh. Right." Her grin was a bit sheepish as she held up his keys.

Alex's lips twitched, too tired to manage a grin. "Nice catch."

"I've always had good eye-hand coordination. I kick butt at *Mario Kart*."

Maybe that's where she got the idea to ram the little piece of crap. He opened his mouth to tell her she should confine her ramming to games but stopped. Sounded too much like something his old man would say. She grinned, as if she knew, then turned to check her bike herself.

He was a guy, so he studied the rear view. A bit of skin showed where her top and calf-length pants didn't quite meet. Her pants fit fine over a nicely formed caboose—she kicked her bike stand and swung a leg over. The scuffed cowboy boots were a surprise, but not as much as the realization she was going to just ride away.

"You can't leave," he protested. "You're a witness. I'll need a statement—"

"I have to go to work." She dug in a pocket, extracted a battered card and held it out.

Alex accepted it, but that didn't stop him from trying again as she lifted a foot to a pedal with clear intent to push off. "I can call your employer and explain—"

Her smile silenced him. The grin had been engaging, but the smile—had he thought her ordinary? He blinked. Tried to remember what he'd meant to say, but before he could she said, "You can't call the muse. It calls you."

He should stop her, would have if he'd shot the kid. Instead, he watched her go. Caboose looked even better straddling the bike. When she'd pedaled from sight, he extracted his cell and rallied the troops, before looking down at the card she'd given him.

By Whitby.

Then in smaller print, her name—Eleanor Whitby—and other relevant details, next to what looked like a tiny vegetable, only with eyes, nose and huge teeth. Opposite that, in fancy script he read....

"Alfonse the Artichoke?" Alex rubbed his aching head.

"Alfonse? The artichoke? *The* Alfonse? That's so sick!" The groggy carjacker lifted his head. Alex looked at him, both brows arched, and the kid said in a defensive rush, "Dude. Alfonse is happening." He looked down the street with a look that was almost awe. "Was that Whitby? I was sure he was a dude."

Alex gave a brief summary to dispatch and rang off.

"I got knocked on my ass by Whitby."

Apparently he missed the part where his chin connected with Alex's fist. But he'd be less likely to file a complaint with IAD if he blamed her, so Alex let it pass.

"Wow. She was kinda sick."

Alex shook his head. So the carjacker had a crush on the artichoke author. Just when he thought New Orleans had gotten as weird as it could get. They should call this place the Big Uneasy.

"She gave you her card? Could I get her address—"

"You have the right to remain silent. I'd suggest you exercise this right until you're in the presence of your lawyer or I might just forget I'm a good cop and kick your skinny ass up over your pointy head."

When Alex finally got clear of the crime scene—something that took way longer than it should have—and made it into his house, he found his dad sitting at the kitchen table, the *Times-Picayune* spread out in front of him.

"You know they are going to quit printing that, don't

you? You'll have to go online to get your news." Alex was pretty sure the neighborhood wouldn't mind missing his dad in his ratty robe collecting the newspaper every morning, but he didn't say so.

He'd outstripped his dad in height but the old man could still take him down. And if that stare meant what Alex thought it did, he'd have heard the shot. He sighed. Couldn't stop shifting from one foot to the other. "I'm fine." Dad eyebrows arched, still packed a punch, even sprouting white and gray. "Truck needs a new window."

And his temper needed an adjustment. Sleep should take care of that, though it would be harder to get to sleep now that the sun was fully up. He gave the rays streaming in the window a baleful look, which didn't faze it at all.

"I know someone who can fix it cheap, bubba." Zachariah Baker called all his sons bubba.

It was faster than working his way through all seven names until he hit on the right one. His six daughters, Alex's half-sisters, were all "honey," except for the youngest, who was "baby," in spite of her shiny new law degree.

Alex wasn't that fond of lawyers, but he could see the value of having one in the family.

"Fixing it cheap would be good." Especially with his insurance rates about to take another hike.

Satisfied, Zach returned to his newspaper.

Alex removed his gun and stowed it in the same locked cabinet that had been his dad's.

Zach had started out as a street cop with the NOPD

and had managed to make it to retirement with his integrity intact, no mean feat in the scandal-ridden police department of the past. A hair shorter than Alex, he was a bulky, large-boned man's man with a weather-beaten face and gray hair. He'd married and buried two wives.

There were signs number three might be incoming, now that his thirteen children, his Baker's dozen, were grown and mostly gone.

Alex considered his current residence at home a temp situation, though his divorce had gone through four years ago. It hadn't been a surprise when the ex served him the papers. He knew she didn't believe him when he told her he'd raised enough kids.

Women. How could she look at this place and not believe?

The kitchen looked like it had been scoured out by gale force winds—something not far from the truth. You couldn't funnel thirteen kids through a room for that many years without leaving a mark.

The long, bruised table was the same one that used to be as crowded—and as noisy—as a bird's nest at feeding time. Mornings, which he still didn't like, were spent racing from open mouth to open mouth, shoving food into them in a vain attempt to close them all.

Feeding was followed by the mad, whine-intensive scramble to find schoolbooks and lunches and get everyone out the door and off to school. And then getting out the door, too. Zach must have been there sometimes. Not even he could work all the time, but it never seemed to make any difference.

"Anything interesting in the news?" he asked. His body might be ready to get prone, but his brain was still too active.

Zach folded a section of the newspaper and shoved it toward Alex, opened a new section. Alex settled in opposite and studied the headlines without taking anything in.

"Rough night?"

Alex shrugged. "Had better. Had worse."

"Shouldn't bring your work home with you."

Alex glanced up, not sure why he felt defensive. Not like he planned it. He rubbed his face tiredly as his stomach rumbled insistently. "Want some eggs or something?"

Zach shook his head. "Leslie's picking me up. Doing breakfast bar at Shoney's."

"Do I need to start looking for an apartment?" Alex had no problem with his dad remarrying. He'd spent plenty of years alone, not through lack of persistent effort. What woman wanted to take on thirteen children or risk increasing that number?

"You wouldn't have to move out. House is plenty big, bubba."

Not that big. Alex realized his dad was looking at him with an unusually intent expression.

"What?"

"Leslie has this friend—"

Alex pushed his chair back and stood up. "No."

"You need to get out, bubba. It's been a long time since the divorce—"

"I'm going to bed." He was not going on a freaking double date with his dad.

He stomped down the hallway to the bedroom, stripped off his shoes, and sank onto the bed. He hurt all over and his stomach was pissed off, but it would have to wait. He was too tired to care.

The sun poked through the blinds in several places, just in case his brain didn't know it was day. He buried his face in the pillow, but that just shut off his air, not his thoughts. How could he be this tired and not be asleep? He finally rolled over to stare at a ceiling still sporting damage from the time he and his brothers tried to play circus.

The muse. Eleanor Whitby must be an artist. They littered the Quarter, hawking their wares to eke out a living. Only the little crap perp had heard of her.

He gave a shudder. Last thing he wanted was to get mixed up with a woman who had anything to do with kids, even if she did have nice eyes and a mouth that looked—he dropped the card, rolled over and punched the pillow. She was a witness. End of story.

He did give her chops for not looking the other way, even if she should have. He'd have taken the perp down, of course, but it might have been a bit messier. The kid had definitely pissed him off. She might have saved him face time with IAD was his last thought as he finally drifted off to sleep.

CHAPTER TWO

It took a couple of blocks for the post-traumatic shock to hit. Had she left her brain at home this morning?

She was too old to be riding to the rescue of a seriously cute, not to mention obviously capable *cop*. Of course, no man was truly capable, or they wouldn't need wives, girlfriends and secretaries—did he have a wife or girlfriend? The television cops didn't have secretaries—

Not her business, she reminded herself with some firmness.

For a moment there it had seemed—but cute guys, even recently rescued ones, didn't have "moments" with her, not even teeny weeny ones.

That didn't stop Nell from thinking about him as she pedaled her way through the early morning traffic. It was spring in New Orleans, the perfect time for a woman to think about a man, even if she was plain as the first Jane.

And it wasn't like there was much else she could do,

other than try not to get killed. Besides, she was an artist. Faces were her business. Okay, her business was mostly cartoons, which he wasn't. And, she conceded a bit ruefully, she hadn't been thinking just about his face.

He's what old Mrs. Higgins would have called a fine figure of a man. Outdated phrase, but Mrs. Higgins had been a bit outdated. Didn't make her wrong.

Nor did it seem to matter that every finely formed inch of him had vibrated with annoyance. Broad shoulders had hunched. Short, impatient steps had started from narrow hips, which she might have accidentally noticed when he bent over to pick up her bike.

He had the height and build to inspire confidence in a gal, despite the fact that her first sighting was him with his hands in the air looking down the barrel of a gun wielded by a kid.

As an artist, she enjoyed a good contrast, especially the ludicrous ones. They were grist for her sketch mill. That scene would end up as a sketch, even if it was too violent for an Alphonse story. Alphonse needed fun vegetables, not awesome butts—

Her bike wobbled a bit and she decided she'd better redirect her thoughts higher before she ended up a statistic. Her cycling skills weren't great even when she wasn't distracted.

Faces, she reminded herself. He had a nice one. The jawline had been strong with a whole lotta stubborn in there, but Nell didn't see that as a downside. It helped that the stubborn chin needed a shave. His upper face had brooding, blue-enough-to-dog-paddle-in eyes, though they were a bit on the cynical side.

She'd rather liked the touches of silver in the close-cropped, brown hair. He was taller than she was, which was a nice change.

She could have been bitter that God had made her tall and undeniably ordinary, but she could reach the high shelf and, for the most part, see where she was going.

She sighed. It wasn't like her to look at a guy and ponder kissing him on the mouth, except...it had looked like that mouth could go from cuss to kiss in a heartbeat. Too bad...her bike wobbled again, worse this time, so she searched for something less...volatile to think about.

Like teeth. He had nice ones. Lined up like proper soldiers, pristine white, top and bottom. She tended to notice teeth. She used them a lot in her drawings. Nothing personalizes a carrot like a good set of choppers.

She had good teeth, too, though no one noticed except her dentist, and he tended to see them as a personal affront, as if she kept them cavity-free on purpose.

She rather thought he—the cop, not her dentist—had almost grinned at her at one point. He'd had the air of a man accustomed to getting what—and who—he wanted.

A pity he hadn't wanted to kiss her. Sad as it was, she'd have let him. Hey, if she weren't a believer in expanding her experience, she'd still be in Wyoming checking out books to bitter teens.

Being ordinary had kept her from expanding her kissing experience too much. Because Nell took after her mom, she didn't mind. Not even when that enormous—from her child perspective—lady called her homely outside the Wal-Mart.

"What's homely?" she'd asked.

Before her mom could come up with something soothing, the lady had said, "It means plain, dear. Not pretty."

"Neither are you." Plain hadn't left her free of the devastating honesty of being four.

Her mom had stuffed her in the car, where Nell had picked up a pencil and her pad and drawn her first vegetable person. The lady made a great eggplant.

Mom and Dad had laughed, and Dad taped it to the refrigerator door—her first, and still her favorite, showing.

She wasn't sure why her brain turned people into vegetables, and she'd not considered it a marketable skill. It was more an aberration.

Besides, her parents had been into "real" jobs, so she trained to be a "real" librarian and kept her doodling to her off hours. She'd still be conducting story hours and cataloging books if fate hadn't stepped on her life with both its big feet.

Nell pushed those clouds away, focusing instead on the silver lining that was her best friend. Without Sarah, well, Nell wasn't sure where she'd be, at least, she knew she wouldn't be living in New Orleans, for sure wouldn't be a published author of an actual book, and wouldn't be following the muse to the French Quarter for a morning of sketching.

It was a fortunate side benefit of having a muse that

often summoned her to the French Quarter. Selling sketches supplemented the modest salary from Sarah's fledgling catering business.

Sarah had gotten some nice contracts in the last few months, a couple from the socially important people with deep pockets, but the competition was keen, and the lagging economy kept the business teetering on the knife edge of disaster—though Sarah seemed to like dancing on the knife edge.

Nell grinned as she turned onto Decatur Street, dodging cars and carriages.

The smells got richer, and the sounds got more complex, despite the early hour. Traffic sounds, both car and pedestrian, blended into those from the street performers, and there was always the calliope from the *Natchez* warming up the pipes.

And if the sights and sounds weren't enough of a kaleidoscope, there were those smells. Car fumes, hot sauce, a mix of flower scents that she was still trying to learn, musty river, food cooking, and her personal favorite: the bakery smells. French bread, pastries and Café du Monde.

She couldn't always afford a beignet, but there was no law against inhaling their sweet scent as she pedaled past.

Nell had a little money in her pocket today, so she locked up her bike, extracted her portfolio with her sketching supplies from the attached basket, and got in line at the Café.

When her turn came, she exchanged some bills for a fragrant bag of three fresh-from-the-hot-oil beignets and headed for the Moon Walk. Her spirits rose as she climbed the ramp up the first flood wall, then down across the railroad tracks.

The steps to the Moon Walk weren't busy yet, though she did have to dodge one set of eager tourists before topping the levee.

She paused a moment to let the barely cool, deeply humid air flow soft as silk across her arms and face. When she first moved to New Orleans, it had felt as if the air was mostly water, but her lungs had eventually adjusted, and her skin lapped up the moisture like a kitten over a bowl of milk.

People who haven't been raised inland didn't, maybe couldn't, appreciate the appeal of water to those who'd grown up landlocked.

Wyoming was known for many things, but water wasn't one of them. The thick, silver expanse flowing past, almost at her feet, both soothed the spirit and enticed her to take the roads not traveled, looking for the sights not seen.

There was something about stepping outside the safe and familiar into the unknown that altered not just her view of the world, but the essential her.

She was still Nell, but when she walked into a French Quarter shop and the mysterious, spicy smells closed around her, she became "baby", "sugar," and sometimes "*cher*" to the store clerks.

She'd been raised to be uptight, but with each day in New Orleans, her insides relaxed more and more, mellowing into something more in keeping with the Big Easy that wrapped a body into its warm, wet embrace.

After a short debate with herself, she turned in the direction of the Natchez steamboat. She liked being alone with her sketch pad, but she needed the money—always did—and was more likely to make some where the tourists gathered to board the paddle-wheeled ship.

She settled on an empty bench and opened the bag. She'd need to eat fast. It never took long for children to collect around her like ants around a crumb. She didn't know why. Maybe she had more in common with kids.

The world of adults perplexed her as much now as it had when she was short. Real grownups always seemed to know exactly what to do, whereas she felt like she groped her way through her life.

Nell scarfed her beignets, enjoying the way the powdered sugar formed a small, puffy cloud in the air around her head before settling onto her clothes.

When she'd emptied the bag, she pulled out a wet wipe—it paid to know her personal weaknesses and prepare for them—cleaned the sticky from her hands, and then flipped open her sketch book and stared at the river.

"You got a blood."

Nell pulled her gaze from the long to the short view and found a little girl studying her.

She'd pulled her thumb out of her mouth just long enough to point out Nell's "blood," then put it back. She was cute and chubby and looked like a sunflower.

Despite a certain grubbiness, Nell could tell she had a

fond mama picking her clothes. They matched, right down to the socks and shoes.

Nell hadn't added flowers to her repertoire, but maybe she should. While she mulled the merits of flowers as characters, she did a mental sort through her various bumps and bangs from her fall until she identified a particularly insistent stinging sensation on her elbow.

A quick examination did indeed reveal a "blood."

The kid and Nell studied it together for several seconds. She suspected the kid was studying it because kids just liked to look at other people's "bloods."

They also liked to look at their own. And pick their scabs. Nell didn't admit it socially, but she liked to pick her scabs, too. She didn't, of course. She knew about scarring, but the temptation was always there.

It looked like there was a bit of gravel mixed into the blood clot that had formed over her "blood," so she pulled out another wet wipe and applied it gingerly to her wound.

It stung fiercely, but she felt a responsibility not to wince in front of the kid. The "blood" cleaned up, Nell looked up to find her audience of one had expanded to six. All were in the six-to-ten age range.

Kids made great veggies. Their bodies were always trying to burst their seams and full of interesting angles and curves. For the most part, their parents liked her sketches, too, a happy accident since many were willing to cough up cash to get one of their particular darling.

She'd picked up enough of this unofficial income to almost close the gap between what she needed to survive and what Sarah was able to pay her. The release of her first Alphonse book had been moderately successful, according to her publisher.

The *Alphonse the Artichoke* tee-shirts had received an unexpected boost from some of the tween set, for reasons neither of them could figure out.

Nell didn't expect it to last, so it was a good thing her art was a labor of love, rather than her only income.

The blood dealt with, Nell studied her sunflower girl, then, in a few swift strokes, captured her personality—and her semi-toothy grin on paper.

She showed it to her—making sure the semi-hovering mama saw it, too. After that, time passed quickly until the *Natchez* called all her customers and their parents for their journey down the river.

She packed up her gear, did a surreptitious assessment of her take—because getting mugged was clearly a dangerous possibility—and headed back along the Moon Walk toward the stairs.

She'd made enough to feel comfortable about grabbing herself a shrimp po'boy or maybe a plate of catfish and fries for lunch, before heading home. She caught the scent of sugar in the languid air and decided she'd have to detour past one of her favorite pastry shops, too.

It had been at least two hours, maybe more, since the beignets. The *Natchez's* whistle announced its imminent departure and she stopped to watch the colorful scene, a breeze off the river easing the heat of the sun.

The shifting combinations of people, the interesting

faces and colors became snapshots in her head that she'd try out for book three, while she waited for her second book to release.

With a sigh she turned from the bright scene and checked her watch. She had to cover the phone for Sarah, so if she wanted lunch and a treat, she'd need to pick up the pace. Her thoughts on food and timetables, she didn't see him until it was too late to change direction.

Today he sat on the bench closest to the stairs she needed to descend, his gnarled hands resting on his cane. As was his custom, at least the few times she'd noticed him, he had a stone-faced, scary-looking bodyguard standing behind him.

It was a different guy from last time—both faces difficult to erase from a memory geared to storing faces. This was the third, maybe the fourth time she'd seen him up here, though he usually sat further along, away from the stairs, more toward the end of the Walk, where it tended to be less crowded.

She'd noticed that the crow-like figure contrasted sharply with the bright bustle around him. She'd been surprised—and not in a good way—when she realized he'd noticed her back. Unless she was sketching, people usually didn't, and even then it was the drawings they remembered more than her.

He'd met her look, then smiled at her. Wasn't a nice smile, but her mom had taught her to be respectful toward the elderly, so she'd smiled back, and gave him a wide berth just in case. Her Mom also told her not to talk to strangers.

This was her first time to see him since the day of the creepy smile. And now he was in her path to lunch. Great.

It was possible he was a nice man who just didn't look like one, but she couldn't quite sell her instincts on that one.

His clothes were understated, even tasteful, but still made him look like a bad guy for some reason. Today he had on what she was sure was an expensive gray suit. Sometimes it was black. Never warm brown, though it could have been a good color for him.

Warmer would have been less creepy. There was something not quite real about him, as if he were a caricature from *The Sopranos*. She didn't know he was a wise guy, of course, but she didn't know he wasn't.

Despite his age and slight figure, he bothered her. Age had not carved kind into his face, and his brown eyes were as chilly as his suit. Even in the light suit, he was a dark spot in the cheerful scene, and she wished she had the nerve to stop and sketch him.

Contrast interested her, even when it probably shouldn't. It wasn't just that she didn't have time that kept her moving. He didn't look like someone who would be happy to be portrayed as a villainous bok choy in a children's book.

Too late to change course, she pressed on, debating which side of the bench to pass on. He didn't seem to have seen her yet. If she went behind, there was the bodyguard creating a different kind of menace.

Her fingers twitched, and she was glad her portfolio

was under her arm and somewhat out of reach. Her stomach rumbled and her mental clock ticked against the insistence of the muse, helping to boost her resolve not to piss off the scary guys.

The old man didn't move or look at her, as she closed on him. She pretended to look at the river as she drew level, sensed the moment the bodyguard noticed her. She felt the chill from his gaze riding beads of sweat down her back.

She angled her head a bit more, her sight and sound heightening, as she drew level with the pair. There was a scraping sound against the path's surface and then her shins connected with something hard and narrow.

No time to wonder how anything came to be in her way. She was going down again.

Portfolio flew one way.

Her feet went the other.

Her tush made painful contact with turf for the second time in not enough hours. And it wasn't even Monday. Some stars did a little dance before her eyes before fading out of view.

"I am sorry."

He didn't sound sorry, and how had his cane—the only hard, narrow thing around—got in her way?

The chill of his eyes extended to his voice. Cliché, bad guy voice. He could have air conditioned a room just by talking.

She accidentally looked up, met the gaze. Oh yeah, he was worse up close. Her her eyeballs felt dry as they did a deer-in-headlights thing. It had never been a good look for her.

"Are you all right?"

He almost sounded anxious. Or like someone trying to sound anxious. He needed more practice, but she gave him a point for trying, then took it back for sucking at it.

"I'm fine."

A large, beautifully manicured hand entered her sight-line. A big, gold ring winked at her, but she didn't follow it up to the face. The bodyguard gave off a worse vibe than the old man—

The bodyguard must have lost patience. His big hand grabbed hers and she was yanked upright hard enough to almost send her staggering into a powerful chest wrapped in cliché black on black.

A cloying scent made her eyes water. She would have slammed into his chest if he hadn't been strong enough to halt the collision he'd almost caused.

In the yin-yang moment, she accidentally caught a glimpse of his hard face. There would probably be some nightmares in her future. If they didn't kill her for tripping over the cane and forcing the creep to help her up.

His grip eased when she steadied, though her heart thumped like she'd been chest to chest with a killer.

"I am sorry."

The old guy still didn't sound sorry. Repeating the words didn't make them so.

"I'm the one who is sorry." Boy, was she sorry. "I should have watched where I was going."

She opened up some distance between her and the bodyguard, still not quite making eye contact with either of them. His cane was pulled back where it had been when she first saw them. Had he, could he have tripped her on purpose?

She couldn't think of any reason he would have, but she also couldn't figure out how it got in her way.

"You should wear a hat." His aged hand flicked his nose.

Nell's immediately glowed like Rudolph's. She touched the end, felt the heat, though it might be from panic.

"You're right. I'll get right on that." She glanced toward Jackson Square. It, and the throng of people there, seemed too far away. She'd lost her mind and something else—

The old guy held out her portfolio. She might be surprised he'd managed to pick it up. How had he moved so fast without her noticing? He had to be over eighty.

She took the portfolio, with another, quickly averted, glance. "Thank you."

That felt weird and wrong, even if it was polite. Like she was thanking him for tripping her.

"Are you sure you are all right?"

Something in his tone caught her attention and she looked at him, full on looked at him.

There was something about his eyes...

The bodyguard grunted.

She jumped. "I'm fine. Great. Hardly felt a thing."

She backed away, almost fell down the stairs. Grabbing

the hand-rail, she tossed an uneasy smile toward them both, then turned and headed down, resisting the impulse to scamper as she felt a bullet-sized hole bore into the center of her back.

The feeling followed her down the suddenly long staircase, across the tracks and back up again, stayed with her until she could drop out of sight on Decatur Street.

As if she'd been temporarily rendered deaf, now the comforting sounds of the Quarter washed over her again. Someone calling them to repentance because this year, for sure, the world would end. A little rap music, a little rock n'roll, some jazz, and just a touch of Zydeco.

She felt better, though the hand she raised to push damp strands off her forehead trembled. She caught sight of her watch. Well, bang went her lunch, not that her appetite had survived the encounter. She just had time to get back and cover the phone so Sarah could make her appointment.

She headed for her bike, but couldn't stop herself taking a quick look toward the ramp. There was no sign of either of them, which shouldn't be a shock.

So why did she feel watched? She did a quick survey—biggest waste of a minute ever.

The Quarter was already crowded with people. So she had an overactive imagination which she should keep focused on her books. It wasn't as if tripping was a killing offense or she'd already be dead.

NOT MUCH GOT in Dimitri Afoniki's way. There were good reasons he'd been nicknamed the Russian Tiger.

When something or someone was stupid enough to get in his way, he had people to remove it, people who acted without having to be told once, let alone twice. If they forgot that, they got removed and new people took their place.

There were those rare times when removal wasn't possible. The world didn't revolve around him. Yet.

He stared out the tinted window of his limousine, one long finger tapping the arm rest, frowning as he considered the problem that had taken him from his office and loaded schedule.

He'd demurred, tried to delegate. His great uncle had accused him of being spoiled. He'd acted as if he should be embarrassed about it. Naturally he was spoiled. Why should he not be?

He had money. Power. Good looks—looks that had gotten him out of trouble more than once when he was young. He had charm, too, when he cared to use it. He only did when absolutely necessary, using it tended to create other complications.

And if all that failed to impress, which it rarely did, there was his name. His great uncle might be three thousand years old, might not have left his house for a decade, but the smart people still feared him.

The stupid people, well, the world was better off without stupid people, wasn't it? Everyone but his great uncle rushed to make him happy. Age, his uncle asserted with tedious regularity, had its privileges. How fortunate it also made the old man tired.

His demands were less frequent with each year that passed. That they were less frequent did not make them less inconvenient or annoying.

This particular task was both. He frowned. Dimitri's growing dominance over the family empire might have made him a bit, he considered a variety of words before settling on, complacent that there would be few bumps—

The vehicle chose that moment to go through one of New Orleans' many potholes. Almost he chuckled. He had a sense of humor. It was part of his charm. He could even appreciate irony. It eased his boredom. Not that boredom was his current problem. It wasn't even that someone had failed to do exactly as he wished. It happened. Rarely, but it happened.

No, it was not the what in his way, but the who. The she. Had he ever been troubled by a she? He considered the question, but he could not recall any woman making more than a mild ripple in his life. Women had one purpose, then were...nudged on. Attempts to linger were dealt with by his people.

The finger tapping tempo increased. What did the old man expect to come of this meeting? What outcome did he desire? The nature of the task was too ambiguous, too lacking in direction.

"Find out why she is here," his uncle had ordered.

With an irritated shift, Dimitri pulled the folder close and opened it, staring at the face of the woman. Bland, beyond ordinary, a librarian from Wyoming? No one that mattered came from Wyoming.

What interest could she hold for the old man? Why did he care to know why she was here? It wasn't the usual interest. She wasn't young or pretty enough for that. His uncle had tried to hide it, of course, but he was very interested. Unnaturally interested.

Sadly, that meant Dimitri must pretend she interested him.

"She shouldn't be hard to charm into talking," the old man had said, as if Dimitri's charm were tonic easily and carelessly dispensed. "No competition noted."

Of course no competition had been noted. She was an ordinary woman in her *thirties*. The trick wouldn't be charming her into talking but getting her to shut up. He frowned down at the photograph. What could she possibly know? The report was so bland, it had bored him to read it.

Was the old man finally losing it? He'd thought so, had delegated the job until, well, the old bear still had some teeth. Uneasy, and not sure why, he'd crafted a plan, certain the problem would be ticked off his to-do list with only a small disruption to his schedule.

The woman would be charmed to meet him and spill her secrets with no muss or fuss. Women always were easy. She worked for a catering company. He often needed a caterer. So he arranged to need one. She was the personal assistant. In his experience, the assistant was the first person one met, not the last.

Two weeks later, he still had not made contact with the

most impersonal personal assistant he'd ever *not* met. If not for the photographic evidence that she did indeed exist, he'd have begun to wonder if he was the one losing it. The impasse might have continued if not for two events.

His uncle had demanded an update, with a look in his eyes that boded trouble for Dimitri, the kind his people couldn't manage. It was not a good moment to realize that not only was the old man spoiled, too, he had also been spoiled longer. And there were many others waiting in the wings for their shot at being the right-hand man to a dying old man.

Even that might not have mattered if not for the clincher in the latest report from the investigator, a report that included a photograph of St. Cyr giving the woman his crocodile smile. This sent her to the top of his to-do list. If St. Cyr was interested, so was he. It was time to force an "accidental" meeting with this oddly elusive quarry.

He'd waited until the Burland woman was too far away to get back and then called and asked for an urgent meeting. And he'd agreed—after a short pause—to make do with her assistant. There was no other personal assistant on record, so he was reasonably confident this time—though not confident enough to update his uncle just yet.

Now his limousine drifted to a smooth halt in front of the stately residence that housed Blue Bayou Catering and, he hoped, his soon-to-be-solved problem. His driver ignored the traffic that quickly piled up behind them while Vlad slid out of the front seat to open the rear door for Dimitri.

Indifferent to the cacophony of honking horns or the waiting Vlad, Dimitri studied the house through half lowered lids. If he owned such prime real estate, he'd bring in a bulldozer.

He understood there were rules, but he'd been driving over them for most of his life. Forgiveness was much easier to buy than permission. And he was weary of the old, most especially weary of catering to an old man clinging with claw-like hands to his power.

Was this the chink in his aging armor? A way to finally bring the old buzzard down? What was it about this woman that brought an avid gleam to the rheumy old eyes of both men?

It certainly wasn't the usual reason. Neither man had ever dallied with a female over twenty-five. Sadly, there was only one way to find out. He must be brave and gaze upon ordinary and pretend to like it. Possibly even charm it.

Dimitri stepped out into the annoying humidity, giving a slight shrug to rearrange the line of his suit. He was Russian by blood, if not by birth. A creature of the cold, he wondered, not for the first time, why the old man chose to headquarter his empire in a humid swamp when he had most of the world to choose from.

He trod the short, curving path to imposing doors, and Vlad stepped up to press the bell, then shifted to the side, his stance alert as his driver put the car—and traffic—in motion once more. The door swung wide, the shadowy interior somewhat impeding his view of what he presumed

was the source of his great uncle's—and very much his own
—discontent.

"Mr. Afoniki?"

At least her voice did not grate. He nodded a greeting,
stepping into the cool hallway without waiting for permission. Out of the bright sun, his eyes adjusted, allowing him
an opportunity to assess his quarry.

"I'm Nell Whitby. Sarah's been delayed, but she
should be here soon."

Not too soon, he hoped, producing a practiced smile
for this easy prey. With a small measure of curiosity, he
compared reality with the photographs. Like a properly
demure personal assistant, she wore a slim black skirt,
white blouse and low-heeled shoes.

There were signs she'd tried to tame her hair, though bits
of it drifted around her face, because of the humidity he
presumed, having endured countless complaints from various
women on the subject. Her voice was pitched low and was a
bit on the cool side. He couldn't mind. At least she didn't gush.

He extended a hand with a gracefully studied flourish.
"Thank you for seeing me on such short notice, Miss
Whitby."

She matched his move, minus the flourish or the grace.
She wasn't clumsy, just prim, librarian-ish, he supposed.
His fingers swept around hers in a gentle caress, the tips of
his fingers settling on her pulse. A bit disconcerting to find
it placid and unaffected.

He held back a frown, rather proud he'd managed it.

He started to lift her hand to his mouth, but it somehow slid free of his.

She had already begun her turn to lead him to the office. "Please call me Nell, Mr. Afoniki."

Had he been glad she didn't gush? He halted her move by not following her. She paused halfway through her turn, one brow lifted in inquiry.

"You must call me Dimitri," he said, shocked by his tone. It wasn't gushing. He did not gush, but it was...rather friendly. He would need to be careful. Too much friendly gave women ideas.

She blinked, the slow sweep of her lashes softening the austerity of her face, but when the lashes lifted again, the look in her eyes showed no inclination toward getting ideas.

He had a fleeting feeling of *déjà vu* from her steady brown gaze. As if this had happened to him before, but that was not possible. Women fell at his feet, had for as long as he could recall.

"If you'll come with me, I'm sure we can get your issue sorted out." The tone held gentle prodding, but not much else.

He'd have been piqued, but then he recalled he'd seen the tactic once or twice before. This pretended indifference to get his attention. He would allow her to continue the charade. For now.

This time he allowed the change of location by following her down the cool hallway. She led him without the usual self-conscious shimmy. She faked indifference very well. Almost her games amused. Almost.

Her figure was not up to his standards, the rear her best side, even minus the shimmy. She had the height for a few adjustments, some enhancements, though the face would take more than a little work to bring it up to code. Not that he planned to try. This game they played was not the usual one. Information, not sex, was on the table.

She turned at the door to the office. "Can I get you something?"

The provocative question was so prosaically offered, he was genuinely amused, he noted, rather surprised. Few men had managed this level of composure in his presence, the women never.

His certainty faltered briefly. It was possible she did not know—but her gaze found him, studying him like a policeman. Or, it came to him in a flash, that assistant principal.

He had not thought of her in years. The private Catholic school was, for the most part, run by nuns. Easy prey. Even at eight he knew how to make them giggle and blush.

He'd caused the fight that had landed him in her office, but he knew teachers weren't allowed to assess blame or disbelieve him. It might damage his tender psyche. Oh, he'd get punished, but so would his victim. A win-win.

He'd been laughing inside until that calm, stern gaze latched onto him. This one sliced and diced him with the same calm, seeing dispassion. Oh yes, she knew exactly what she was doing. Her eyes lost focus for several seconds. Not a good idea in the presence of the Russian Tiger.

She blinked, returning to the present, with no sign of discomposure. "Sorry, was just thinking about rutabagas."

He frowned. Did she plan to offer him a vegetable tray? He replaced the frown with a smolder. "I prefer the sweet to the savory." He waited for her to return this serve. Or at least blush.

She studied him thoughtfully, distantly. "I'm afraid we don't have a lot of variety. Just bottled water and maybe a soft drink or two, but I'm happy to check."

Was that a return of his serve or—it was his turn to blink, trying to connect the proper dots. Rutabagas to drinks? She was not what he'd expected, despite keeping his expectations low. Not that he was disappointed. He was not entirely sure what he was. Nothing felt familiar, a novel sensation that he hoped never to encounter again.

"I'm fine." He wasn't, exactly, but he would be. Ordinary women were not on his radar, but she was a woman. The management of an ordinary one couldn't be that different.

"Right then, let me pull up your uncle's file." She crossed to the chair tucked in behind a small, but well-crafted desk and sat. "Please." She gestured toward the wing back chairs in front of the desk. "This will just take a minute." Her hand covered the mouse, waking up the computer screen, then attacked the keyboard with an economy of movement.

Her fingers were long, nicely shaped and showed some care. No polish or talon nails. They were her only good feature, so she might have enhanced them with an understated polish, but she hadn't.

She'd accepted her ordinariness, he concluded. He lowered himself into one of the chairs, studying her with professional curiosity. She made no effort to flirt or acknowledge him as a man, because she knew what she was and what she wasn't? Would that make her vulnerable to a modest charm offensive? Would she know the basic moves? Almost, she'd seemed to look through him—but that would be a feint, a pretense. No woman looked past his face. Ever.

He relaxed in the chair. "You don't sound local." Idle conversation first. A circling of the prey before moving in.

The shift of attention toward him was brief. "No. I'm from Wyoming." A pause. "Not Star Valley."

He felt free to frown at this, her attention wholly on her screen. "Of course not." Why did he feel as if he'd missed a cue? He never missed cues. "You're very far from home." A slight nod, something that might have been a smile. "What brought you to New Orleans?"

That pulled her attention off her screen. The careful way she considered her answer confirmed his suspicion that they played a game.

"Sarah—Miss Burland—was my roommate in college. When she started the business, she asked me to come help out."

Cagey, very cagey. Seemed to deliver information

without delivering. A clever woman. He supposed it was the fallback position of the ordinary, but it gave him no hint to her purpose. Did she seek to hide her past? Or her reason for being in New Orleans? He'd read her file. She seemed like an open book...

Was that the key? "Don't you write books or something?"

This nudged a smile out of her, one that improved the austerity of her features, but it faded quickly. "I've published one children's book."

She followed this with a look that made him add, "I was looking for a gift for my...cousin's child and..." He realized he was explaining—which he never did—so he smiled. It was what he did.

She seemed about to comment, but she gave a sort of nod instead. When she did speak it was to offer, "I'm sorry. The computer is a bit slow today."

Was she uneasy? No sign of it on her face and her gaze appeared singularly untroubled. In profile she seemed less, well, it verged on—he shook his head, not sure what he thought. Which was not typical.

He was spoiled, he realized, hovering between amused and annoyed. He'd come here expecting easy. It had been some time since he'd faced a real challenge. Not that he considered her a real challenge. Not yet. His thoughts kept circling back to: not what he'd expected.

When he took her features, her figure apart, there was nothing special, and yet...somehow the sum was something more than not-special. Was it her eyes?

There was intelligence in them and humor. Not the malicious kind, but he did resist a need to shift in his chair. If she was here for some hidden purpose, why wait two years to act?

Unless...was that her aim? Force them to make their move? Or perhaps her plans were long term? If so, she was a cool customer. Very cool.

"There." A final tap and she looked at him. "What seems to be the problem?"

Besides her? He shifted, leaning in so that his arms rested on the desktop, pretending an intention to look at the screen, but instead he looked at her. His eyes, he'd been told, were more dangerous than his smile. And his smile was most dangerous indeed.

"Miss Burland mentioned something about the date?"

Most women could not construct a coherent sentence while he looked at them. Except that assistant principal. He'd stopped picking fights that year, waited until she'd changed schools. "Yes."

He leaned closer and asked, "Do you like New Orleans? It must be very different from Wyoming."

She leaned back in her chair, as if giving the question serious consideration, not putting distance between them, her retreat so smoothly managed it didn't look like a retreat at all.

"It's almost completely opposite. But yes, I like it." Then she grinned. "I love the food. The heat, not so much."

He could not pretend the grin was for him. He might

have—regretted how quickly it was gone. When she smiled she was almost...

"I, too, do not care for the heat." He boosted the accent. Women liked it and she was a woman. Now they would chat—

"It's a beast." She turned back to the screen. "According to your file, we have your dinner booked for the nineteenth."

It seemed casual chatting was not her game. Was she afraid of what she would betray? She should be.

"My uncle insists he told me the twelfth, but I checked my notes and I have the nineteenth as well." He moved his shoulders in a "what can you do" shrug. His shoulders were broad, and he moved with tigerish grace. At this angle, he could see her pulse, see it not change. Surely even ordinary women had biological responses to wildly attractive men?

"The twelfth. Let me see..." Her right hand moved the mouse, clicked.

Did she swing the other direction? Sarah had not acted indifferent to him, though she had taken care to remain professional, but the two women did live together.

"We are booked for the twelfth, and according to Sarah's notes, that booking was made before your initial visit. With our system, it isn't possible to double book."

He fought the odd sense of being pulled into the unfamiliar as she continued—saying, while managing to not say —that if a mistake had been made, he'd made it.

"We can try to find you a different date or cancel the

booking. You will," she looked professionally regretful, "have to forfeit your deposit if you cancel."

The brown gaze was sympathetic, regretful, but devoid of all the things he come to take for granted when a woman gazed at him. He summoned another smile, though it felt off, unfamiliar. For the first time he understood what an alternate reality might be like.

"I am going to risk my uncle's wrath and hold the current booking," he said. That she didn't look away this time helped, for it seemed to him that finally she looked, and in this looking, finally saw him.

He boosted the smile with *I'm bad and spoiled, so why fight it?* His lids half-masted again. He was a very bad boy, quite possibly the worst she'd ever meet.

Nell didn't blush. Or wriggle. Or giggle. She blinked, the thick, silky fan almost endearing as it made the trip down to her cheeks, then rose again. "We are happy to hold your booking while you check. Just don't forget there are additional cancellation penalties if he changes his mind later. The sooner you confirm or cancel, the better."

He'd have liked to pretend there was a double meaning in there, but he hadn't risen to second in command of his uncle's empire by pretending. That also meant he knew when to push. "I can take my punishment." He gave her a wicked, intimate smile—

And she *chuckled*. Her tone both dry and librarian-ish, she said, "Because men are so good at taking their punishment."

She was very like that assistant principal.

"You should laugh always." The imperious tone brought her gaze back to his, her brows shooting up. "It is most pleasing."

Another of slow blink. "Thank you."

He waited for a laugh or a smile. Instead she sobered, her gaze turning more librarian-like. What did she think of—

"Though sustained laughing might be annoying. And it would be difficult to sustain," she pointed out quite seriously. "There is that need to breathe…"

She did not seem to be making fun of him, but seriously considering the problem. He tried a different tack.

"Have we…met before now? You seem familiar?"

She considered this question seriously as well. "I don't think so, unless, have you been to a party catered by Blue Bayou? I pass out the canapés and petit fours and such." Her hands lifted from the keys and she fluttered her fingers in the region of her shoulders. "This is my wait get up, too. Most waits dress like this, only pants, not skirts."

It was his turn to blink. Had she truly missed his point? Did she think he noticed the wait staff? Or did she choose to ignore it? He summoned a smile, though it was getting more difficult. "I doubt I could forget you, even for canapés."

It was clumsy. He knew it. She knew it. So the kindness in her slight smile surprised him. Was this, could this be his opening? She turned back to her keyboard.

"I'm putting a note in the file for Miss Burland." She

finished and hit "save," then leaned back once more. "Was there anything else I can help you with, Mr. Afoniki?"

It was an opening—or a trap. He could admire her skill, even though he was seriously unhappy. His uncle would not be pleased. He was not pleased. Usually all he had to do was look at a woman and she did what he wanted. They were, after all, the intuitive sex, though this one made him wonder.

A distant sound of a door closing and footsteps approaching brightened her expression. "Miss Burland's back."

He nodded, as if pleased, while inside he cursed the timing. As the tap of heels against wood grew closer, he rose, trying to frame a question that would provide an opening.

Nell rose, the principal manner back. "It was nice to meet you, Mr. Afoniki."

So polite. Like a child. And yet, her eyes were wiser than a child's, older. Was that what made them so unsettling? The mix of innocence and old? His window of opportunity was closing.

"I asked you to call me Dimitri," he reminded her, moving to block her escape.

She had the height to almost look him in the eyes, though she stopped further from him than most women would have. Usually they came right up, tipping their chins up in invitation. No sign of inviting in her old-young eyes.

He held out his hand, determined to get some reaction

from her. When she reciprocated, he gripped it, lifted it to his lips, his mouth lingering against skin that tasted unexpectedly sweet. His fingers wrapped her wrist again, settled where her pulse should race to betray her—

Before he could find a flutter, her hand was gone once more and she'd moved past him.

It felt like rejection, though it couldn't be. Must have been a retreat. She'd not known what to do with a man such as himself. Of course she wouldn't know what to do. He turned and saw Sarah looking at him over Nell's head. Her appreciative gaze soothed—not that his ego was bruised. Not by an ordinary, clueless, annoying female.

He smiled at Sarah. To show chagrin was to expose weakness. He widened it to include Nell as she half turned to offer a prim, "Good-bye."

"Until we meet again," he corrected, waiting for the blush—which wholly failed to appear. She did pause, her head tilted, her gaze once again curious and assessing, then, with a quick half smile, she passed from his sight.

Her retreat sounded different, not like retreat at all. He'd heard many women walk away from him. None had sounded quite so...indifferent.

FROM HER ATTIC EYRIE, Nell saw Afoniki leave, moving with a long, confident stride toward the street, a broad-shouldered man falling into step behind him.

Once he'd slid into a limo and pulled away, Nell

grabbed her portfolio and clomped downstairs, happy to be back in shorts and boots. Sarah, who had to have heard her coming four flights away, waited at the bottom.

"Well?"

Nell grinned. "Rutabaga."

Sarah's brows shot up. "But the guy is—"

"There are very handsome rutabagas." Probably. "You should study them instead of just whacking them to bits with your seriously huge chef's knife."

"I don't have time to study my veggies when I'm cooking. Or when I'm not." Sarah turned, heading back to the office, her cool summer dress a perfect frame for her tall, slim figure.

Nell followed her, fingers itching to sketch, though her muse was torn between capturing her "rutabaga" on the page or going for a classic, semi-vintage of Sarah. That twenties style and Sarah were a match made for a muse. And then there were all the other images tumbling in her brain, not unlike how her body had tumbled this morning. Twice.

Unable to sort through it all, Nell sank on the arm of the chair recently occupied by the rutabaga, wrinkling her nose at the heavy scent still lingering in the still air.

"I don't know what the big emergency was." Nell tossed the portfolio into the other chair, rather pleased at its perfect landing.

Sarah half shrugged from her spot behind the desk. "He didn't tell me when he called."

"Maybe he just wanted to see you?" Sarah made a face, prompting to Nell to add, "He is rather gorgeous."

Sarah leaned back. "And?"

Nell traded chairs with her portfolio, which reduced the scent intensity to bearable, and considered the question. "A bit brooding. A bit...creepy." Now that she thought about it, more than a bit. If she drew animals—which she didn't—she'd have cast him as a tiger. She didn't say it. He was a client, and she could be wrong. She often was. "You looked him up."

Sarah looked everyone up. She and Google were besties.

She nodded. "Add womanizer and ruthless to creepy." Sarah frowned. "Hints of something more. The stench of not quite legal hanging around. If we lose the booking, I won't cry." She straightened. "What was that 'til we meet again' about?"

Nell chuckled. "No clue." She frowned. "I have no experience of course, but it did seem a bit plummy, over-done. Maybe he thinks chatting me up will help him with you?"

Sarah laughed as she shook her head. "He's not inter-ested enough in me to work that hard. Maybe it's a Russian thing."

"And my inability to understand it is a Wyoming thing." And a lack of experience thing. Nell grinned and then stretched. Rubbed her temples. Too many images vied for attention inside her head, the clamor growing almost to the point of giving the muse a headache. And she needed to eat. But the muse was usually harder on her head than her stomach.

Sarah knew the signs. "You'd better go do some dump sketching or you'll be mainlining Tylenol."

Nell collected her portfolio and headed for the door, remembered she hadn't yet told Sarah about her adventures in crashing, but when she turned back, Sarah was already focused on the computer. She hesitated, but it wasn't like there was anyone to tell on her. She could fess up later. And speaking of up, she needed up and sketching. In that order.

HELENNE ST. CYR sat in the chair that overlooked her garden and waited, with the calm knowledge that she waited for the last time. She was not impatient. The long years had bled it out of her.

If she'd known how long when it started she might have turned aside. The young did many things they should not because they did not know better, because, even as they believed they'd live forever, they did not know how long forever could be.

She was supposed to remember her youth now that she was old. She did not remember anything but hating Phineas. And him hating her.

For so many years they'd been locked in a silent war to survive the other. To win. Neither dared to kill the other until—her lips curved in a smile. Today, she sighed, today he lost it all. How he'd hate losing. He'd hate that more than dying. He'd hate knowing he couldn't take her down with him

It must be done by now.

Done. A small, neat check on the to-do list she'd almost despaired of finishing. Her revenge wasn't just cold, it had almost dried to dust. Almost she'd given up.

Phineas had kept his secrets well, had never trusted her or liked her. Oh, he'd wanted her for a few minutes. He was a man and she'd been beautiful. She hadn't minded when he'd moved on. She'd never wanted him, just his power. Had needed it to strike at the man she had wanted. The man who hadn't wanted her even briefly.

If either of them had wanted anyone but *her*. Eleanor. Ellie. Her other mistake.

How ironic that Ellie had been Phin's mistake, as well. Now, at the end, she could be amused by that.

If he hadn't tried to match her son with Ellie's child...

No, she'd still have wanted him dead. Her hand trembled a bit and she gripped the sides of her chair. Even if her beautiful Phillip had—if, if, if. What was the point of looking back?

What couldn't be changed had been endured.

And she'd made sure Phin hadn't enjoyed the years either. She smiled, wondering what he'd thought today when the blow had fell. Had he known it came from her? His stupid, sentimental decision to take the sun in the French Quarter had made him vulnerable just when she needed it. How exquisitely ironic was that?

She shifted her arm, just enough to see the time on the very expensive watch Phin had bought her for her last birthday. She'd hoped to feel it, to sense the moment his life ended, but she felt nothing, not even relieved. Perhaps she no longer could feel. She did not mind. Feeling was over-rated.

She lifted her chin, as if sensing an errant breeze. Almost she laughed. It seemed she could feel one thing. The tremor as Phin's death swept out to take down Aleksi and Bett. She felt again the flash of anger that she'd almost missed it, too. But she hadn't. The weapon was in *her* hand, not theirs.

Speaking of which, he should be here soon—ah, yes, here he came.

He moved through the garden with surprising grace for a man who had none, for one so different from her beautiful, dead son. He was not really a man at all. He was a hammer, and he did not know it.

He didn't knock, just slipped in a gap in the door, then shut it behind him with a care unusual in a hammer.

She didn't look at him. One didn't look at tools unless one had to. "It's done."

"It's done." He was terse. "Loose ends tied."

She liked him terse. Was pleased he knew it. She looked then, bestowing approval. It would be his only reward. A pity, but he'd become a weak link, a loose end.

"You saw it."

He nodded, something flickering over his usually blank face.

"What?"

"There was a contact—" He frowned. "I took a picture with my cell." He extracted it, tapped the screen a couple of times, then handed it to her.

She stared down at the tiny screen, adjusting it until the blur cleared. The tableau was small, but the body language was interesting. She knew every nuance of Phin's. She'd had so many years to study him. She messed with it until his companion came into view—her whole body went stiff. How had he found out? She'd been so sure he hadn't—clever bastard. He'd given no sign. None.

"How...interesting." She directed a look at him. "I think, yes, I very much think I need you to do one more thing for me today, dear boy."

"Of course." His face was impassive, but his eyes gave him away.

She smiled at him, the mothering one that made him stupid. Tools sometimes needed that extra care to do their best. "I do not, I really do not know what I'd do without you."

CHAPTER THREE

Alex woke with a jerk, the sun stabbing through the gaps in the blinds into his eyes.

He muttered a curse and then rolled over to look at the crooked wall clock. Four hours of sleep wasn't going to do it. He closed his eyes, but it was too late. Tired but not sleepy. How did that work? He sat up and rubbed his eyes.

The silence of the house didn't soothe. Why should it? He'd been raised in chaos, probably forever ruined by it. A quick shower took the edge off tired. He already had a bunch of texts from the sibs about his early morning adventure, which for some reason made him think about Eleanor Whitby.

He should have mulled the crazy parts, but he found himself stuck remembering her eyes. Wondering what it was about them that he couldn't forget. Not that he was interested in her or anything. Curious. Yeah, that's what he was. Curious was logical. Curious was not even first cousins with interested.

He left his room, his ears tuned for signs of life. His dad was still out. That felt normal. He opened the fridge. Shut it again.

He should go eat.

Maybe if he saw her, he could figure out why she bothered him, put it—and her—to rest for good. He did need to get her statement. Okay, someone did. Technically he was the victim, not the arresting officer, even though he'd made the collar.

Still debating with himself, he went outside, unlocked his truck—his most useless act of the day so far—brushed the glass off the seat, and got in.

He made a mental note to do something about the window before his radio disappeared. As he drove the few blocks to her address, he used the time to argue the pros and cons of seeing her again.

She had perp-fans and wrote what looked like kids' books.

Counter that with memories of her eyes and lips...

The fact he was thinking of her as anything but a witness almost made him drive past—but there was a great parking place in front, right on St. Charles. That never happened.

He had to take it, if only to be able to tell the story later. And he could save some poor slob in a uniform from having to get her statement. Yeah, that was it. He was doing a favor for a fellow officer.

He approached the double wood doors of the rather imposing house. Next to the doors was a small plaque that announced to the curious that Blue Bayou Catering could be found inside.

He checked the address. It matched, so he knocked. When he heard a distant, "Come on in," he pushed open the door and stepped into a hallway that belonged to a distant, more gracious past.

Cool enclosed him. Peace, too. Kids may have played here in bygone days, but unlike the Baker house, they hadn't left their mark.

The wood floor was smoothly pristine. It swept the length of the house, crying out for the swish of long dresses. From its heart, a stairway curved up, the banister inviting him to take a slide—even if he was in advanced years and wouldn't survive impact with the wood floor.

"Give it a go," a cool, amused voice said from his right.

Alex looked and found the owner of the voice, leaning against a door jamb. She was everything he most liked in a woman. Tall, cool and blonde—with just a hint of red in her hair.

He couldn't picture her riding a bike, let alone running into a carjacker with one. Her eyes swept him, sparked with interest. He waited for his libido to kick on, but it just sat there. "Excuse me?"

"The banister. Everyone wants to slide down it."

Okay, her apparent ability to read his mind went into the minus column, but when she started toward him, one hip at a time, her body all fluid and sexy, he added a few more ticks to the plus column and told his libido to get cracking. It was really letting him down. Out of habit, he produced his badge and showed it to her.

"Miss Whitby here?"

Her perfect brows arched perfectly. "Nell?"

Nell suited her. Sounded more friendly. "If she rides a bike and has a muse."

Her lips twitched slightly. "That's Nell." Now her brows pulled together in a frown. "Why would you be looking for Nell? She is the most law-abiding person I know."

He could see she was going to get all protective, when it ought to be obvious that it was the world that needed protection from Nell.

"I just need her statement. About the carjacking."

That popped her brows up again. Interesting that Nell hadn't mentioned it.

"Nell doesn't have a car."

Alex sighed. "She witnessed a carjacking but left before I could get her statement. The muse is, apparently, her boss."

She laughed and smoothed down her hackles. "That sounds like Nell. I'm Sarah Burland. Nell's other boss. And friend."

At least she hadn't tossed lawyer in there. She shook hands with him. Her hand was cool and slim as it settled inside his. He enjoyed the contact, but his libido remained stubbornly unaffected. It had never let him down before. Was there a place to get it checked?

He met her rueful gaze and half shrugged. Why did he feel like he should apologize?

She grinned, but it turned into a frown. "She didn't mention anything about it."

It wasn't his job to fill her in, so he asked, "Is she here?"

"In the garden. Second door on the right, then out the terrace doors. She's probably up a tree."

Alex had started to move but stopped at this. "Up a...tree?"

"She likes being up." Sarah paused her own retreat to add, "Check the oak in the middle. It's her favorite."

"Thanks. I think." The second door opened on a living room, a tidy and welcoming room with terrace doors that opened onto a small, not so tidy garden.

Several old oak trees cast their shade on the enclosed space, but there was a particularly fine specimen in the center, its branches reaching close to the ground, as if in invitation.

It reminded him of the tree in *Swiss Family Robinson*, only without the treehouse. In a particularly complex juncture between several branches, he picked out what looked like a reclining figure. She'd picked a spot a serious distance from Mother Earth.

He walked to the base. From this vantage point, all he could see was her butt, surrounded by branches and leaves and one foot dangling over the edge. So he hadn't imagined it. She did have a nice caboose. His libido gave itself a shake. Glad it was still around, but now was not the time.

Nell was not his type. Not the time to recall that his ex had been his type...

"Miss Whitby?"

There was a pause, then the foot was pulled in and the body—and the caboose—turned until he could see her face peering down at him through the branches.

She didn't say anything, something he found a bit unnerving. She may have arched her brows. It was hard to tell with the shade playing games with her face.

"I realized you live pretty close and thought it would simplify things if I stopped by and got your statement. From this morning."

"Oh, right. This morning. Sure. Come on up."

He wanted to but felt like he shouldn't. Tree climbing was for children, not homicide detectives. He studied the arrangement of branches and trunk. It was a great tree.

"It's lovely and cool." Her face disappeared and her caboose reappeared in the juncture. "Unless you're afraid...."

Her voice had just enough imp in it to provoke—if the taunt wasn't enough.

He started up, half expecting gravity to be bitchy about it, but it must be snoozing in the afternoon sun, too. In short order he'd clambered up beside her.

Close, but not too close, was another branch arrangement where he could settle quite comfortably. She was right. It was nice up here. Relaxing. Like he'd left his worries and frustrations back on the ground. And his hang ups. Air moved softly through the leaves, their rustle just enough to mute distant car sounds and cool the sweat from his climb.

He turned and studied her, curious to compare memory with reality.

She'd changed into a pair of shorts that showed off a rather well constructed pair of legs, though she still wore the cowboy boots, so he didn't get the full view.

She'd tucked her portfolio into a branch close by her, had a closed pad resting on her lap. One knee was scrubbed, probably from this morning. Her hair puffed out around her head, the ends curling in a variety of directions.

She fingered the end of a strand. "It increases exponentially, in proportion to the humidity level."

He chuckled and was rewarded with a smile that put crinkles around her eyes. He shifted uneasily. "They smile."

"Excuse me?" She blinked, though slowly, her lashes drifting down and then up as if that was all she had energy to do.

"Your eyes. They smile."

"Do they?" She touched the edge of one, as if feeling for the smile.

"Inside them." He knew he was being...something. He should shut up.

"Oh." Her lips curved up to match her eyes. A slight breeze made the shadows on her face shift, revealing, then shading her mouth.

"How was the muse?" he surprised himself by asking.

She made a face, punctuated it with a lazy shrug.

His libido kicked it up a notch. Odd to feel that slow slide now. He dealt with the aftermath of human impulse at work all the time. Saw a butt load of human impulse—and some he considered not-human—helping to raise his siblings.

He should understand it. He didn't. He didn't know why he'd come, though he wasn't sorry.

He found himself remembering the moment when he'd almost kissed her and hadn't. Maybe he should give into impulse every now and again. He sure couldn't make a move now when they were up a tree. He found he was kind of sorry about that.

She shifted position, uncrossing her booted feet. She leaned forward, stowing her pad in the portfolio and securing it.

"You're not from here, are you?" The question came out conversational, rather than cop-like.

"Wyoming." She turned her head, just enough for her sleepy gaze to meet his. "Not Star Valley."

He grinned. "How did you know—"

"Almost everyone's 'I know someone from Wyoming,' is someone from Star Valley." An amused frown pulled her brows together. "Not sure why. It's not huge."

"Not many towns in Wyoming are," Alex pointed out, which was almost all he knew about the state. And that most of Yellowstone was in Wyoming. Okay, he just thought he knew that.

Her tiny nod conceded the point. It was followed by another lazy smile that made his insides relax some. He liked that she didn't fidget or chatter. She looked at him straight, her gaze clear and honest. And smiling. There really was something about her eyes—

"So you're from not-Star Valley."

Her chuckle was engaging.

"Waipiti. I'm from Waipiti."

"Wa—what?"

"It's a little place between Cody and Yellowstone. A really little place."

"How did you get from there to here?" Her perch suited her, New Orleans did, too, but at the same time...he tried to picture a little town in Wyoming behind her, but he'd never been to Wyoming. Were Wyoming small towns like Louisiana small towns? Her eyes shadowed some and she looked away.

"Sarah was my college roommate."

"College?" Alex probed. He'd have pegged Sarah as a local, in habitation and with her college selection. But what had brought Nell to Louisiana—

Nell grinned. "University of Wyoming."

His brows shot up. "Seriously?" He did not see that one coming.

"She won't admit it, but I think she did it to piss off her parents. When my parents—she's the one who hooked me up with my publisher. He's local, too. When she inherited the house, she decided to try her hand at catering and she invited me to come work for her."

He didn't have to be a cop to note the quick subject change or to fill in the blanks. He didn't need to be a metro-sexual either. "How long ago did your parents pass?"

Her lashes shot up, her gaze on his for a long moment before she said, "A little over two years."

"No siblings?" She shook her head. Did he envy her? Probably not, though ask him tomorrow. The answer changed with the day.

"No family." Her smile was overly bright and not that happy. "I'm relying on the kindness of strangers these days, though," her tone softened, "Sarah's not a stranger."

"You must have left a lot of friends back in Wa —Wyoming?"

"Of course, but—" she shrugged again. Her lashes drifted to half mast, her mouth drooped.

"A clean break was probably a good idea." It had worked for his ex. She and the new hubby were in Saudi Arabia or maybe it was Dubai. He didn't keep track, but one of his sister's had mentioned seeing something about it in her Facebook status a few weeks ago.

Sometimes it bothered him how little he missed her. Mostly he was relieved. Nothing more depressing than a guy who couldn't get over the ex. It annoyed his sisters that he forgot he had an ex. Maybe it was having so many siblings. He didn't have room in his brain to remember an ex. "How long you been here?"

Her face relaxed at the change of subject. "A couple of years."

"That kid, the failed carjacker? He wants your auto-graph. Didn't realize I'd been rescued by a celebrity."

That made her chuckle a bit ruefully. "Only with tweens, I'm afraid. It's the strangest thing, but Alphonse has been deemed totally sick, only locally of course. Kids that age won't even eat vegetables, but apparently they like wearing him." She grinned at him, then shook her head. "I'm still a bit shell shocked thinking about trying to ram him. I do not know what came over me. I'm not usually reckless." He trotted out a skeptical look and she grinned. "Truly. I'm a librarian. Until today, the boldest thing I've done was move here. My first and last rescue attempt. My bike was not happy to be turned into a weapon. Or attempted weapon?"

His turn to laugh. "You see a nail, everything is a hammer."

"My dad would tell me to not make eye contact with the nails if I'm feeling hammer-ish."

This time no shadows, Alex noted.

When was the last time he'd been this relaxed? It was spring, so the air wasn't too humid, though the sun was high enough he'd bet it was eighty on the ground. The leaves probably reduced the temp some.

He gave his gaze permission to linger on Nell, trying to figure out why it felt longer that he'd known her. That they weren't strangers.

He didn't usually think this much around a woman, he thought, with a wry inside grin. Added to the odd, no doubt. His brothers—he felt a flinch and realized he didn't want his brothers to meet her until—what?

He wasn't here for personal reasons. He was up this

tree for police business. Okay, even he knew that was weird. Might even be a big, fat lie. He looked around, mostly to look away. "This is nice."

"I like being up."

It didn't sound so weird this time. Maybe the world needed more up. A change of perspective didn't hurt once in a while.

"Would you like something to eat?" He heard his voice say the words, without a bit of cop in the question.

He told himself it was to stop his dad from trying to set him up. He told himself it wouldn't matter if she said no. He told himself a lot of things while he held his breath waiting for her sweet, slightly husky voice to say no.

"Okay." She looked and sounded as surprised as he felt at her agreement. "I'm a much better witness with food in my stomach." As if to prove her point, her stomach rumbled. With a rueful grimace she covered it with both hands.

He chuckled, a bit relieved at the out she'd given him. A business dinner was less risky than a date. At least that's how he explained it to himself as he got his feet back on the ground.

Trouble was, looking into her eyes as she climbed down to him, he still felt up in the air. She handed him her portfolio, then dropped to the ground and stopped, as if caught by something in his face or his eyes.

She met his gaze, not obviously uncomfortable, even as the silence drew out. With the leaf-filtered light playing on her face, he revised her looks up again. No one could call her beautiful—except when she smiled.

Her smile changed everything about her face, though if he had to explain why he'd be stumped. Her face was as uncluttered as a kid's. Now that he thought about it, her steady gaze reminded him of a kid's. It seemed to look right through him.

As if he'd made it happen, he realized there were two children standing on either side of her looking right through him. It gave him a bit of shock to see them, so much so he actually took a step back.

"Nell," the girl said, importantly. She seemed sure of her welcome.

With good reason it seemed. Nell's smile wasn't exactly like the one from this morning, or directed at him, but it still made Alex catch his breath.

She knelt down, her face now level with the children. "Hi, Fancy. Georges. What's up?"

"My cat," Fancy said, turning her small body to point to a tree in the next yard. The foliage was dense, but Alex did spot a bit of white in among the green. "She won't come down."

Since Fancy was holding a doll dress, Alex was not surprised. He remembered all too well the attention his sisters had lavished on the various cats that had passed through their lives. Their favorite thing was to dress the cat in baby clothes. This caused the cats to meow piteously.

Alex could see the baby carriage at the foot of the tree.

He knew just how that cat felt. In fact, at this moment, he wouldn't mind being with the cat.

"She ran right out of the dress," Georges said, his admiration evident in his face and his voice. "And up the tree."

"Now she can't get down," Fancy said sadly.

Won't was more like it.

"I could go up and get her," Nell said, "but she'd probably just go higher now that she's scared." She lowered her voice as if sharing a secret with them, "Do you know what a lure is?"

Fancy's eyes got wide and she shook her head. Georges small round face brightened with interest. Alex felt his senses stir at the way her lips pursed.

"A lure is like bait. Fish like worms, so fishermen use them to lure the fish to the hook and catch them. What does your cat like?" Nell asked.

Fancy's small face screwed into a tiny frown as she pondered this. Finally she said, "Tuna?"

"Yes, cats do like tuna. So I'd move the baby carriage where your cat can't see it, then put a can of tuna at the base of the tree and lure her down."

"Lure," Fancy said, with relish.

Alex could tell the word delighted her. His libido shared that delight, though for entirely different reasons. It gave a little kick every time Nell said it. He looked away, but he couldn't escape the sound of her hushed, husky voice.

"Lure," Nell said. "And if you don't want her up there

again, maybe you should put the dress away. I'll bet your cat is tired of playing dress up."

"Oh," Fancy drew the word out, her expression wise and knowing. "Okay."

She and Georges took off running, their small bodies thrusting through the humid air with youthful zest. At the gate, Fancy turned to cry, "Thanks!"

Nell waved and smiled as she rose from her crouch. The requirements of etiquette satisfied, they disappeared from sight.

"Cute kids," Alex said, aware the words came out a bit flat.

Once again, her gaze assessed him. It seemed to see through him and inside him, all the way down to the parts he wasn't that proud of, to his fear of being back in that kid zone.

A familiar panicked feeling rose inside him, one all too familiar. All those eyes, all those gazes assessing him and finding him wanting. All those years of never being quite enough. He wasn't mom, or his sisters' mom. They were both gone, and he'd missed them, too. He'd never been able to take their place.

Nell's mouth curved slowly into a smile that was new and just for him—though he didn't know how he knew it. He might be deluding himself. Odd, he didn't mind.

Delusions had their place when a day started out like theirs did. Her eyes reflected the new smile, too. She took her portfolio back, tucking it under one arm. She took his hand in hers, sliding her fingers between his with the inno-cent trust of a kid and said, "Two questions?"

He couldn't speak yet, his throat was still tight, though tight was easing, as if the palm of her hand was absorbing the panic and neutralizing it. He arched his brows, giving her tacit permission to continue.

"I didn't catch your name earlier?"

"Oh. I'm sorry." It was habit to pull out his ID and show it to her. "Alex Baker."

"Homicide." Her eyes widened briefly.

It felt like she took a step back though she didn't move. So, he inched closer. "You said two questions."

The tension inside him was almost gone now. Her face relaxed a bit, her lips trying to curve.

"Where are we going to eat?"

There was a nudge in the question, he felt it, and heard her stomach growl again. He grinned. "Have you ever been to *The Italian Pie*?"

"No, but I love pie." Her eyes invited him to stay in her comfort zone as long as he needed. With a sense of relief, he accepted—while also reminding himself that he didn't have to worry about kids. Not anymore. He was done with that. He was having lunch—not babies with her.

With a pause to leave her portfolio on a table by the door, they went outside. Nell waited while Alex inserted the key into the lock of the passenger side of his truck.

"Wow, great parking place. Are you sure you want to give it up?"

He grinned. "If you're going to drive in this city, you have to learn when to let go."

"I suppose so."

There was no come-hither or sexual undertone in her eyes, but he felt heat build in his mid-section. They weren't up a tree now.

He wanted to kiss her, just to know. No, that wasn't all of it. He didn't know what it was, or why it was, but whatever it was, it dried out his mouth. It left him wanting to know the taste of her.

Her eyes widened, as if she'd joined his wavelength. She licked her lips. He wasn't sure if she knew it was provocative. She appeared to decide something and he braced for it.

"If you..." Her voice faded and she had to clear it, the husky sound incredibly sexy when taken with the innocence in her eyes. "If you want to kiss me, I wish you'd just do it," she said in a rush, "because the suspense is killing me."

Her chest rose and fell in a quick breath. Maybe that's what made him notice the tiny red circle of a targeting laser right over her heart.

He knocked her to the ground. Above their heads, the passenger window of his truck shattered, spraying glass all over his back.

CHAPTER FOUR

Nell was about ready to eat her own arm. Seriously. She didn't get the kiss or the pie. And she'd hit the ground three times in one very long day.

It was an ironic twist on third time's the charm.

Third time's the harm?

She winced at the cliché, and from the sting of alcohol as the EMT re-cleaned the "blood" on her arm, then gave the same painful attention to her knees.

At the apex of the confusion, Alex presided over a scene filled with flashing lights, yellow crime tape, the neighbors, random ghouls, and one or two press types.

He hadn't answered her question—which she couldn't believe she'd asked—but she'd sensed a yes, a little mouth-to-mouth incoming.

Instead she got a crime scene she couldn't pedal away from and some more bruises. She shouldn't have changed into the shorts after the creepy encounter with Dimitri. She felt—and probably looked—about five with her thoroughly scrubbed knees and elbows.

At least Sarah was away, meeting with a client. It was a target-rich environment for an artist, but not the best advert for a caterer.

"You hit your head?" the EMT asked, sounding like she was going down a mental check list.

Nell considered the question. There had been a tree root. They ran along the top of the ground. The water table was barely under the ground in the city, except when it rained and then it was above ground.

The roots were very Middle Earth and rather cool— until your head got slammed into one. Her back, too. Nell half nodded. She felt the urge to apologize, though she wasn't quite sure why.

The EMT was gentle, but it still hurt like a son of a gun. It was probably a good thing she hadn't eaten yet, since the pain induced a wave of nausea that popped up beads of sweat along her upper lip.

"So how long have you known Alex?" Her voice was pitched low, and Nell saw her glance dart briefly in Alex's direction.

Her cheeks warmed. "Since this morning." It felt longer, though she didn't say it. So this EMT—Nell's gaze did an up and down—this very attractive EMT, knew Alex.

The EMT's eyes widened. "Well, how interesting."

Nell couldn't argue that.

The whole day had been interesting in a bruise-inducing, bat crap crazy, creepy guy overload kind of way.

Was this gal a girlfriend? Past, present, or hoping to become one?

The hands fell away, the EMT stripped off her gloves and tossed them into the van. If she was a girlfriend, she didn't look bitter or worried. Not that she needed to be. She was beautiful, even rigged out as an EMT.

With the added distance, Nell studied her like an artist instead of a girl. Mostly. There may have been a bit of a green filter over her eyes.

This EMT was everyone's girl—tall, but nicely shaped, and blonde—wait, was there something familiar about her?

"I think you'll live."

Nell might focus on sketching vegetables, but she also sketched people in their original form. She was capable of doing family facial math, once she dumped the green filter. "Are you related to Alex?"

Her brows shot up. "I'm his sister, Laura."

The last of the green faded into relief she had no right to feel. Laura's head tilted, the careless knot of blond hair flopping to the side.

"Most people don't see a resemblance." She didn't sound thrilled Nell had.

Nell wasn't most people, but it wasn't a blessing.

"Nell Whitby." It kind felt like she should add a qualifier or identifier, but she wasn't Alex's friend, hoped she wasn't his foe. *I'm his witness* just sounded weird. *I'm an artist* was too pretentious.

They shook hands. It was something to do in the awkward search for follow-up comments. Neither found one, so this was followed by an extension of the silence, not helped when Alex made a beeline for them, his gaze clearing a path ahead of his body.

Nell gave him a careful smile, one with lots of neutral in it. The sister's eyes had turned into lasers. She saw him frown, but at the sister or her?

"You have a sister. Cool." As in not really cool, but she needed something at the end of the sentence so it didn't sound accusing.

"He has six sisters." Laura's grin was wicked. "And six brothers."

Nell felt air hit parts of her eyeballs that had never felt air before, as those eyeballs bugged. Seven plus six wasn't a difficult calculation, even for a gal who didn't like math. That was a lot of sisters. And a lot of brothers.

"None of us wants to meet or beat daddy's record," Laura added, perhaps to soothe the bug-eyed shock.

It didn't, though it rather explained the way Alex had looked at Fancy and Georges. She studied Alex profession-ally, okay, not completely professionally, but long enough to decide, "You're the oldest."

She was not sure how she knew this. It's not like she was an expert on birth order or anything. And she did not know Alex, even though it felt like they were friends who just hadn't met before now.

"You have siblings?" Laura asked.

"She doesn't. Lucky her," Alex said. "Is she all right?"

Laura stared at her brother for several seconds. "She's fine, Alex. A few cuts and bruises and a tiny bump on the back of her head." Her gaze shifted to Nell. "But you should see a doctor if you feel dizzy or the *headache* persists. Mine keeps coming back, but you might have more luck."

She shot a look at her brother that was thick with sibling rivalry.

Nell's lips twitched. She'd keep the headache if he'd kiss it better. If he had been planning to kiss her. She kept swinging between certain he meant to, fear he hadn't meant to, and certainty it would have been a pity kiss because she'd asked for it.

This though train made her feel dizzy, which didn't help when she noted the sulky curve of his mouth. Pouting shouldn't be so cute. And sexy. The shadow of a beard and the pout, yeah, definitely sexy.

She ran a finger along her lower lip, wishing...his lashes flickered. In books that meant something. But in books everything meant something.

"She might be a bit shocky." Laura spoke, rocking Alex back on his heels. She added, "Sibling shock, big brother." Her grin was wicked, then turned wry. "I'm all too familiar with the condition."

His jaw clenched. A couple of deep breaths that expanded his chest quite nicely—Nell thoroughly enjoyed the sight from her vantage point—and then he gritted out. "Thank you, Laura. I'll return the favor. Soon." On this clear threat, he turned to Nell. "Can you stand? Walk?"

Nell blinked, wondering why he'd think she couldn't. She wasn't on a stretcher. And she'd been certified fine by a professional, well, mostly fine.

She stood, instead of answering, then dipped her chin to hide the wince as stiffened muscles protested. Okay, walking was more challenging than she'd anticipated and might involve some zombie-type limping.

Alex's hand lightly gripped her arm above the scuffed elbow. The warm grip eased the muscle gripe a little. It would be a great time to do the helpless female routine.

It was a pity she didn't know how.

She'd made her best pitch for the kiss, so the ball was in his court. It was just that guys didn't always seem to recognize when the ball was in their court. One might conclude their balls—ouch. She had not meant for her thoughts to go in that direction.

She didn't want to look or sound desperate, so she proffered a friendly smile. This had the added benefit of requiring her to look at him. It was rather nice looking up into those blue eyes, being in the range of his musky scent. It could make a girl dizzy and not because she'd got her bell rung yet again.

Alex's mouth opened. Closed. There was a pause. His hand dropped away, leaving her elbow both sad and chilled. "We need to talk."

"We could go inside," she offered. It was cooler and there might be bread or something left over from their last gig. Her stomach—now that it was back in place after dropping to her feet and then jumping up into her throat—

had joined the grumble parade with the rest of her muscles.

He didn't touch her again—a change from when they'd headed to his truck on their way to not get pie. Then his hand had rested against the small of her back. It had stayed there even when she turned, it had given her the courage to ask the kissing question.

Maybe he was relieved that he didn't have to answer? Guys were deep into avoidance. The most interesting ones had sure managed to avoid her for a great portion of her life. Her knowledge of them was mostly culled from books, movies, TV, and girl chats with her friends. Some field observation. Amazing what couples got up to in a library.

It was a sad fact that she and Alex would never have met if she hadn't ridden her bike into his carjacking. He'd had to notice her. It had felt like he'd considered the question before she asked it, but it was also possible her imagination had run away with her. It had been running a lot today.

The running of her imagination led her thoughts to the hot Russian. There'd been, like a second, she'd thought he'd been flirting with her. Yeah, the imagination had been on a roll today.

Her practical side, the librarian, agreed that the imagination had been out of control, though that librarian also wanted the kiss. The artist, well, duh, she wanted the kiss, too. She was the one who'd asked the question.

Her thoughts got her to the front door, helped her sort of ignore the feeling of being heavily watched by the mass of police and sundry others who had collected to observe, assess, report, and block traffic.

She got the door unlocked, and Alex pushed it open, angling so she could pass him. With a last look back, Nell noted that the chaos seemed to have gotten worse during the short walk. Now there was a TV news crew in the mix.

"Slow news day," Alex said, nodding for her to go inside.

"Slow would be nice." Nell clumped across the wood floor, her ungainly factor increasing exponentially with each loud, painful snap of boots to wood. It was a relief to finally reach the kitchen. These old houses sure had long hallways. Pity the poor servants of the past. "I know you're hungry—"

"Nell."

The insistence in his tone turned her from the fridge and the edible something in there calling her name. It might have been something with mold, but at the moment, she didn't care.

"I'm sorry, but we need to talk. Could you take a seat?"

She could but she didn't want to. Her tush was still bitter from the triple slam. If she'd known he'd make her sit down without eating being involved, she'd have taken him to the living room and the soft chairs.

She eased down, managing to hide most of the wince.

Alex seemed distracted, though, studying her with a frown that had her shifting in unease, which also hurt, by the way.

"What?"

He pulled out a notebook and a pencil. The artist saw "cop" drop over him like a shroud. The librarian wondered why.

"Can you think of any reason someone would want to kill you?"

Neither artist nor librarian saw that question coming. Her jaw sagged. The cop who pissed off criminal type dudes day and night thought someone wanted her dead?

For a second, she replayed her encounter with the creepy guys on the Moon Walk, but even her imagination failed to supply a reason for that to be life threatening. "Not to be rude, but isn't it more likely to be you?"

"The targeting dot was on your chest."

He had been looking at her chest? She looked down. A targeting dot was the most interesting thing to happen there...ever.

"It's not like the shooter couldn't see who to target."

Okay, it was a fair point that still didn't make sense. She was a former librarian, current wait in a catering company, sometime sketch artist, and author of one children's book. Not the résumé to attract a killer. Or a date.

"Maybe I was just the first place the dot landed. It might have been getting ready to move to you. Or it was a mistake."

It was kind of a pity she wasn't interesting enough to kill. Not that she wanted to be that kind of interesting, but the notion she might be that kind of interesting had Alex looking at her like she was interesting.

Alex frowned. "Mistaken identity does make more sense."

He didn't have to agree so fast. He could pretend she might be interesting enough to kill. Only he was a guy. He couldn't.

He shifted in the chair, as if settling in for a long haul. "But we need to be sure."

Making sure was a plan she could support, though she'd be more supportive if there was food involved. She tried to compress her stomach so it wouldn't whine.

It had been bad enough that it whined while they were up the tree, but in the deep silence of the kitchen? What if it sounded like a different body sound?

He half frowned. Nell could see ideas ticking through his oh-so-blue eyes. She could sort of figure out his thought processes. Thanks to TV and movies and, of course, books. A lot of mysteries had passed through her hands, most of them pausing long enough for her to read them.

"No," she said.

"What?"

"No one to leave me a large fortune. A pity, but there it is." It didn't need to be a fortune, just enough to stabilize her situation would be nice, but not so much someone needed to kill her to take it. That was just ostentatious.

She held up a hand, ticking off the mystery plot motives. "Don't know any secrets. And I write kids books, not tell-alls."

How sad was it that she didn't need that many fingers. Her life was not that interesting.

This did not stop him from trying to find a crumb of lethal in her life.

He found no rocks to turn here or in Wyoming, where they had actual rocks. When he paused to regroup, she sighed yet again.

That left someone gunning for him. She'd suggested it without really thinking about it, but all of a sudden it felt real. Scary real.

"What?" Alex asked.

"Well, I just realized that someone might be trying to... kill you."

He shrugged. "It happens."

Okay, that was seriously sexy. So wrong to go there, but hard not to when she was weak with hunger.

He tapped fingers on the tabletop. "Maybe you saw something?"

"Something?"

"Something or someone—you shouldn't. Maybe you sketched the wrong person?"

She'd been tempted, but tempted wasn't doing it. "I mostly sketch kids, and their parents buy the drawings..."

"None of them seemed...upset by it?"

"One mom didn't like their kid being turned into a radish. But the dad thought it was funny."

"If they don't like the sketch?"

"I tear it up." That had only happened once. It wasn't her fault the kid picked his nose the whole time. She'd thought it funny to turn him into a comic ear of corn picking its nose from a line of five different noses. His

Mom wasn't a fan of irony. Or maybe she didn't get the joke.

His fingers tapped some more, until he realized what he was doing. He flexed the fingers, then lowered them to the wood. "Anything seem out of the ordinary in the past few weeks?"

Nell couldn't help it. She had to give him a Look. "I moved here from Wyoming. Everything is out of my ordinary."

He grinned, the cop dropping away for several very heady seconds.

Her toes curled so tight she almost couldn't straighten those piggies out again. And they sure didn't want to go to market. She leaned her elbows on the table to stop the lean toward him. Her fingers slid into her hair, started twisting strands.

"Let me rephrase that. Anything sinister?"

That brought back the creepy old guy, but other than the fact that he looked sinister, she hadn't seen him do anything sinister. Not even a shady meeting for her to accidentally observe. And she was one of thousands who had seen him, since the *Natchez* sailed past his perch several times a day.

It wasn't actually a crime to misplace your cane, though they'd both acted like she committed one tripping on it. She gave a small shrug but felt a need to try. Not that she actually thought someone had tried to kill her.

No, she just wanted the cute cop to keep looking at her like someone in need of protection. For that, she flipped

through her mental portfolio for anything she could prof-
fer. And came up with zip. Nada. Bupkis. Whatever
Bupkis was—

"Sorry."

"What about the past week?"

"Week?"

"Takes time to set up a hit."

Well, wasn't that a lovely thought. "Last week was
spent cooking with Sarah, handing out canapés, and
washing dishes." That's why the muse had been so insistent this morning. Usually she didn't roll out quite that
early.

"What about today? Anything interesting happen?"

She waited for him to look up so she could give him
another Look. She got another grin, which was pretty
much the goal. The grin faded into a thoughtful frown. He
made what looked like random doodles on the paper.

"What's bothering you?"

He glanced up, gave a half shake, then a wry grin.
"Wish I knew."

She shifted her chin to one hand, started tracing
patterns on the wood with her other. "Wish I could help."

"You have helped." She must have looked skeptical,
because he added, "Eliminating possibilities helps."

"Okay." She hesitated. "You'll...be careful, won't you?"

Before he could respond, they heard footsteps in the
hall.

"Detective?"

"In here," Alex called, half turning in his chair.

The uniformed cop peered inside. "They need you outside, sir."

"Right." He pushed his chair back. It looked like he wanted to say something, but if he did want to, he decided against it. "Excuse me."

He strode out and she didn't know if he would be back. Her sigh was on the shuddery side, but a rumble from her stomach helped redirect her thoughts. She got up, felt free to groan now that she was alone, then headed for the fridge.

This time she flicked on the small TV sitting next to it. She glanced at the clock and realized she was just in time for the news. She flipped to the channel that she'd seen lurking outside—maybe they'd be on the news—and opened the fridge, randomly shifting through containers as the announcer did a recap of the stories to come and then launched into the top one.

"In a bizarre twist, wealthy businessman Phineas St. Cyr was shot to death on the Moon Walk—"

It was the location that made her look at the screen just in time to see a photograph replace the announcer. She straightened and stared. If it wasn't the creepy old man who tripped her, then it was his twin.

ALEX WATCHED the tow truck drive away, taking his wheels to an uncertain future.

It wasn't just the windows that got hit this time. The

shooter had taken out his engine, which was better than taking their lives—though he had a feeling his insurance company wouldn't agree.

Techs were rolling up the tape, uniforms had thinned to just those trying to untangle the snarled traffic. Laura had been gone when he came out, but she must have started texting the family as soon as she and her partner drove away.

His cell had started buzzing like angry bees. Even ignoring them hadn't stopped it. At least the press had cleared off.

He looked at his watch. He and Nell might make it on the end of the broadcast. At that point, he expected the texts to graduate to a call from his dad, who never missed the news.

Eventually he'd have to call someone, unless he wanted to walk home. He looked at the house, wondering why he didn't make the call. It was past time to leave.

It's not like Nell would go out with him, even if he had a way to take her somewhere. Getting shot at twice in a single day had probably cooled her jets. Wouldn't take her long to figure out that hanging with a guy like him was a bad idea.

Too bad. It had been awhile since he'd kissed a girl. It had been longer than that since he kissed one he liked. And he couldn't remember when a woman had asked for it. He liked that.

He should make sure she was all right before he left.

He knew it was an excuse, maybe even a stall. So far he was the only one who knew it.

If the signs looked good, maybe he could still get in the lip action...he climbed the shallow steps but before he could knock, the door opened.

For some reason, seeing Nell there in the open made him uneasy, so he stepped inside, like she'd invited him, and closed the door. He didn't really believe someone wanted to kill her, but...

"You all right?" He studied her. She looked a bit pale.

She rubbed the back of her head, creating more disorder in her hair. It was kind of cute.

"I'm fine."

She wasn't. With six sisters, he knew when a woman wasn't all right. He'd never known the exact what—he'd never expected to because he was a guy—but had learned to recognize the signs. "Did you remember something else?"

She shook her head. "It's just...well, odd." She hesitated, then asked, "Do you have time to come back in the kitchen?"

"Of course." The trip felt short, though the hall was long, and not unpleasant following Nell. The boots put a nice sway in her caboose. Inside, his gaze swept the room, stopping at the small television, an image frozen on the screen. They must have a DVR. "Someone capped St. Cyr? Well, that was a public service."

"He's not...nice?"

"No, he's not nice."

"I didn't think he was, but then I thought, well, I do have an imagination. It's kind of obligatory for an author, you know."

He frowned, unease creeping in and making itself at home. "What?"

"I think I...actually I don't think, I did see him today. In the Quarter. On the Moon Walk. Where they found...him —he wasn't dead when I saw him," she added hastily.

"No, of course not."

She shifted from one foot to the other. The move was not unfamiliar to a guy with six sisters. He jerked his head toward the table.

"Let's sit and you tell me what's worrying you."

"It's probably nothing." She didn't protest when he pulled out a chair for her and only winced a bit when her ass hit wood.

He took the chair next to hers, angling so he could watch her face. He settled back, his feet planted, but relaxed, like his dad. He even heard his dad's words come out his mouth. "Tell me."

So she did. She was a natural storyteller, guess she would be since she wrote stories, but he could tell she tried to stick to the facts.

Almost enjoyed her recital until she got to the part where she tripped over the wise geezer's cane. He straightened some, even though he could see no possible connection between that and the recent shooting. Or the wise geezer's timely demise.

It was weird, though.

"So the bodyguard helped you up." That made him itchy, not sure why. She nodded. "St. Cyr say anything to you besides sorry?"

"Told me I should wear a hat." She touched the end of her lightly sunburned nose.

He studied her, trying to figure out if it meant anything. "I'll make some calls, see what I can find out. Don't think a chance, one-time—"

She twitched a bit.

"This was the first time?"

She shook her head. "Not the first time I saw him. It was the first time we talked. I notice faces, it's kind of my thing when I'm not doing Alphonse, or even when I am because—" She stopped. "Sorry. Anyway, I noticed him before today. I guess he liked to come sit on the Moon Walk. That's where I saw him."

St. Cyr liked to sit on the Moon Walk? Since when? "You say this is the first time you talked?"

"He sort of smiled at me once." She made a face.

"Sort of?"

"He's not—he wasn't good at it. Kind of creepy, actually. Like a crocodile."

"He probably didn't get much practice smiling," Alex pointed out, a bit dryly.

That made her smile, though it faded too fast. "I felt a bit guilty. I didn't like him. When I saw him after that I'd avoid him, but today—"

"What about today?"

"Today he was between me and my lunch. And my

bike. And I didn't see him until it was too late to find an alternate route. And I was running late—" Her gaze turned distant. "It was probably a good thing I was late. I wanted to sketch him, but I didn't think he'd like being a bok choy."

Had he missed something? "A...bok choy?"

She blinked and distant disappeared. "It's a Chinese cabbage."

"I know." Maybe. He knew that it was a vegetable anyway. "So you didn't sketch him?"

"Not as a bok choy." She turned and grabbed a sketch pad he hadn't noticed laying on the table. She flipped through the pages and then handed it to him. "Sometimes I just need to do a mental dump, to clear my head. So I sketch my day."

She'd had a lot of material today. He looked down, not surprised he'd made the mental dump.

She was better than he'd expected. Not sure why he hadn't expected it unless, maybe it was the whole vegetable thing. Following the muse on a bicycle. But she was published. Someone had invested money in her books, and she had at least one creepy little fan, so he should have expected her to be decently good. But she was better than that. Not that he was an art critic, but he liked what he saw.

It wasn't just the white of the page and gray of the pencil that made it so surprising. The sketches were small, but well done. There was one of him getting jacked by the kid. She'd caught the humor of it. The contrast. He gave her a quick glance and got an apologetic grimace. His gaze got caught by another sketch, across from his. He blinked. Tapped it.

"What's this?" he asked, even though he knew.

She angled her head to look. "Oh, a client. Sarah had an appointment, so I had to meet with him."

"Dimitri Afoniki was here? In this house?" It had to be a weird coincidence.

Her brow wrinkled. "His uncle hired us to cater his dinner party."

In one day, she'd had contact with a wise geezer who died and the evil nephew of another. And got shot at. His gut twitched, but it refused to tell him what or why. And his brain couldn't find the connection between the three events, though he pressed it.

"You ever met him before?"

She shook her head. It helped. Some. Though his gut still twitched with unease.

"Why does it matter?"

Alex hesitated. "New Orleans has a mob trifecta we call the three wise geezers, or rather we did," he added, casting a glance at the frozen television screen.

"Geezers?"

"They're really, really old."

Nell straightened. "St. Cyr, Afoniki and—"

"Calvino." He half expected to hear she'd met him today, too. She frowned. "Don't tell me you met him?"

Nell half grinned, shook her head, then paused. "Might have served him canapés, but not even sure about that. We did this big fundraiser last week with some other catering companies. Seems like I've heard the name, but it doesn't mean he was there..."

Not sure whether to be relieved or not, he returned his attention to her sketched mental dump—yeah, that was St. Cyr. No question. She'd managed to capture the moment. And the sinister quality of both men.

The river, the Moon Walk, the old man on the bench. He even got the impression of light and dark, of sun and cloud, all with a pencil. In one cameo, the old man leaned toward her.

The angle was from the ground, the other man standing aloof, behind him, though his hand was outstretched. Reluctance in every line. Hard-faced, cold eyes.

Alex shifted his attention to the old man. She'd caught something in his eyes, though he didn't know what—the more he looked, the more the drawing flattened out. It was like he had to glance, then look away, and think about it.

He leaned back, trying to figure out what he'd seen. When he couldn't, he sighed, looking down again. Something bothered him— "His cane was tucked in." He tapped the drawing.

Nell shrugged. "Maybe he'd started to stand. I was looking at the river when it happened, trying to get by without making eye contact."

"He wouldn't have stuck it out to stand up." If anything, it would have been closer to his body. "You sure you didn't trip on his foot?"

She tipped her head to one side. "Only if he has a wooden leg."

Could St. Cyr have tripped her on purpose? But why? Nell wasn't a stripper or under twenty-five. Not remotely St. Cyr's type. But he'd smiled at her. Noticed her at least once before tripping her. He looked at the drawing again, and this time he caught it—the look that puzzled him.

He'd known he was going to die.

Alex had seen too many men on the brink of death not to recognize the look. So he could have tripped Nell to— what? Tell her she needed to wear a hat?

"This is going to sound weird," Nell said, shifting uneasily in her chair, "but I thought he did it on purpose. It's like he knew I didn't want to talk to him, so he made me stop."

Now that sounded like St. Cyr. He couldn't have hoped she'd help him. Still, it was odd. "He didn't...look worried or anything?"

She frowned. "You think he stopped me—but the only person around him was the bodyguard guy—" Her eyes widened. "You don't think—"

"I don't know what to think, Nell. I have some contacts I can call." Most of them relatives. And someone needed to know Nell might be a material witness.

At the very least she might help them fix the time of death. And at worst?

He looked at the sketch of the bodyguard. He could be a steely-eyed killer and a bodyguard. For St. Cyr, that would be a requirement for the job. And if he was the one who'd tapped St. Cyr? Survival of the fittest.

Was that what amused St. Cyr? He didn't seem the type to want to die, but he wouldn't mind going out causing lots of trouble to lots of people. Which brought him back to, why Nell? Had he tripped her because she wouldn't look at him? To make her? Was it that simple?

He didn't like that she'd become a witness. Again.

But it did give him an excuse to hang around while he figured out why he wanted to hang around. If he had wheels, they could still go get food. As if on cue his stomach complained.

She grinned. "I'll fix our stomachs something while you make your calls."

WHERE A MURDER INVESTIGATION STARTED, and who ended up with it, depended on how high-profile it was likely to be.

St. Cyr's getting tapped was almost as high as it could go. It wasn't just his wise guy status. His death was bound to cause some ripples in the criminal underclass. Maybe shift the power balance. St. Cyr would have an heir apparent who would have to prove he was tough enough to keep it together.

Feds would be interested and so would the Organized Crime Unit. He had a brother in either place, but in the end, he decided to follow the body and called his sister, Hannah.

If she wasn't digging through St. Cyr's brain, she'd know who was—and where they'd be sending the pathology report. He needed to talk to whoever would get that report. She was—he flipped through the texts—the only one who hadn't texted him. Either she hadn't heard about the shooting, or she was digging through someone's brain.

He went into an unoccupied room to make his call. Shut the door, just in case he had a lot of explaining to do. He half expected to get her voice mail and had his pitch ready. It took him a minute to realize he had the voice, not the mail.

"Alex?" This was delivered with a hint of impatience.

"Yeah. Sorry." Funny how almost every conversation with his sisters started or ended with an apology. Ninety percent of the time he didn't know why. It was a bad habit. Sometimes it saved time, though he suspected his sisters had started to figure it out. When they did, it wouldn't be pretty. "Long day."

"Really? I wouldn't know."

"Sorry." Really bad habit.

"I've got a corpse waiting."

"Not St. Cyr?" Would the cutters fight over the body? Or try to pass the brain?

"Yeah. Lost the toss."

"He's one of the three wise geezers." It was historic. Not to mention a happy day. One down, two to go. He felt a twitch again at the thought of Nell having contact with two out of three. In one day, too. Had to be some kind of record.

"It's a bullet to the brain." A pause. "You'd better not let Dad hear you call them geezers."

"They're older than he is." He did some math. Okay, a little older than Zach. Not that old age had made them less deadly. If anything it had made them worse. But they'd been around longer than Alex had been alive. He tried to think of a way to ask that wouldn't catch her interest. Figured out there probably wasn't one. "Who you sending the autopsy report to?"

He swore he heard her straighten to attention. Or maybe he just felt it coming across the ether.

"Why?"

"I might have some information relevant to the case."

"You sound like a snitch."

He did. "Need to know."

She sighed. "The Feds and OCU are still duking it out. Last text from Ben, he'd offered to arm wrestle Frank for it."

"Frank won't go for that." He'd lose. This brother didn't like to wrinkle his clothes.

"He is less susceptible to the taunting dare than most of you."

Alex let this possible side swipe pass since "most" might exclude him. Frank was a cerebral s.o.b. Good fit for the feds. "So for now, it's Ben's case."

Frank probably had someone working on a court order.

That was at least one Baker too many on the case. Bad enough when a case was twice "Baked," but a triple?

None of them would want big brother sticking a toe in. They wouldn't believe he didn't want to be all up in their business. He had plenty of his own, not to mention keeping off his Lieutenant's bad side long enough to get a good night's sleep.

Complaints from other divisions or the feds would not help him achieve this goal. He looked at his watch, tired hitting him like a bat now that he thought about sleeping. "Look, Hannah—"

"How come everyone is texting me about you? Why do they want to know if I heard from you?"

He tapped the phone. "Sorry, what was that? Losing signal or battery or something. Bye."

"Alex—"

He disconnected and dialed Ben before Hannah could call him back. Since Ben was one of the sibs that had texted him, Alex wasn't surprised when his brother answered. Or his WTF greeting.

"I'm fine. And Laura knew that when she sent out the all points bulletin."

"You shouldn't have cut that hunk out of her hair, bro."

"She was eight and she needs to learn to forgive."

"Yeah, that'll happen."

Alex could hope. "You still on the St. Cyr case?"

"Your district doesn't have enough bodies? You gotta come looking for one of mine?"

"I don't want your body." He rubbed his face. "I have a

witness, someone who saw the old fart and his bodyguard, maybe not long before he got capped, but if you're not interested..."

He heard Ben's chair give a loud squeak. "The bodyguard got capped, too. Found him stuffed in the trunk of the geezer's limo."

Alex felt a mild stirring of interest and stomped on it. Not his problem. "My witness has a sketch of them both. She's one of those French Quarter artists."

"She?"

Alex ignored that. Gave him the address and rang off. Then he studied the messages that had piled up while he was on the phone.

Yeah, he'd made the evening news. The last was from Zach. He'd have ignored it, but he needed that ride home. He tapped his dad's name on the tiny screen. One ring and his dad was on the line, going from zero to chewing his butt in two seconds.

"How come you can't go a whole day without getting shot at?" He didn't wait for an answer. "I got everyone and their dog calling me, and what do I have to tell them? My son has not bothered to call and tell his old man he's still breathing. I realize you're all grown up, too big for your britches is more like..."

Alex waited it out. His laconic dad didn't get wound up often and he only got this pissed when he was worried.

"And why the hell is Curly Gastonieau burning up my line trying to reach you?"

Alex straightened. It was a good question. He wished

he had an answer. Gastonieau was his dad's old partner. Not only that, he'd been retired longer, so he had less reason than most to be burning up phone lines.

Alex lowered the phone and did a quick scan of his missed calls. There was one number that showed up a lot. No ID since Gastonieau wasn't in his contacts. No reason for him to be there. Those calls hadn't started until after the news, though.

"Maybe he's worried, too," Alex offered without conviction. "If he calls again, tell him I'll get back to him when I can."

"Look, bubba—"

"Dad. I gotta a few more things related to the shooting to deal with and I'm done." Boy was he done. He rubbed his face again. "I'm gonna need a lift. Might be able to catch one with Ben—"

He stopped but not in time. At least he hadn't mentioned Frank. He might be meeting him before the night was over if he got his court order tonight.

"You're meeting Ben."

Could almost feel the old man's brain spinning with questions. He knew what Ben did, knew what Alex did. Knew when their twains should meet and when they shouldn't.

"Nothing to do with the shooting. Something else. But if he's busy—I'm not far from the house. I'm on St. Charles. If you're not busy." With Leslie is what he didn't want to say, so he didn't.

"What's the address?"

Alex gave it up again. Almost he asked his dad about the three wise geezers, but caught himself in time. It would just stoke Zach's curiosity, keep them on the phone longer. Not that he knew what to ask. It was a pity they didn't all shuffle off together.

Two wise geezers didn't have the same ring. Afoniki might be too mean to die. Word on the street was Calvino had been trying to clean up his image. He'd been in the paper a lot surrounded by kids. If Alex had any kids—which he wouldn't—he sure wouldn't want them around that creepy old geezer.

It made him want to snort to hear the press call St. Cyr a "businessman."

Guess it was libel to call him anything else, since he hadn't done time since juvvie. None of his people had ever flipped on him or managed to get the drop on him. Until now.

He could almost feel the unease in the air from the sudden power vacuum. He tried to remember if he knew who was St. Cyr's next in line, but his brain slowed to a tired crawl. He needed food and sleep.

He sniffed. Food. He had just enough strength to follow his nose...

CHAPTER FIVE

"**D**oes he have a brother?" Sarah murmured, when Alex stepped out to take another call.

She'd come home about halfway through the cavalcade of leftovers Nell had dug out of the fridge. Her brows had risen, but she'd tucked in without doing more than murmur a greeting.

"He's got six," Nell told her, "and six sisters."

Not much surprised Sarah, but that did. "You're kidding."

Nell gave a shrug. She'd had several hours to get used to the idea, well, as used to it as one could. She went back and forth between wanting, and not wanting to meet the dad. It felt historic and awkward. Already she pictured him as a zucchini, which made her blush before she met him. So yeah, be better if they didn't meet.

"Wow."

Their gazes met and they both grinned.

"Seven brothers. They can't all be single."

Nell didn't know the relationship status of his brothers. She didn't know Alex's status, though he seemed single. He hadn't mentioned a wife when she asked for the kiss. He hadn't kissed her either. Which brought her back to uncertain. She looked up and caught Sarah on her smart phone. "What are you doing?"

"Looking them up on Facebook."

"Oh." Of course she was.

"Says he's divorced. Doesn't seem to post here himself. Just his sisters taunting him."

"So why don't you make a move on him?" She hoped the question sounded casual. This wasn't the first time she'd had to watch a guy she found interesting go for Sarah. It was the first time it mattered. She'd get over it. Sarah was more family than friend.

Sarah looked up. "I gave him my come-hither look when he came looking for you. He didn't."

Nell found this a little too heartening, so she rose and started clearing debris. Usually Sarah didn't have to get to the hither part of her come-hither look. She opened the dishwasher and started loading plates. "Are you sure?"

"Oh, sweetie."

"Then he must be involved with someone." Or he swung the other direction. Which meant she'd imagined everything and totally embarrassed herself...

"Usually don't like *spoilers, sweetie*, but in this case..." Sarah drew the moment out. It was what she did. "It's you he's interested in."

Nell spun around, found Sarah looking at her with amused affection. "Because of the shooting, not—" She stopped. "It's been a strange day. I'll be glad when it's over."

She almost meant it. Ninety percent meant it. Ten percent kept hoping—well, that ten percent needed a reality check. Dang, she was tired. She checked the time. It wasn't as late as it felt. The aches and the scrapes launched a cacophony of complaints about that, too.

"Do we have any ibuprofen?"

Sarah indicated a location and Nell crossed to it.

"They're all varying degrees of not married," Sarah murmured, her attention directed down at her phone.

She heard the sound of footsteps in the hall. Nell turned, the bottle in hand, as a strange guy peered in.

"I knocked. The door wasn't locked..."

Nell studied him. Not completely strange. "You're one of the brothers."

He was a variation on a theme. He had almost the same build as Alex, though he was younger, a bit leaner. His coloring trended fairer, though he wasn't blonde.

He grinned. He had the charm down pat. Was it from the dad? Was that how he'd convinced some woman to pop out thirteen kids?

"I'm Ben." His gaze assessed her, a bit cop, a bit brotherly curiosity, and a little bit of something she didn't recognize. "You the she who might have seen something?"

Nell nodded, though not with certainty. What had Alex told his brother about her?

"You going in or coming out?" Alex appeared behind Ben, giving him a brotherly nudge into the room.

Ben turned and gave him a once over. "No visible holes."

"They're all in my truck."

"Any idea who you pissed off?"

It wasn't that much comfort that Alex's brother thought the bullets had been meant for Alex, too. Not that she wanted them to be for her. She didn't want anyone gunning for either of them.

She blinked. How was it she'd wandered into a mystery? She wasn't Miss Marple. She was too young and not nearly nosy enough.

Sarah put her phone down, rising from her place at the end of the long table, her come and her hither both fully deployed. It hit an unprepared Ben, who hithered her direction with admirable dispatch.

"Ben Baker. And you are—"

"The roommate of the she who might have seen something." He blinked. She took pity on him. "Sarah Burland. This is my kitchen."

Ben didn't look at the kitchen. He did take the hand she'd extended. "Very nice."

Sarah flicked Nell a brief, satisfied grin, before turning back to Ben. Alex gave his brother an irritated look. Nell used the distraction to knock back the pills, then returned to table clearing.

When Ben gave the debris a longing look, Sarah

shelved the come hither for the practical. "Would you like something to eat?"

"I had a bagel at eleven." He added a pathetic look.

"Grab a chair."

While she made her food magic—and it was magic—Alex showed Ben the sketch of Nell's far too interesting day. Ben's brows arched and he studied Nell with professional interest.

"Afoniki and St. Cyr?"

Sarah spun around, but Nell shook her head, with a "later" look.

Sarah wouldn't be happy to find out her client was some mobster guy. Though it did explain Dimitri's bad boy vibes. And possibly his odd behavior. She considered it and decided, no, it didn't.

Ben studied the page for what felt like a long time, then glanced at Nell.

"You're good."

"Thank you." Nell felt her cheeks warm.

"I told you she was," Alex said.

He had? Nell's cheeks warmed some more.

Ben shrugged. "But that's not the bodyguard."

"He's not his usual one," Nell objected.

"You didn't mention he wasn't the same guy—" Alex interrupted.

"I didn't think about it until now." At the look on his face she added, "How would I know the turnover rate for bodyguards?"

"Could be the shooter," Ben interrupted. He tapped

the face. "This sure isn't the guy we found in the trunk." He frowned. "I wonder if he sucked at his job or—"

"—he was the one who capped him," Alex finished.

It was a good thing she was already sitting, because her knees went soft. Nell looked at Sarah. Had she been yanked to her feet by a killer? It was bad, very bad to see killers, before or after they did their killing. Sarah looked worried now, too.

"Do you think Nell is a witness..." Sarah stopped, as if she couldn't finish.

"But he didn't act like a killer." He'd been annoyed, no doubt about that, but he hadn't looked—wouldn't he have done something? Maybe tried to find out who she was? Not hurried her along so he could get to his killing. "He acted like a real bodyguard."

Both men gave her a look.

"Well, he looked and acted like I'd think a real bodyguard would act. And he didn't act like I'd foiled his evil plans." Which she hadn't foiled if he had been the killer. "I couldn't have been the only person to see them there." Though she might be the only one to draw them together.

"It's a fair point," Ben admitted.

Nell felt compelled to point out, even though she shouldn't have had to. "He's probably on someone's YouTube channel by now."

"Look at the drawing again," Alex told his brother.

Nell, Sarah, and his brother bent over the drawing. Nell looked at Sarah who shrugged. To Nell it just looked like her drawing. Ben met Alex's gaze, a frown between well-marked brows. In that instant, they looked very alike. Nell itched to grab the sketchbook and draw them.

Ben leaned back in his chair, his gaze stabbing her way, then at Sarah. "Let's start with Afoniki, if you wouldn't mind?"

Sarah's expression cooled. "Dimitri is a client, or rather his uncle is. Dimitri is the go-between."

"Aleski Afoniki is—"

"—giving a dinner party. We cater dinner parties." Her gaze had narrowed considerably.

"He's also a mobster, a wise guy, Sar," Nell broke in.

Her brows shot up. Then lowered as her expression shifted to thoughtful. "That would explain it."

"Explain what?" Ben asked.

"His bad boy thing." Sarah frowned. "Didn't know he was that bad, though."

It was weird that Nell hadn't liked him, but she also hadn't gotten the same level of creepy from him as she had from St. Cyr and his henchman. Right off they'd made her think *Sopranos* and she'd never seen the show. While Dimitri just made her want to send him to the principal.

"Do you think there's any risk for Nell?" Alex asked.

She looked from one to the other with an anxiety she couldn't hide.

Ben considered the question, half shrugged. "I'm going to take a picture of this," he pulled out his cell and focused in on the face of the so-called bodyguard, "and shoot it off to Frank. Save him the trip here and he'll owe me."

He grinned. Nell heard the whoosh of it leaving, then he put his phone back in his pocket.

"I got a heads up from a contact at the courthouse that he got his court order. His sup and my lieutenant are still arguing it out, but I'm too tired to care. Been a long day." He rubbed his face, letting a bit of tired show through. "What's this about you almost getting your truck jacked in the a.m.? And something about a girl—"

He stopped as a flush rose in Nell's cheeks. He looked from her to Alex, his brows doing a fast hike toward his hairline.

"I forgot I wasn't playing *Mario Kart* and tried to ram the boy," Nell admitted.

"What—" It was obvious there were still dots to connect, but his phone shrilled. He looked at the screen. "Frank. Excuse me." He rose and left the room.

Nell and Sarah looked to Alex.

"Brother. FBI."

"Oh. It's a jurisdiction thing." Another thing one learned reading mysteries. She studied Alex a bit thoughtfully. That must get interesting with a sibling. Or two. Or more?

"We're all in it, one way or another," Alex said, as if he read her thoughts. "Even the girls."

"Intense."

"Oh yeah." Now his phone buzzed, but it seemed to be a text. He scowled. "My dad. He's gonna get something to eat, then come get me."

Nell exchanged a look with Sarah, saw "awkward"

echoed in her gaze. Hopefully, if she did meet him, she'd be too tired to blush.

BEN HAD an odd look on his face when he came back into the kitchen. He stowed his phone and sat down.

"What?" Alex asked, wary, not to mention wasted, after a day of shock piled on weird, then covered with crap.

"They'll have to run ballistics, of course, but they think the douche bag in the sketch is the shooter. Had the same weapon on him."

Alex blinked. Did it not make sense because he was tired, or was it just that it didn't make sense? "They caught him already?"

"Someone did." Ben paused. "He's dead."

That was good news, well, three bodies wasn't good news for the people who had to process them, but three dead bad guys was better for the rest of the world. And it wrapped the case up in a neat package. He rubbed his face. He should be happy. He was too tired to be happy. "So Nell's sketch—"

"—connects the dots." The odd look didn't fade. "And she might be the last person to see them both alive."

"Except for whoever killed the killer," Sarah pointed out, a hint of steel in her tone.

"Of course." Ben offered the agreement a bit too fast.

Did he think Nell could have anything to do with those two? Alex studied his brother.

Yeah, he wondered. Alex supposed he'd have wondered too if—he hadn't known her a full day, he reminded himself. But—no way. She could have kept quiet about it all. She had no reason to tell him she'd seen St. Cyr. Almost no chance someone could have connected her to either of them.

"You didn't see anyone else around St. Cyr?" Ben asked.

Nell's brows arched. "It was the Moon Walk," Nell pointed out. "In the French Quarter."

"Lurking," he amended, looking as embarrassed as he should for asking such a dumb ass question, "or showing special interest in them?"

He wanted to tell Ben to look at Nell, really look at her, but at the same time he didn't want Ben to really look at her.

What if he noticed that there was, well, something about her? Ben had turned the charm on Sarah, which suited Alex just fine. Not that he was—okay, he might be interested. He was also too tired and too sore to sort it out.

Until he did, he would rather not have to fight his way through his brothers to get her attention. And if they thought he was, they'd delight in clouding the issue. No honor among the brothers. And the sisters would bet on the outcome—all of them against him.

He was the oldest and he'd changed their diapers.

Alex watched Nell consider the question. She opened her mouth. Shut it. Finally shook her head. "I don't even know how to answer that question."

Her blink was a bit owlish. He noted the signs of tired in her face, too, signs she hurt from the body slams they'd shared. And it wasn't fun sharing them either. It was a bad time to remember the kiss she'd asked for. Did she still want it?

"Surely you can't believe Nell had anything to do with this, other than as a witness?" Sarah's eyes narrowed.

"I have to consider all possibilities—"

"Really? They were total bad guys, so you have to consider the innocent bystander, instead of the hundreds, possibly thousands, of really bad people who had good—and bad—reasons to want both of them dead?" Sarah demanded.

Ben swallowed.

"Not to mention, it's not your case anymore," Alex pointed out. Hey, if the shoe were on the other foot, Ben would have taken the shot.

Ben's eyes narrowed a bit, then he shrugged and finally grinned. "I think I'll stop now." He looked down, realized he hadn't taken more than a couple of bites and dug in again, quickly cleaning his plate.

Sarah waited until he was done before slanting a look at Nell. "I'm feeling a need to get a little crazy."

Nell's eyes widened, she shook her head. "I'm too tired and too sore—"

Alex exchanged a puzzled look with Ben. Maybe one mixed with unease. He had that buzz in his ears that said he was between the second and third wind—and maybe the third wind wouldn't reach him. A bit like being drunk only without the painkilling effects. But not so buzzed he didn't sense danger incoming. Tired, drunk or sober, he knew women were always dangerous.

"One should never be too tired or too sore to get crazy." Her smile was slow and evil.

Alex might not know Sarah, but he knew the body language of a woman on the mischief war path. Nell stared at her friend, her look one a guy with six sisters was all too familiar with, so he was not surprised when her mouth curved up into mischievous as well.

He didn't expect the jolt to his gut from the smile. Cute. A cute woman could be the most dangerous kind of woman, except maybe one with a yen to get maternal. And cute often led to maternal—damn. He gave a mental shake. He should quit thinking now. It was starting to hurt.

Sarah considered them all, a finger tapping a pointed chin. "What do you think, Nell? Vocals or air instrument?"

Alex exchanged a glance with his brother. Way in the back, behind the buzz he heard: *Danger, Will Robinson.* But the sight of Nell's pursed lips as she gave amused consideration to the inexplicable question muted the warning.

"Vocals might hurt less, but," she waved her fists like they held something, "drumming is both cathartic and crazy fun."

Sarah grinned. "Excellent choice." Her gaze shifted to them. "Air guitars or vocals—keeping in mind that singing along is required, while staying on key isn't. In fact, we adore dreadful. It's crazy making fun."

Ben exchanged a puzzled look with Alex. "Um, air guitar?"

"Yeah, that for me, too." Alex wasn't sure what he'd agreed to. His tired brain was slow to assemble the clues. Crazy. Vocals or air instrument. Drumming...surely they weren't planning—Sarah made her way to a drawer and pulled out a spoon.

"I'll do vocals then." She struck a pose, the spoon angled like a...microphone. Then dropped it to tap the spoon against her grinning mouth.

"We don't usually have a four-person band. Need to pick the right song..." She headed for a small speaker set up and inserted her smart phone. She appeared to consider and discard several choices. "D'oh!" She flashed Nell an impish look. "So obvious."

His brain said no way in hell, but the words didn't make it out of his mouth before the music started booming. He wasn't tired enough to not care, Alex noted, but he had been side-swiped by something worse. He wanted to kiss the girl and was willing to play air guitar to do it. It was crazy, but Nell's grin was an invitation to crazy he couldn't turn down.

Ben rose, giving himself a shake, as if it loosen up. Alex shot a warning look at his brother. "Cell stays in your pocket." He wanted no YouTube videos or pictures on Facebook.

The look Nell exchanged with Sarah reminded him of his sisters. They'd made a sort of family, he realized. He knew Nell had no one, but if Sarah had family, she'd still made room for Nell. Family wasn't all bad. His would like this—he blinked.

Yeah, tired was a lot like drunk. Only tired hurt more. He was a bit surprised to find himself standing, too, taking his place in the "band." His thoughts started to spin off as the music for *Bad Moon Rising* began to thump out of the speakers, loud enough to rattle the cups on the table.

It should have hurt. It didn't hurt enough. He could have left. He was a grownup. No one could make him do things—okay his sisters made him do things all the time. Was that why he started to "play" his guitar? Might be. And it might be a bad case of crazy. Or it might be Nell.

He'd sort of figured a librarian would be shy, maybe a bit inhibited. She didn't look either as she kicked in with her air drums. Good sense of comic timing. Seemed like they all vied for truly awful.

It was as infectious as a cold. Something you caught whether you wanted to or not.

Ben, who never minded what anyone thought of him, riffed like he was a member of CCR. And suddenly it didn't matter that they were awful or goofy or tired. It was fun. And it probably hurt less than if he'd tried to slide down that banister....

He and Ben did rival air riffs, his eyes closed as he felt the music. And when he opened them there was his dad. And Curly Gastonieau.

The band froze, but the music kept going, a perfect compliment to the look on Bubba's face. Why did he look so grim? It's not as if air guitar was a crime. If anything

Curly looked more shocked than Zach. Damn near white as a ghost.

The music cut off, the silence both deep and weird.

Curly swallowed, tried twice before he managed a hoarse, "You look just like your mama."

Nell shook her head, frowned. "What?"

"Is your mama," he had to swallow to finish the question, "where is she?"

"My *parents* passed two years ago."

He half flinched back. "I need—"

The look in her eyes should have dropped him where he stood. It did rock him back on heels, clearing the way so she could stalk out.

"That went well," his dad said into the uncomfortable silence, giving Curly his destroying angel look that Alex had been on the receiving end of a few thousand times. And a few seconds ago.

Alex felt a need to get away. To help Nell. He made a move to follow, but Sarah held up a hand.

"I'd better take this one." Her gaze shifted toward his dad, studied him for several seconds, then shifted Alex's direction, her brows lifting.

"My dad," he muttered, not sure why he felt awkward or why that put a slight flush in her cheeks.

"Indeed." She followed Nell out, leaving behind a deep, and uncomfortable silence.

～

NELL STIFFENED at the sound of footsteps coming up the stairs toward where she sat, tracing the patterns in the spindles. She'd run out of steam just past the second landing. She relaxed when she saw Sarah, who sighed, then lowered herself onto the stair next to Nell.

"I told you not to choose the attic."

Nell nodded sheepishly. She shifted her tush a bit. "Thinking of sleeping here tonight." Her butt was already asleep. One of her legs, too.

Sarah angled, so that the wall supported her, her expression a bit too complicated to parse. What was worse than tired? Because she was so there.

Nell studied the spindle she fingered. Unlike the two men, it wasn't hard to parse. She wrapped her hand around cool wood and stroked up, then down. Saw cartoon eyes and a toothy scowl form in the spindle shape.

"You all right?"

All right was so subjective. She'd met people who thought it was a tragedy if they broke a nail. On the other hand, her mom always told her, "If you're not dead or hungry, then you're all right." By those criteria, she was freaking awesome.

So why had she felt so desperate to get away from that man? It wasn't what he said, at least not totally. She did look like her mom. The fact that they were in New Orleans, and he knew that didn't mean anything.

Lots of people passed through Waipiti on their way to, or from, Yellowstone Park. And a bunch of them had shopped at the Wal-Mart where her mom had worked. A little weird for one to notice her mom and then notice she looked like her...to remember...

No, the panic hadn't come from what he said, but from how he looked at her. As if the sight of her horrified him. Scared him in some way.

She half-shrugged, half nodded. "I'm fine. Tired."

Done getting knocked down. Done getting up. She might have to crawl to her room or maybe just to the next landing.

"Speaking of people looking like people, did you see their dad?"

Nell looked over at that. "Does he look..." ...like the father of thirteen...

"You'd never know his still waters ran that deep."

"Thirteen kids, his waters don't get to be that still," Nell had to point out. "Did you blush?"

She nodded.

"Awkward."

"Truly." Sarah chuckled.

Nell giggled. It helped ease the knot in her tummy. "That might be our most embarrassing moment ever..."

Surely a record? They'd been a band a long time, so there were lots of contenders for most embarrassing.

They'd started after surviving the worst run of finals ever. After days with no sleep, they were maybe a step from zombie-ness. They'd had to do something or burst. They did both. Half the dorm had pelted them with popcorn for being so bad, the other half had joined in.

One thing she knew to her toes, was if you did bad

karaoke in your underwear with someone, you were friends forever. Over the years, they'd worked the kinks in, milking it for maximum embarrassment factor. Tonight might have been the pinnacle.

Sarah laughed. "It was a score. The guys helped boost our suckage factor by a really big number."

That made Nell laugh and then wince. It hurt, but not so much she stopped, at least not until Sarah sobered. "What?"

"Alex started to follow you, but I told him to let me."

Good choice. "Not going back in there. I'm done. Three times is more than enough for one day."

Sarah frowned. "Three...what?"

Oh yeah, she'd missed the *Cliff Notes* on her three impacts, so Nell caught her up.

Sarah stared at her. "Someone shot at Alex?"

"He is a cop. People do shoot at them."

"Indeed. In that case, I can see why Alex is worried, but why is the guy who isn't the dad so freaked out?"

Unease spiked again as Nell remembered the look in the guy's eyes as he asked about her mom. She shrugged.

"Did you ever wonder..."

Nell shifted so she could look the question she didn't have the energy to ask. The world had gotten fuzzy around the edges. Seriously fuzzy.

"...why you never managed to visit here until..."

Nell considered the question with as much energy as she could muster. Had she wondered? Yeah, but not nearly enough. She didn't remember thinking their opposition was about New Orleans. She had wondered if they had issues with Sarah. Or cities.

"They didn't like cities." She frowned, traced some more patterns in the spindle. "You'd think they'd gone to Oz on a tornado as kids. No place like home was their mantra."

Weird that two home bodies had managed to have a daughter with a secret longing to fly to the moon—or at least the coop. A coop that turned out to be rented. Had they left her a house, it would have been harder to leave.

The lack of money, well, that wasn't a surprise. There'd never been a lot of that. She shifted uneasily. Did it matter? The look in that man's eyes seemed to say that yes, it did.

"I thought it was me they didn't like," Sarah admitted, her look a bit wry.

"There were times when it seemed like they didn't like much," Nell admitted, "but they never minded when you came to visit me." That she knew of anyway.

"Aren't you curious to know why he's here? Why—" Sarah stopped.

"I'm too tired to be curious." Okay, not the whole truth. Sarah's gaze called her on it. "Okay, maybe a little," she hesitated. "I guess I thought all the people who knew them were in Wyoming." She made a frustrated sound, rubbing her face. "It has to be a mistake." She looked at Sarah. "Did you see how...freaked out he looked?"

"Yeah." She tipped her head to the side. "I'll make him

go away until morning. If that's what you need. If you'll get any sleep."

Nell didn't have to say it. Sarah knew her capitulation look. She rose, held out her hand. "Come on. Let's shrink this problem down to a manageable size."

CHAPTER SIX

Left alone in the kitchen, Alex looked at Zach, not sure what to ask.

"I did knock," Zach said. "Guess you didn't hear it."

Color scored Alex's cheeks as Curly grabbed a chair, sank into it like he needed it. Without consultation, he and Ben chose the opposite side of the table, where they could keep an eye on the door, even though it was too little and way too late.

Zach picked the head of the table, his chair squeaking when he pulled it out.

Alex had questions, but Curly Gastonieau looked like he'd aged twenty years in two minutes. Lines cut deep into his gray face and sweat glistened on his bald head. His mouth was set in grim lines. He didn't look at anyone, just stared ahead like the zombies were coming for him.

He rubbed his upper lip, his hand showing a tremor when he lowered it back to the table.

Without speaking, Alex rose, found a glass and filled it with water. He carried it back and set it down in front of Curly. He looked old and tired and scared and his hand shook when he lifted the glass to his mouth, but it seemed to help.

Just when Alex had decided that Nell did not intend to come back, he heard footsteps out in the hall. Sounded like two sets, but his insides didn't ease until he saw her with Sarah. They all scrambled to their feet, his dad and Curly moving a little slower.

Nell's gaze met his as she paused in the doorway, a slight flickering of something across her face before this who-yelled-in-the-library look replaced it.

He ignored the shiver of remembered trouble snaking down his spine, reminded himself it wasn't for him, and pulled out a chair for her. Ben pulled out one for Sarah, putting them all on the opposite side of the table from Curly.

It felt a bit unfair, but Alex got a murmured "thanks" from Nell when she'd made her way past Curly to the chair. Silence settled over the room once more. Nell appeared to gather herself in, and only then did she look at Curly, who had watched her with a weird mix of horror and fascination.

"Maybe you could do some introductions, Alex," Zach prompted.

"Nell Whitby. Sarah Burland." Alex knew he sounded

terse. "Nell, Sarah. My dad, Zach Baker. And Curly—William Gastonieau. They were partners when my dad was NOPD. They're retired now," he finished, not sure why.

Zach looked annoyed, and maybe worried. Curly just looked shell-shocked.

No one said hi or how do you do. Nell did take her gaze off Curly long enough to nod at Alex's dad.

Maybe two old cops couldn't help putting on their interrogation faces, though Alex wasn't sure who was supposed to talk or what they planned to ask.

Curly lifted the glass again, with one hand this time. His color went from dark to light gray. "Damn, you look like—"

"So you said." Nell's voice cut him off. Her tone encouraged him to move on. "They say everyone has a twin."

Something like respect filtered into Curly's eyes. "Some of your daddy in you, too."

Alex watched her pulse give a kick just under her chin. He realized that he'd stereotyped her again, equating librarian with gentle and a bit frail. Not sure why he'd done it—at their first meeting she'd tried to ram a carjacker with her bike. She kept surprising him. In a good way, but he didn't like surprises, even good ones. He liked to see stuff coming.

Curly looked down, his hand turning the glass with his thumb. He licked his lips before asking, "What did she tell you—" He stopped, rubbed a forehead gleaming with sweat.

Alex shot Zach a look, wondering if they should call an ambulance. Zach stared at Curly, his gaze on his "bore to the core" setting. Curly didn't seem to notice. Or didn't seem able to take his gaze off Nell.

Nell took a long, slow breath. She must be bursting with questions, but she didn't speak. She looked and then arched her brows a little, like she didn't know how it was his business.

She would have made a good cop. She'd have perps spilling their guts in record time. Curly cracked first. He rubbed his face. Alex could almost hear the gears turning inside his head.

Curly hesitated, then pulled out his wallet. He thumbed through the contents and extracted what appeared to be a small photograph, which he flipped at Nell. She didn't reach for it, didn't look at it at first.

Alex slid it close enough so he could see it.

Sarah leaned in to look, too.

It was small, aged, and creased. Color had faded a lot. The girl in it looked like Nell, though younger and like it had been one of those pretend vintage photographs. Except it wasn't pretend and the shot was candid, the girl's head half turned as if in answer to a hail, but not from the photographer. Wrong direction.

"She looks like you," Sarah offered to the silence gods, her tone mild.

Nell's lips tightened, but she didn't pick it up.

Alex did that. The background didn't look like Wyoming. Wrought iron gate, lots of flowers, big house almost hidden by trees and crap.

Ben reached out. "May I?"

At Nell's slight nod, he handed it to Ben, who studied it. "Could be wrong, but that looks like Calvino's place in the background."

Nell inhaled, to speak or protest, he wasn't sure, but her lips clamped shut. Zach took the photograph from Ben. He didn't look happy. He also didn't look surprised. What did he know that he wasn't sharing?

"Antonia Calvino." Curly twitched as Zach added, "I remember—that case."

Curly's chin lifted, though his color had gone bad again, apology and defiance in his eyes. Then he seemed to deflate, his gaze settling on the glass he had both hands wrapped around.

"What case?" Alex managed to bite back the swear words that tried to crowd out after the question. Ladies were present and he wasn't sure his dad wouldn't put his head down in the sink with some soap. He'd have to let him. It looked like the old man had a head of steam with nowhere to go.

Zach's voice was grim as he set the photo down and pushed it toward Alex. "According to the newspapers, public records and the police file, Antonia—Toni—Calvino died in a car bomb. Along with her lover, Phillip St. Cyr. Both of them are tucked away in a couple of crypts last I knew."

There was a long silence as their side of the table processed this.

"*Romeo and Juliet?*" Sarah looked from Zach to Curly.

When Zach didn't speak, Curly shook his head. "It wasn't the love affair that bothered St. Cyr or Calvino."

"It bothered Afoniki. It threatened to upset the balance of power among the three families," Zach said. "One third of the empire was all right as long as no one else had more."

"Is that what set off the turf war?" Ben put in. "I remember hearing something—"

"It was short, but ugly," Zach said. "There were rumors at the time that the families came to some sort of peace deal after Pavel Afoniki got taken out."

Weird how the three names seemed to be linked, as if something more than crime kept drawing them together.

"Pavel was the heir apparent for Afoniki," Zach added.

"Balance was restored. Each family lost an heir, though —" Ben stopped, earning a questioning look from Nell. "Pavel was a nephew, not—"

"Bone of his bone?" Nell finished for him.

Zach half shrugged. "Criminal accounting is always on the fuzzy side."

Vague memories of hearing the story niggled at the edge of his tired brain. An heir for an heir. If that had been a flash point, then the families had gone to their corners and stayed there for over thirty years. Oh, the minor thug, here and there, had tried to dent the edges of their empires and fatally failed. Honor of a sort among thieves—until now? But if Nell was the pebble in the pond that Curly seemed to think, why did it take two years for any ripples to be felt?

There was more. Alex felt it. He saw it in Zach's gaze. And in the way Curly avoided Zach's gaze. Could a cold case ever really be cold in New Orleans? But even if something was trying to bubble up out of the ooze, what could it have to do with Nell? Unless she was the best actress ever, she hadn't known about her parents—if this was about her parents? He didn't blame her for not being convinced. People did sometimes have twins.

Nell leaned forward, cutting into the thick atmosphere to assert, "Whatever you think, you're wrong. That's not my mother. She worked at Wal-Mart. My dad fixed cars in a garage. They were high school sweethearts. None of this has anything to do with them. Or me."

Curly leaned back. He half shrugged. "Might be a coincidence. Stranger things happen. It doesn't matter. It's what they think, it's who they think you are that matters."

Curly had a point. It didn't matter what was, only what all the players thought it was, who they thought she might be. She might not know anything, but if she was the granddaughter, the lost heir to two very wealthy, very criminally minded families—all the sudden it didn't seem so crazy to think someone might be trying to kill her.

∾

IN A HAZY WAY, Nell knew that Alex and the others were discussing options. Arguing. Barking and puffing at each other. She wanted out, wanted to be alone more than anything. Well, except for getting that kiss. It was kind of shallow to be thinking about kisses right now.

The chance of it happening was beyond slim but it still seemed more likely she'd get kissed than turn out to be some kind of lost mafia kid.

It was too incredible, too improbable, too interesting to be true. She put a finger on the corner of the photo, as if touching it would make the unthinkable real, and pulled it to where she could see it again.

Something about the shot bothered her, though she was too tired to figure out what. Was it remotely possible that her mother had given up the mansion for a cabin in Wyoming? For a job at the Wal-Mart?

She looked up, caught hairless Curly staring at her.

Even if it were true—which it couldn't be—why did it freak him out so? Why would it matter now, so many years later? He didn't look worried. He looked scared to his toenails. Why had he kept that photo? Had this...Toni mattered to him? That made it even harder for her to believe this was about her mom.

She could accept that a child could never truly know a parent, but there was nothing in memory that could connect the mafia with her mom and dad. This Toni looked so young, so hopeful, and happy. The photo blurred, not unlike the past, Nell's aching head was almost a dead weight on her neck.

"I need to go to bed." She pushed her chair back and realized everyone was now staring at her. "Sorry."

"I'll walk you to your room." Alex rose, holding out a hand.

She took it. She needed it. She hoped he wouldn't regret the offer. It was a long way up. They took the first flight without speaking. He looked around.

"Where's your room?"

She pointed up. His brows arched. "Three more flights."

He might have sighed. Her vision was a bit wavy. "You really do like up."

"Not so much tonight." It was lovely when his arm slid around her waist. She leaned without shame. That she liked it didn't mean she didn't need the help. Her head drooped against his chest. She might have slept through a flight or two. She blinked when they stopped moving, a bit startled to find herself outside her door.

"Mind if I take a look around?"

Odd question, but she nodded. It had been a day filled with odd. Might as well end with it. He propped her against the wall, opened the door and reached in, flipping on the light. He stepped in, out of her sight. She gave in to the insistence of heavy lids, but she jerked them up when he spoke.

"Nice. I can see why you like it up here."

She blinked. He looked, she considered him a bit distantly, cop-ish again. Pity. Cop was even less likely to kiss her good night. He was rather dreamy as a cop, though.

A real mafia princess would know how to get a cop to kiss her. A real mafia princess wouldn't mind the danger, might even like it.

She studied him through half-mast lashes. He'd worn jeans this morning, too, but also a jacket and shirt. Didn't she remember a tie?

Now a tee-shirt hugged his chest. Alex's hands settled on the wall by her head, his dreamy self angled in a way that put his face closer to hers and everything melted away but him...

"Are you all right?" he asked, this cute frown between his brows.

"Would you kiss it better if I wasn't?" She jerked out of dreamy as the words kind of echoed in the hall. "I am so sorry. I did not mean to say that out loud—"

"Yes," he said, cutting her off. His mouth curved up, but his lids did this sexy droop. "To both questions."

It took Nell a minute to sort that out. She might have blushed a bit, as she considered a couple of responses. Thankfully she did not share them with the hall or him. Instead, she smiled, hoped it was inviting. If he didn't make his move, she was liable to drift off to sleep again.

She felt the shift of his gaze from her eyes to her lips. They parted, but not to talk. She was unable to take her eyes off his face as one hand settled on her waist, warm and firm. Then the other. Working together, they drew her away from the hall wall, toward the chest wall. Tiny bump as chest met chest. Nice bump. Her head tilted to the side, following an instinct as old as time.

His head, his mouth appeared to approach. Slow though. She hoped he wouldn't take too long. A of wave of tired was incoming like a tsunami—he got it. Or he got tired of slow, too. His mouth landed, fast and with just the right amount of hard. It didn't feel like a pity kiss—

Thinking sputtered. Or maybe it crashed and burned. She didn't need it anyway. Thinking was overrated. His arms tightened. Her arms snaked up around his neck, and maybe did a bit of tugging.

It was hard to know details as she spun off into a lovely swirl of sensation. Sort of like the Fourth of July. The kiss had some rockets red glare in there for sure.

He eased back. She was too tired to whimper. He smoothed her hair back, grinned a bit ruefully.

"You're done, aren't you?"

"I was done hours ago."

He opened some space between them but kept his hands on her waist. Good decision. Her knees had turned to overcooked noodles.

"Are you going to be okay?"

"You kissed it better. I have to be."

He chuckled, the sound of it both warm and husky. She had questions but was too tired to put the words into their proper order. "I guess I'll see you—"

"Yes," he said. He kissed her forehead, turned her door ward, gave her a gentle shove into the room, and then pulled the door closed.

She didn't move until she heard him leave. It felt kind of like a romantic movie moment, and she didn't want to spoil it just because she needed the bathroom down the hall.

BEFORE HE'D MADE it down one set of stairs, Alex knew one thing. He wasn't leaving. He'd kind of known it when he did a quick search, not just of Nell's room, but the whole floor. He knew it for sure when he searched the floor below and then the one below that.

He didn't know what the various crime families might do about Nell. He was pretty sure he knew what the various law enforcement agencies would do. Not much. Not without more information. A twitch in his gut would not be sufficient cause to deploy resources.

Alex had vacation time and he'd only recently been advised to use some, with forceful emphasis in fact. He wasn't worried about that. He was worried about being able to stay awake. He'd started stake outs with a bigger sleep deficit, but he'd been younger. He sighed. He'd sure been looking forward to a good night's sleep.

When he reached the kitchen, he was surprised to find Ben there, was even more surprised to find him alone. He arched a brow.

"Dad talked Curly into going home."

Alex nodded. It meant he'd have to call his dad and explain. Well, that would keep him awake for a while. He studied his brother, considering his approach.

"Been thinking," Ben said, shooting him a wary look, "I

might hang around for the night. Just in case you need some back up."

Alex was too tired to summon up more than mild relief. Wasn't so stupid tired he didn't know it had more to do with Sarah than him, but he was too stupid tired to feel offended. Or maybe he was stupid tired smart? And a little bit grateful for the backup?

"Does Sarah know we're staying?" He blinked a couple of times. "And dad?"

"I told Sarah—she's sorting out some pillows and blankets—and I'll call dad when he's had time to off load Curly."

Alex sank into an askew chair and rubbed his face. "Curly." Still having trouble wrapping his brain around Curly.

"Yeah." Short silence. "Do think he—" He stopped. "I looked it up. Antonia Calvino was seventeen when she died."

Alex frowned, not quite up to doing math. "Maybe he had a thing for Antonia's mom? She would have been about the right age, wouldn't she?"

Ben frowned. "Wasn't her photograph he's been carrying around for years—" he stopped. "Unless..."

Alex was a bit surprised to find he'd followed his brother's thoughts without too much trouble. If he was Antonia's real father....wow. Risky move.

"Hard to imagine, but I suppose it's possible." Was Curly shocked that Nell was in New Orleans or that he'd just found out Antonia Calvino didn't die thirty plus years ago? Nell didn't believe Antonia Calvino was her mother, he reminded himself. But if she wasn't Nell's mom, that was one big coincidence.

Ben was quiet for a minute, then he shrugged. "Not sure it matters..."

Alex didn't want to think about that. It opened up too much more to think about. Like, who had died in the car if the two wise kids hadn't? Who had lived? Both kids or just Toni? How much had Curly known?

No question he was involved in some way. There was no way to find out tonight how this might affect Nell. Her world had been rocked pretty hard today. Had he only known her one day? It didn't seem possible. It felt longer. It felt—crap, he was thinking about feelings.

He was just tired, punch drunk was all.

Sarah returned to the kitchen, worry knitting a line between her brows. "Are you sure you don't want to use a bedroom? There are plenty."

"Couch is fine," Alex said, pushing upright like the old man he was.

"Well, I piled some stuff on the couch in the small living room, the one you turned into phone central." She hesitated, then said, "Thank you." Both of them shifted. "If you need anything, I'm on first floor, second bedroom on the right." Another pause. "I'll see you in the morning and I promise you an awesome breakfast."

She left with a backward look at Ben.

"I'll take first watch," Ben said, then added in case Alex was inclined to argue, "I've not been on nights."

"I nosed through all the floors but this one on my way down. We should do a walk around. Been a lot of people in and out of this house today." Practically a parade. All that was missing was the brass band—he gave a mental twitch. If he wasn't careful, that might be the next air band. Brass instruments were, in his opinion, a lot harder to air play.

Aleksi sat at the back of the cold, gray room, his body curled in the wing backed chair like a spider in its web.

Dimitri always had to fight a sense that he was young again, small and back in his uncle's power, even after so many years, and so many of these visits.

Outside this room, he felt powerful. Outside he could forget he was the replacement heir. But once inside...at ninety the old man still had presence, Dimitri could concede as he strolled forward and settled in a chair without waiting for the gesture that had been permission in the past.

A gleam in the almost dead eyes had him leaning back, his legs crossed with seeming casualness, though he'd never be at ease, not now, not when his uncle was dead.

If the years of waiting, the years of watching his uncle watch his back, had taught him nothing else, it had taught him that there would always be someone watching for weakness. Waiting for a relaxing of the guard. Someone like him. The old man annoyed, but by damn, he had to respect him for surviving for so long.

He met the old man's gaze now, playing their little power game, determined not to be the first to give in. He had a feeling he'd win this one.

For once, he had something his uncle wanted more than he wanted to win.

In the silence, the old grandfather clock counted off the seconds, since not even traffic penetrated to this inner room. When he'd first come here, he'd hated that clock. Now he appreciated the power of that steady sound in a waiting silence.

"You are late."

"I had business. You will have seen the news." And if he hadn't, his sources would have fed him the news of St. Cyr's death. Like a deep, dark well, the muck at the bottom had been stirred by St. Cyr's fall.

It had erased the illusion of balance, the pretense that there was peace between the three empires. Whatever had held the three old men in check for so long was gone.

A turf war would not be good for business in the short term, but for the chance of picking a few plums off the St. Cyr organization, Dimitri might risk it. The locals and the Feds had made a point of letting him know they wouldn't like a turf war, of course. As a professional courtesy. It was all so civilized, except when it wasn't.

For the long term, they'd all need to flex their muscles. How far Dimitri got to flex his was, regrettably, still up to his uncle.

Dimitri brought the tips of his fingers together and considered the old man. It was possible he was involved in the hit, though he couldn't see a reason for him to disturb the balance of power now.

There was no reason, no change—except for the woman. She was an...oddity but a catalyst? Based on her file, that seemed improbable, though he wouldn't rule out anything where his uncle was concerned.

"Executed like a senile old man on the Moon Walk. I expected better of Phin," Aleksi said, his voice so low that the comment might be meant for himself.

It was a surprise St. Cyr had gone first. He was not the youngest, but also not the oldest. In their line of business it was not common to die peacefully in bed, but it was an odd move on St. Cyr's part, getting caught out in the open like that.

Dimitri had never heard his uncle call him Phin before. Almost he asked. But when had his uncle ever answered a question, particularly a personal one?

"We all worked for Zafiro, you know."

It seemed the old man was in a reflective mood. It was not a mood Dimitri particularly enjoyed, but this time it might prove useful. In the past there might be clues to the present situation. He nodded, but still did not risk speech.

"He groomed us to take over." The old man's lips twisted in what might have been a smile. "We were supposed to fight for it. He wanted blood, liked the battles. We all wanted it but...we also wanted to live. So we played for it. Poker. We played to a standstill. We were evenly matched. Then, it dawned on us that we didn't have to play it the way Zafiro wanted. If we worked together, we all got something. A gentleman's agreement." He gave a short, nasty bark of laughter. "Of course, Zafiro had to go."

It took all Dimitri's self-control not to react.

The rheumy old eyes from fixed on him. "You wondered, didn't you, how it worked? Only twice before did it almost come apart."

Twice? Dimitri knew about the turf war that had cost all three their heirs. He could guess what had created the uneasy bond that kept the peace now. From what he'd heard about Zafiro, though, he'd have wanted blood. The more spilled, the happier he'd have been. Only he hadn't planned on the spilled blood being his. Had they all been in on the kill?

It was the only way to hold them all in check, he decided. And there'd be a trigger of some kind, an information release when one of them died. They all needed incentive to keep each other alive. But surely, as they aged —they'd grow more paranoid, he decided, somewhat grimly.

There was no statute of limitations on murder. Their age wouldn't protect them.

"They thought I was behind it."

Dimitri blinked. What—? Zafiro? That didn't seem right. Then he got it. He'd moved on to Toni and Phil.

"Who was behind it?" The question flattered, he hoped.

Aleksi smiled grimly. "No way to know for sure, of course, but Phin bit off more than he could handle when he married Helenne."

"Her own son?" Dimitri found the story unexpectedly intriguing, though he knew many parts were missing. And that those were probably the most important parts.

"She wouldn't have liked her son sniffing around Ellie Calvino's kid." The hooded gaze shifted his direction. "Never let business get personal. And never let a woman into your business."

"Business is business." Dimitri said what was expected.

"Exactly." Dimitri endured a long scrutiny, was rewarded with a twisted smile. "You're a cold bastard. Like me."

Something was wrong, off. He'd said the words before, but now he mouthed them, like a mantra, or to keep from saying the wrong thing?

He wanted Dimitri to bring the woman up, so he wouldn't have to. Was this the key? Or a key?

The maze of his uncle's life was deep and dark, no more so than right now, despite this rare burst of confiding. And, for the first time, he sensed that the real power had finally shifted his direction. So he waited, suddenly comfortable with the silence, as he'd never been before.

"You have seen her."

There was nothing new in his uncle's voice and yet...he allowed himself a slight, very slight nod. He'd had time to consider the meeting, to figure out how to turn his lack of success into something that would play better with his uncle. But if he gave it up too quickly, his uncle would know.

"What..." a pause as the old man took a drink of water "...was she like?"

Dimitri did not move, but his eyes widened some. This was not a question he'd anticipated from the old man who never, ever got personal. He sorted through his confused impressions from the meeting, wondering which would play the best. He did not want to lose this edge.

"She was..." he shrugged, "...ordinary, though..." He stopped, as his uncle's hands gripped the arms of his wing backed chair. He did not think he wanted to tell his uncle she'd accomplished something no other woman had. He'd walked away remembering her.

"Though?" His uncle prompted. Surely a first.

He shrugged. "We were interrupted. I believe she'll be handing out canapés at your party, if you plan to go through with it."

His uncle took another sip from his glass, then set it on the table at his elbow. One finger stroked down the side of the glass, lids and stoic expression hiding his thoughts.

Dimitri knew this silence, fought its insistence, the question an irritating itch in the back of his throat. To ask was to give power back to his uncle. Or to let him believe he had it back? Yes, that was it. Something about Nell Whitby had opened a vein of weakness in the old man's fortress.

"Who is she?"

"She is no one." The heavy lids lifted, the cold gaze stabbing bright into the dim room, daring him to argue with the words.

"It is as I thought," Dimitri said, and knew he lied. That they both lied.

She was not yet someone, but she was not no one. The deep well of the past shifted again, uneasy as it had not been in memory. Because his uncle watched him, he could not shift against the chill creeping down his back.

He did not know how or why she mattered, just that she did. And the answer lay not in her life, or in her file, but in his uncle's past. It was a dangerous place to probe but this time, it might be worth the risk.

CHAPTER SEVEN

Nell woke to pale sunlight trickling through gaps in the blinds. She eyed it with disfavor. It felt kind of pissy of Mama Nature to weigh in with sun today. The least she could do was throw some clouds into the sky. Maybe a little storm action. Not that unusual-for-spring heat was exactly the cheerful choice, but...

Nell sat up before she remembered why it was a bad idea. She rode the waves of ouch until everything settled into a low grumble. Then she rested her feet on the cool wood floor. That felt rather good.

She might have tried it for other achy body parts, but she wasn't sure she could get up twice. And her bladder had a standing date with the porcelain throne down the hall. It, more than the sun, was what had pulled her from sleep.

It was true that her dreams had not been so great she'd wanted to linger there. Waking or sleeping, she felt dogged. A cat person should not feel dogged. Particularly one who did not, at present, have a cat.

In the bathroom, she avoided making eye contact with herself in the mirror. She didn't need to confirm the bags under her eyes when she could feel them dragging down the upper part of her face. She concluded her date with porcelain, then turned to the shower. Maybe it would help ease the ouch factor.

When the water turned as cool as it could this time of year—didn't even need the hot water heater—she stripped and climbed in. She found it a bit win/lose. The water eased the sore muscles while making the scrapes sting fiercely.

Without enthusiasm, she applied soap and shampoo to the appropriate places, inducing another round of stinging. After rinsing and repeating, she leaned her aching head against the side, and while the water beat into sore spots, she eased open the angst flood gates and let herself think about yesterday.

Instead of a flood, angst trickled in a bit half-heartedly. Nell sighed. She'd always sucked at angst.

She turned her back to the wall now, shifting so the water didn't hit her face. She should have been able to get some good angst going. She'd dang near died yesterday.

She stared down at her chest. It looked the same as it had before she'd almost died. Not a lot there. She touched the targeted spot, but it didn't feel real. None of it felt real. Not the possibility someone might be trying to kill her or bald Curly's—why were bald men always called Curly —revelations.

Declarations? On the one hand was the photograph he had showed her. It could have been her in vintage get-up, she had to concede. But when she tried to picture her mom as a wise kid, her brain slammed into memories of her extremely ordinary, a bit on the plump side mom in her Wal-Mart checker uniform.

Those twains did not want to meet. They sure as shooting didn't want to shake hands or sit down for a catch up.

And how did her dad fit into bald Curly's reality? The one where her mom was a wise kid with a—she did not even want to think the *L* word.

She'd had no doubt her parents had loved each other, sometimes to the point of embarrassing. She had no desire to consider anything beyond that. Parental sex was—meh. Of course one knew it happened, but one didn't want to think about it.

Was it possible that her Dad wasn't her father? If her mom were this Toni, how likely was it that her dad was the...boyfriend? Wouldn't there have been some evidence of it?

The obligatory confession when she attained her majority? There were health history issues, and besides, her parents and secrets—there was that ordinary wall again. Hitting it hurt almost as much as hitting the ground.

Was she crazy? Or was bald Curly the crazy one? She knew who had her vote.

And—this was why she sucked at angst—why was her brain trying to bring in Alphonse? Maybe work on a story about, well, not wise guys. She wrote kids' fiction, but what if Alphonse had been adopted? Maybe his dad wasn't an artichoke after all?

Nell turned off the water, with another sigh. No wonder she couldn't get a good angst wallow going. But was it reality? Or denial?

Not without some reluctance—okay a lot of reluctance—Nell considered St. Cyr while she mopped water off her parts with a towel.

What had he believed? Had he believed she was his granddaughter? Was that why he'd come to the Quarter? Smiled at her? Tripped her? Yeah, that was grandfatherly. He had told her to wear a hat. That might be semi-paternal in a really lame way.

She rubbed her hair with the towel, then contained the damp strands in it, turban style. She wrapped another one around her middle, tucking it in where she wished she had more cleavage. She rubbed a circle in the steam clouding the mirror and studied her nose. She had gotten a touch of sun. Not what one expected a wise guy to worry about, but what should he have said?

"Nell, I am your grandfather," she intoned. One who wielded a cane instead of a light saber. "Right."

All roads led to ordinary. Even the scenery and signs were boring.

Auto mechanic.

Wal-Mart checker.

Joe and Ellen Whitby.

Mom and Dad.

Small town. Small lives.

Mom had loved lotions and soaps, but no signature scent for her. She went for the flowers. She couldn't grow them—total brown thumb—so she wore them. She used to tease Nell about her preference for coconut and lemon and vanilla.

"Always the food smells. You'd think we didn't feed you."

Mom didn't like flaunting her feelings, was more likely to scold than get mushy, but was quick to defend her family.

Dad had loved to tease Mom, get her wound up and then grab her and spin her around until she'd laughed and told him enough of that nonsense.

Nell had never seen him so much as glance at another woman, though they'd for sure glanced at him. In that unfair way of the universe, his years had rested more lightly on him than on Mom, but Nell had no evidence he'd noticed Mom getting older. He really did only have eyes for her.

At the funeral, everyone mentioned how they'd loved each other, that they'd have wanted to go together. Nell didn't know about that. Going together meant leaving her alone, but it was true she couldn't imagine one without the other. They'd loved each other.

They'd loved her.

She sat on the toilet seat and rubbed coconut lotion

into her skin, her movements as slow as her thoughts. What was fact? What was fiction? What was delusion?

Had Mom—*her mom*—had a first love? If St. Cyr thought Nell was his granddaughter, that meant Mom had gotten pregnant here. And then what? Met Dad after? She could believe her Dad would accept Mom, accept and love Nell as his own. But they'd told her they met in high school. And how did she fit their very ordinary into a world of mob families and, what, faked deaths?

She sighed. When you're little, normal is your world, your life, your family. Even if it was different from other kids, it was what it was. What was normal anyway?

There'd been differences. Things her friends had or did that she didn't. Like grandparents. Family dinners with relatives. Her friend Lil had a grandma who made paper dolls. It seemed like something she'd like to have, so she asked.

"No, you don't have a grandma," her mom had said and handed her a pile of clothes to put away.

Nell remembered thinking it was too bad. And not much else. She'd been six. Mom bought her some paper dolls and ended the longing, which had been more about paper dolls than grandparents.

There was that time she was supposed to bring baby pictures of parents and extended family to school to make a family tree. Then it hadn't troubled her that there were no pictures of extended family.

No pictures of her parents as kids. No pictures as babies.

Her mom had suggested she draw pictures instead. Had the teacher been surprised? Nell couldn't remember. No surprise her family tree had consisted of veggies. It's what she did.

Drew too much, didn't think enough.

Why hadn't she wondered about it? She'd gone through their things after—it was as if their lives started with Nell's birth. Okay, she'd been grieving. And she'd never noticed, so she'd never asked.

There might have been a reasonable explanation. A fire or something. Stuff did happen to fragile things like mementoes. Adults could be orphans.

But it was also true, as Sarah had noticed, that her parents had not wanted her to leave home. They'd raised her to be independent, so it was a bit of a shock to realize how close they'd managed to keep her.

Oh, she'd gone to college. She frowned, still not sure how it was she'd gone for library science instead of the art degree. What had they thought when she met Sarah? She'd wanted to visit her, had planned to several times, yet somehow hadn't. Had she been manipulated? And so skillfully she'd been annoyed, but not suspicious? Or had it been benign clinging? Not relevant to current events?

Singly, each of these oddities were little, kind of frail, pegs to hang a huge conspiracy onto. Together? She still wasn't sure they added up to anything but mildly odd, something they could have explained if they'd lived. People were allowed to be odd, to have quirks. To not be wise kids. To even look like people they weren't.

To look amazingly like a woman she wasn't, couldn't be.

Was this denial? Or inescapable reality? It's not like she could go ask the wise guys for a DNA sample. And what if they did turn out to be her long, lost family—

Family. What if she did have family? They couldn't all be bad, could they? If her mom had sprung from these people, well, look how she'd turned out.

Family. To not be so alone in the world. There was temptation. Was that why they'd kept their secrets? If they had them? Was she starting to believe? Or...hoping?

What did she want?

Wow, there was a question. If she could go back to yesterday morning, to not knowing...hard to believe the genie could go back in the bottle, but if she could, would she? One didn't become even a somewhat reluctant librarian without embracing knowledge, the quest for it thereof. So the answer to the question was a hesitant no. She wouldn't go back. Probably.

So that left forward. What did forward involve? A plan, she needed a plan. Her dad always said, when you feel out of control, make a plan. So...

Hmmm...

What did she need to know? Or what would she like to know?

Well, her dad. If this wasn't some huge mistake, she'd like to know if her dad was her dad and if he was this Phillip St. Cyr. And if he was....it was a story with missing parts.

It was natural to be curious, wasn't it? Was there a picture somewhere of Phillip St. Cyr? There had to be surely. Maybe on the internet, though that was a slim hope, since it hadn't existed when he supposedly died. And if she recognized him, that would make St. Cyr her nasty, and recently murdered, grandfather.

For a moment her mind boggled, literally, trying to mesh her mom with a wise kid on the run.

Did she, could she, have gangster relatives?

Despite the photograph, it didn't seem possible, couldn't be real. She'd browsed through her parents' papers after the accident, not with a great attention to detail since she'd been weeping, but she didn't recall an "open in case we die" letter.

It doesn't matter what you believe. What matters is what they believe.

What did they believe? Why hadn't St. Cyr talked to her if he thought she was his long lost granddaughter? He could have had her followed, she realized with a chill that did nothing to ease the aches or the pains.

The idea she'd been watched, her life turned over, was totally creepy. What had he learned? What did he fear? Could he fear? She bet he wondered what she was up to. He was a bad guy and they always thought people were up to something.

So, somehow, he saw what he thought was a face from the past. And once the look into her life was finished? What had he planned to do with what he learned? And that last day of his life? If he knew he was going to die—

Nell stiffened. He'd done something after he tripped her. He'd picked up her portfolio.

It seemed overly dramatic to think he'd used the moment of inattention by his possible killer to pass on the message he could have passed on when he wasn't about to die.

She jumped up, almost losing her towel. She re-secured it. It was crazy, illogical even, but it didn't hurt anything to look. She flung open the door...

...and came face to face with...

ALEX STARED MOROSELY at the rising sun wondering which would be harder. Getting the kinks out of his back or getting rid of the headache from too little sleep and too much thinking. Thinking was overrated, but in the dark reaches of the night, it was hard to stop.

He'd made the rounds, gone up some stairs, down some others, checked windows and doors, with worry balefully circling through his brain.

Was he overreacting?

Was he under-reacting?

Was he swimming into deep waters? Flailing in shallow?

That the answer to all questions was a resounding *maybe* did nothing for the headache. The darkness, night-time, made everything look bigger or feel worse. Not just because his dad said so. Experience taught the same. This was why he hated nights. Not that he was wild about days when he hadn't gotten enough shut eye. But nights made the bogeymen loom large. At least in the bright sun, problems shrank down to normal. Well, mostly normal. Okay, not very normal this morning.

The pile of troubles looked about as big as it had in the dark.

There was Nell.

There were the three wise geezers.

And Curly.

It was hard to make the normal case with a mix like that.

Three dead bodies—nothing new to a homicide cop—and a shooting.

Did any of that have anything to do with Nell? His gut said not the bodies, and it was conflicted on the shooting. Logic? It was wandering through the headache, looking for a way out. And the doubts kept pouncing. Night made the tired brain easy prey.

He'd underestimated her at least a couple of times. She was hard to understand, easy to kiss. A woman, in fact. It didn't seem to matter that he was crap at picking women. Not that he'd picked—but he had kissed. He wanted to do it again.

His pacing brought him back in sight of the overnight bags Dad had brought over—without comment. Alex rubbed the back of his neck. Why hadn't he commented? Was it because of Curly? Or something else? Yeah, some cases were easy to remember. Or hard to forget. But he'd run the numbers last night. Thirty years ago his dad was still in a uniform. He and Curly weren't partners until Zach got promoted to detective. Now Curly might have been involved in the case. He was older than Zach.

Curly. He'd looked to be in the running for the role of Fourth Corpse. He might wish he'd got the role, if he had been involved in some sort of cover up. Had he screwed up or covered up? Alex was not sure he wanted to know. The department wasn't exactly squeaky clean in those days, so it wasn't a huge shock something had gone wrong.

He paused at the foot of the stairs, his hand on the bannister. He frowned, wondering why it was so easy to believe that Curly might have done something not quite straight?

The shriek shattered all thoughts.

He leapt up two, maybe four steps at a time, rounded the landing, did the same for that set, and the one after that, and saw his brother sitting sheepishly near the top of the last set. Alex slowed enough to realize he was puffing pretty bad. He leaned on the bannister and looked the question he couldn't ask.

"I heard something moving up here and thought I'd better check, make sure Nell was all right. She popped out of the bathroom before I could warn her I was, you know, in the hall."

"And?" Alex managed the single word.

"She didn't drop her towel or anything." He grinned. "And she's fine. Real fine, big brother."

Alex gave some thought to whether he'd caught

enough breath to kick his ass. He decided not quite yet. It wasn't just the stairs, but yesterday, all the body slams. His breathing was still iffy, though the pain report was in. All nerve endings were on duty, sending regular reports.

As if he knew, his brother grinned. "I don't think she knew we were guarding her rest, bro." Something in Alex's face must have prompted a hasty rider to this comment. "I did explain, through the closed door."

Alex sighed and started up the last flight. "I'll wait for her." He jerked his head in the direction of down. Walking and talking was still on the tough side.

Ben looked like he wanted to say something, but he'd decided against it by the time Alex reached his stair. He might have eased past his brother with extra caution, or maybe he remembered what Alex had on him. Sometimes it didn't suck to be the oldest.

None of them had changed his diaper.

Before he could decide to sit or not, he heard her coming. She rounded the corner and stopped, her eyes widening a bit, hair clinging damply to her head and face.

"I stayed, too," he said, giving her a grin that felt crooked.

Her smile was a bit shy, maybe a little embarrassed. "Good morning."

Was that a librarian thing, the prim greeting? Did they learn that in librarian school? Did they know how hot—

"You look—" he stopped. Was it bad to tell a woman she looked better? She'd donned long pants, probably to cover her banged up knees. Her tee shirt had *Bazinga* written across her chest. She looked fresh and clean. She melled good, too.

She smiled. "I am better, thank you." She shifted her shoulders. "Still a bit stiff. You?"

"Oh, yeah." He grinned, then rubbed his rough chin. "Need a shower."

"Don't you know where the bathroom is?"

He nodded. "I'll wait until Ben—"

The color that ran into her face was kind of cute.

"Sorry about that. I wasn't expecting—"

"He's sorry he startled you."

She half smiled. "I kind of startled him, too."

It was not the right time to remember what it had felt like, kissing her last night. Not when they were the same height, because he was on a lower stair—he gave a quick shrug and gestured down. "I think I smelled coffee on my way up."

"Sarah has one of those pots that tell time."

Nell stepped down, Alex turning when they were on the same step. He matched her descent to his, not sorry she took it slow. The silence was okay until she paused and looked at him.

"Am I putting Sarah in danger by being here?"

He didn't rush his answer, took his time before giving a shrug. "I have no idea, Nell. I wish I did."

She turned, continued the descent.

"If you are, it's already done," he added, to a silence not as okay as it had been.

A slight nod gave him a brief glimpse of her nape. "If I

mess up her business—" her lips thinned. "I'd never forgive myself."

More steps. More silence. Then...

"I've been thinking..."

Alex braced. A thinking woman was trouble about ninety percent of the time.

"...wondering, actually, if there was a way to see a picture of Phillip St. Cyr?" She paused, this time on the last landing, a slight flush in her cheeks, as if the question embarrassed her. "This all happened before the internet and all."

The police file would have pictures. Might be tough to get at. The St. Cyrs would have photographs of Phillip, but they couldn't stroll up and ask to see them. But there had to be other sources.

"Some of the old newspaper files might be accessible online. We can check."

Her smile was a bit tense, but grateful, too. "Thanks."

His dad might know something. He preferred to keep his questions unofficial for now. Part of him wanted to throw Curly under the bus, part of him wondered if the old buzz killer's pension could be saved. Most of him wondered why he felt so uneasy about Curly's attitude toward Nell's mom, thirty plus years later.

"I did wonder..." she trailed off this time, her gaze a bit distant.

"So much news reporting has been digitized, it's possible there's a picture of him out there."

She nodded, then her gaze moved past him. "Oh, there's my portfolio. I wondered where I'd left it."

She sounded a bit odd, but bound to be off balance, after all that happened in twenty-four hours. He was still shocked that it had only been one short day. It felt longer. A lot longer. He'd need to call in.

Should he ask for leave? He watched Nell cross to her portfolio. She moved good, real good. Her feet were bare so it seemed she had no muse to answer yet. With any luck the muse would keep its mug shut until they sorted this out.

She paused by the portfolio. He couldn't see her face with her head bent just enough to swing her hair forward over most of her face. Her shoulders moved in a slight sigh, then she picked it up and turned to face him. It seemed like her smile was a mite over bright, but she'd had a heck of a twenty-four hours.

"I think your sketch pad is still on the kitchen table," he offered. And if he was lucky, some coffee. When they reached the kitchen, he found Sarah pouring some, his brother standing near her with a hip propped against the counter. They both turned as they entered.

Like Nell, Sarah wasn't dressed for business, not in a pair of shorts that showed off her long legs. Her tee shirt was festooned with flowers and bling.

He could thank his sisters that he knew about bling. And festooning. Sarah shot Nell a concerned look, but didn't comment as she sank into a chair, lay the portfolio on the table, and pulled her sketchbook toward her. Alex wasn't surprised when she flipped to the page of sketches that included St. Cyr. Was he her grandfather? She looked up, caught him watching and half shrugged, as if she'd caught his thought.

A cup in each hand, Sarah joined them at the table. Sarah set one in front of Alex and he muttered thanks. Sarah took the seat by Nell, her head tipped so she could study the drawings. Ben strolled over and grabbed a seat next to Alex.

"Creepy," she said, into the silence.

"Yeah," Nell agreed. "I was wondering if I could use your desktop to look—"

Sarah pulled out her smart phone, activated the screen and handed it to Nell. "That's Phillip St. Cyr. Not the best picture, but all I could find."

A brief hesitation, before Nell took the phone. There was nothing in Sarah's tone or face to tell if she knew the answer to the question. It seemed likely she'd met Nell's parents though, them being good friends and all.

Nell stared at her friend for what felt like a long time, then lowered her gaze to the small screen.

Alex exchanged a look with Ben while they waited for her to react. Again she surprised him by not reacting. Okay, her shoulders might have got a tad straighter. Sara's hand covered Nell's free one.

"I'm sorry."

Nell half shrugged. "They should have told me." A sigh with a bit of a shudder to it, then she added in surprise, "I'm angry."

Alex looked at Ben again. "Did I miss something?"

"Did *we* miss something?"

Nell pushed the phone toward him, waited while he picked it up, studied the handsome, somewhat willful face. Then looked at Nell, giving her an I-don't-get-it shrug.

"It looks like you have two missing wise kids."

"Two? You mean that's—" he stopped.

"That's my father. Or at least a younger version of him."

Sarah nodded agreement.

Ben stared at him. "So who—"

Alex was glad when he stopped. Time enough to wonder who had died in that car.

"They should have told me—warned me."

"Maybe they meant to, Nell. It's not like they planned —" Sarah hesitated. "Are you sure they didn't leave any...clues?"

"Obviously I need to go through their stuff again." She rubbed her face with her free hand. Alex must have looked curious. She added, "I have a couple of boxes in the attic." She flipped the sketch pad closed and slipped it inside the portfolio.

Alex eyed that uneasily. Surely she wasn't thinking of leaving? Before he could protest, she slid her hand deeper into the depths, apparently feeling for something.

She froze, her eyes widening a bit, then her hand emerged, with something clutched in her fist. She stared at her closed fist, sighed, then let her fingers flower open.

In her palm lay a ring. Heavy, gold, a signet with a sort

of crest. And a single diamond winking at them like a baleful eye.

"Holy—" Ben cut off the swear word Alex had a feeling he'd been about to let out. "May I?"

Nell, wide-eyed, nodded. Ben took it from her as gingerly as if it were explosive.

"What's wrong?" Sarah asked. "Is that yours, Nell? I've never—"

Nell shook her head. "It's not mine."

"It's St. Cyr's," Ben said, examining it with a look of near wonder. "I've seen pictures, but as far as I know, this is the first time it's been off his hand since Zafiro died."

Of course Alex had heard the Zafiro stories. The old timers brought him up when one of them complained about their organized crime problem. If half of what they said was true, he made the three geezers look pretty good.

The two women exchanged puzzled looks.

"Zafiro is the guy our three wise geezers used to work for. He's the one who gave them their start. The story is that Zafiro groomed the three men, planning on one of them, the strongest, to take out the other two and take over for him."

Alex snagged the ring from him, studying the crest with more interest.

"Everyone thought—" Ben continued, but paused

"*There could be only one?*" Nell's lips twisted wryly.

Ben grinned. "Exactly. But when Zafiro...died..."

Was murdered, Alex amended silently.

"...they claimed he'd divided it between them. The proof was the rings. Zafiro used to have this huge—"

"Ring of power," Sarah said, taking her turn.

"Maybe he saw the *Godfather* movie with all the ring kissing," Alex said. Or he had a secret desire to be Pope. "Rumor has it that he liked the drama." And the bloodletting.

"Well, they claimed he melted it down and made them each a ring from his, giving each of them authority over one-third. No one believed them. Zafiro liked a fight, the bloodier the better, but no one inside the organization actively complained. Or if they did, they didn't for long. Zafiro wasn't around to dispute the story and law enforcement couldn't prove they were lying, and were probably relieved the expected turf war didn't happen."

Sarah took the ring from Alex and studied it, then handed it to Nell. "So they each have one exactly like this?"

"Except for the gemstones. Afoniki has an emerald. Calvino has a ruby. That's how I know this one is St. Cyr's." He hesitated. "According to...the people who know this stuff..." Ben's gaze tracked reluctantly to Nell. "...this ring transfers power to the new...heir."

Nell's eyes widened and she jerked, dropping the ring onto the table. It wobbled some, then settled there, winking at them like an evil eye.

NELL FELT that jolt of surprise, yet again, at how quickly —and without fanfare—one's world could change beyond recognition. She'd had a few minutes to be relieved that her parents hadn't lied about everything. They had been high school sweethearts. For whatever reason, that had seemed like the big betrayal, more even than the rest of it.

It was that love, that history of their love, that had made her their kid. It had been the rock on which her life and memories were embedded. It all might have started in a weird place, but the world they'd built, the love they'd shared was real. Who she was, that was real, too. It might be a bit out of focus at the moment, but that didn't mean it had been an illusion.

No wonder they'd been so tied at the hip. Had they done it for her? Or was it something more? Someone had tried to kill them, had believed they succeeded in killing them until she came to town. No wonder her parents hadn't wanted her to visit Sarah. It would have helped if they'd told her.

She rubbed her face, catching sight of the ring in the process. Just because someone gave you something, that didn't mean you had to take it. Her parents were proof of that.

Of course, they'd had to fake their own deaths and hide until they died.

Sarah's hand covered hers. "Are you all right?"

Nell wasn't sure. Her mom's rules of "all right" hadn't covered getting handed a ring of power over a criminal empire. Was she all right? It didn't feel "all right" knowing that creepy St. Cyr had been dad to her dad. And her mom's family? What were they like? Besides creepy. What had really happened all those years ago? And not to be all about herself, but how would it affect her going forward?

"I'm probably okay." Nell heard the doubt in her voice and tried to smile at her friend.

No one knew she had the ring, did they? So no one ever needed to know she'd had—why had he given it to her? Had it been an impulse when he realized he was going to die? Had this been what the killer was after?

She reached over and picked it up again, remembering that moment when she'd really looked at him. What had she seen in his eyes before the bodyguard interrupted them? It would be so easy to imagine she'd seen...something. That he'd felt something for her as a person. As a granddaughter. That the ring wasn't to hose her but to acknowledge her as his son's child.

Wow, she really did have an imagination. Which could be put to better use than trying to imagine what a dead, wise guy might have been thinking when he tripped her. And stalked her. And dumped a hot potato in her portfolio.

Thanks a lot, gramps.

"No one needs to know I have it, do they?" she asked, uneasily. Who had expected to get it? "You could just give it back to, I don't know, whoever was supposed to get it?"

Alex and Ben exchanged glances of a significant nature.

"I'm not sure we can," Ben said, "but yeah, better if no one else knows you have it."

She didn't plan to blab to the gangster relatives. She might not speak to them at all. She wasn't sure what she felt, let alone what she wanted to do. Other than avoid them. Her gaze happened to accidentally intersect with Alex and she almost sighed.

She did know one thing she'd like to do. Very shallow, but there it was. Besides, her mom had once told her there were times in life when you went deep, but also times when it didn't hurt to ride the tops of the waves until the storm passed. That sounded like permission to be shallow every now and again. If she didn't paddle there indefinitely.

Her mom would have liked Alex, she decided, though she wouldn't have approved of his anti-kids deal. Thirteen kids. That had to leave its mark, particularly on the oldest. The brothers tweaked each other as they tried to figure out what to do going forward. She could see the bond of affection between them, even during the mild argument. It had been there with his sister, too. Family affection. Family bonds. She and Sarah were a different kind of family, friends, almost sisters but by choice, not by blood.

It was the almost part that left her feeling a bit blue. Family, the call of blood. Would she feel it with anyone in her parents' families? She sure hadn't felt any call around the old man. Not even a whisper.

Alex would make a great—if reluctant—dad. Cute gene pool. She'd liked to have been a mom, had thought a couple of kids would be nice, but now she had to worry about her gene pool.

As if he felt her attention, Alex looked at her, one brow quirked. "You sure you are all right?"

"I'm not dead."

He grinned. "There are times when that's not the good news."

She matched the grin, surprised she had one in her. The warmth in his eyes made the grin widen—

The front doorbell pealed sonorously. An odd, sad sound for a house that managed to be both old and cheerful. It had a disconcerting effect on the two men. They both shot upright, all signs of softness replaced with steely-eyed resolve.

Yesterday Alex had been brisk cop. This was different. More dangerous. She exchanged a rather wide-eyed look with Sarah.

"What was that?" Alex asked.

"The front door bell?" Sarah said, with a caution Nell shared.

"That's your doorbell?" Ben asked.

Got a nod from them both.

"Are you expecting someone?" Alex asked, rather tersely.

"No, but—"

Alex exchanged a look with Ben. "Wait here." They disappeared out the door to the long hall.

"I hope they don't shoot a client," Sarah murmured. "I haven't got that many."

After a tense wait, one not broken by a gun shot, Ben

returned, with an distinctly odd look on his face. He looked at Nell.

"There's someone here to see you."

"Me?" Had anyone come to see her before Alex? Even her publisher had her come to him. "Who—"

"Helenne St. Cyr."

Her grandmother? She could be wrong, but she was betting this grannie hadn't arrived bearing paper dolls.

CHAPTER EIGHT

The old lady was remarkable, an artist's gift, if Nell could have managed a sketch while that cool, dark gaze scorched over her. The eyes were so like—yet also very not like—her dad's. No question where he'd gotten his looks. She still had the bones, the bearing. There were lines etched in the face and the hair had gone gray without obvious interference.

She sat ramrod straight in the chair, both gnarled hands resting on the impressive head of a finely crafted cane. If Nell had seen her, instead of St Cyr, she'd have known from whence her DNA hailed.

Unlike her husband, she didn't call up vegetable images. Nell might have mulled trees, tall, stately ones with creepy twists, but she didn't dare blink, let alone mull anything. If looks could kill, grandma would have managed it.

Alex standing like a rock at her back helped some.

Kind of funny that the old lady was accessorized with two bodyguards. Or maybe not. She must have trust issues after yesterday.

The artist in Nell picked out the differences in the tall, lean, cliché-clones in dark suits. They periodically scanned for threats with creepy intent, but mostly they glared at Alex. The more goonish one shifted his glare her direction, but removed it when he realized she'd noticed.

The chill receded some, when the old lady looked at her the bodyguards. "Wait in the hall." Her heavy-lidded gaze shifted to Alex. "Go away."

"Nell?"

She managed what she hoped was a regal nod, though she did spare him a quick, reassuring glance. He looked more amused than worried. A heavy silence filtered into the room in the wake of the three men's departure.

She stared past the old lady, her gaze settling on the music box. It was big, ungainly, the craftsmanship rough. Her dad had made other music boxes, better ones, but this was the one she'd had to keep because it was his first.

It would have been upstairs by her bed, but it was a heavy little s.o.b. The sight of it anchored her to Dad. It connected her to her past as she turned her gaze back to his mother.

For a couple of seconds, she didn't know what to say, but then went with the obvious.

"I'm sorry for your loss, ma'am."

The brows arched imperiously. "Are you?"

Nell didn't care if she didn't believe her. The old lady could—and would—believe what she wanted anyway.

"I must suppose that my son is dead." A pause. "Again."

The voice was distant, detached. It kind of made sense. She'd lost him, probably mourned him thirty years ago. The fact that he'd died again didn't change that much for her now.

Nell nodded. It felt weird, it was disturbing, how much she was like Dad. And how very much she wasn't at all like him. It was hard to see her getting warmed up enough to get pregnant. And now she needed to wash her brain out with soap.

"Where did..." Her nose quivered like she smelled something off.

It took Nell a moment to figure out the question. "Wyoming. Northern Wyoming."

A pause. "How extraordinary."

Okay. She did not know what that meant. It was like those nightmares where you had a test you weren't ready for.

"I did not think there was a large city in Northern Wyoming."

"There isn't." There were more people in New Orleans than the whole state.

Another longer pause. "How—I see."

What did she see? Since the old lady had no trouble staring, Nell stared back, trying to connect her dad with this woman in some way besides superficial appearance.

"What was—Phil like?" It was easier for Nell to call him that for some reason.

The precisely shaped brows lifted. The pause long before she offered, "Phillip was a handsome boy. Bright. Charming."

Nell felt the implied *not at all like you* and wondered why his mother had stopped. Her dad had been more, so much more than handsome and bright and charming. Maybe if she could have sketched her...that's how she figured people out—what would her dad have wanted her to do? Besides never meet his mother? It had happened and couldn't be undone. So now what?

"I tried to save him."

The words didn't feel meant for Nell for some reason. She sure wasn't looking at Nell.

"You did save him." Or someone had. The gaze slammed into hers and she suspected that—Nell couldn't think of her as a grandma, not really, so she defaulted back to Mrs. St. Cyr—probably hadn't meant to save him for Wyoming, but for herself.

Nell changed position and managed to sneak a look at her watch. Only three minutes? Seriously? It felt like she'd been in this room a lot longer than that.

"How did he die? When—" Not a muscle quivered in that regal face.

Did she really not know or was this some kind of wise gal game? "Drunk driver." For the first time, Nell felt the irony that his second death was also in a car. "Two years."

And some change, but the old lady wouldn't care about change.

The silence felt longer this time. The old lady avoided looking at her, her gaze apparently fixed on a vase that needed flowers, sitting on a table that needed dusting. Why was she here? What did she want?

The disconnect between her dad and his mother was almost intergalactic. It was hard to believe there'd been a time when both her parents must have sort of fit into this world.

Nell studied the chilly mask of a face. She wasn't here to bond with Nell. There'd been no questions of a personal nature. So what issue was still hanging?

"What did he tell you?"

Everything and nothing. Not that it was any of the old lady's business.

The elegant lips thinned into a sneer. "Were you hoping there'd be money? An inheritance?"

"No." Nell didn't hesitate. Hard to hope for something she hadn't known existed and knowing now, yeah, didn't plan to line up for the blood money.

She met the skepticism in the old lady's eyes without flinching. Not exactly the cozy grandmother she'd wished for once or twice. Not the grandma her parents had wanted her to have, Nell reminded herself. Had she known what she was getting into when she married St. Cyr? She didn't look like the kind to not know what she was getting into.

"Then why are you here?" The old lady turned to give the room a disparaging look. "One hears things, of course."

She somehow managed to make Nell feel like she'd been tacky to get talked about. Neat trick from the widow of a wise geezer. She waited for the gaze to make its way back to hers, then arched her brows. Just a bit. It had worked for her mom when people were nosy.

"Canapés and drinks?"

Her sneer was mixed with disdain. No, not cozy.

"Sarah took me off drink service, so just canapés these days." She also chopped and cooked, but that didn't seem relevant to the moment.

Wow, if her parents hadn't booked it, she might have been on the other side of the trays. Would she have been as snotty? Nell couldn't imagine that, or the person she might have been. Assuming she'd managed to get born, she reminded herself. There were those crypts where her parents weren't buried. But why had it taken all of two years—Sarah's business had only started to make headway into the type of clientele the St. Cyrs most likely frequented. That had to be it.

Her visage on her book jacket was as a green bean. If they recognized her from that—ouch. Unless they'd been watching her for two years? That was a creepy thought, though it seemed unlikely they'd be that patient.

Nell met Mrs. St. Cyr's gaze and retracted that thought. This old lady could be more than that patient. Nell had a sudden sense of a spider spinning a web—

Her cool gaze swept Nell's face. "You're very like her."

"My mom—" Nell began.

"Your grandmother."

Nell had not known that. She hadn't known Mom looked like her mother. It wasn't exactly a shock. Kids did look like their parents. It just felt weird to find out her face was a double hand-me-down. "You...knew her?"

For some reason she'd thought that the families were armed, hostile camps. Wasn't that Wise Guys 101?

The old lady blinked. "I knew her, yes." She did not sounded thrilled so it was a surprise when she added, "We were friends."

"Is she—"

"She died before you were born."

There was something there, a hint of an acid leak, though nothing showed on her face or in her eyes. Was it the family connection that bothered her? The fact that her beautiful son had fallen for the ordinary girl? Some kind of twisted version of housewives of wise guys? It was weird to realize one could have too much family. Was this how Alex felt? Of course, he didn't have Family. Nor did his family have in their trail, clouds of goons.

The silence was a bit fraught. Not even the hum of a clock and the curtains muffled any street sounds brassy enough to attempt entry. Dim and a bit close, the ever-present humidity made the cool feel less so.

The old lady's scent had to be expensive and was on the strong side in the still air. Rather *grande dame* of crime-ish. Was she a power behind the throne or more splendidly oblivious? The spinning spider image came back, stronger and more creepier than before.

Nell's finger tips quivered. She closed them into fists. She'd been known to make air drawings when the urge hit at paperless moments.

Nell still couldn't figure out what the old lady wanted. She replayed their conversation so far. It didn't take long, but she'd missed something. She wasn't sure how she knew, she just did.

Nell's head tipped to the side. "You're angry at him— them." Or just Mom?

It was hard to believe her eyes could get more arctic, but she managed it.

"He was a fool to run away, just because he and Phin didn't see eye to eye about the business."

"The business?" Would that be the murdering and stealing and who knew what else business?

The cold gaze regarded her. "Phillip would have come around."

Nell doubted that. Since he hadn't.

"Toni was naive and idealistic and Phillip—"

"—loved her," Nell cut in.

The old hands may have tightened on the cane head. "So he said."

Nell mainlined her mom's unflinching look. Her dad had *proved* he loved her mom. The eyes shifted back toward Nell, dark, deep and disturbing.

Nell didn't know her well enough to know what stirred down in her depths. She didn't want to know her that well.

She looked like dad but—wow, the apple hadn't fallen close to that tree at all.

Nell wanted to ask stuff but didn't know how to do it without giving away what she did and didn't know, or that she had that ring.

She had a fervent hope that this woman never found out about that. The silence stretched like spandex and was about as comfortable.

Had the scary matriarch really not known her husband was watching Nell? How long had he watched before Nell noticed? What had he planned to do about it? When had the old lady found out about Nell? The timing of St. Cyr's death—Nell realized where her thoughts were going and put on the brakes. If grandma had taken out grandpa, she did not want to know it. Or think it in her presence.

"Has Bett been to see you?"

"Bett?"

"Your mother's father."

She didn't see any reason not to admit he hadn't, so Nell shook her head.

"He will."

"Unless he's the one trying to kill me," Nell said, though she probably shouldn't have. Unless being in someone's gun sights boosted her creds with the fam. The old lady's brows arched. No sign of sorrow or worry. Oh well, she wasn't really looking to boost the creds with this particular fam.

"Why would you matter enough to kill?"

Nell shrugged, not sure why that stung. Yeah, no cozy

grandma there. And she only mattered if someone knew about the ring, didn't she? Which they shouldn't. But someone might know it was missing? Nell shifted uneasily.

"I suppose Aleksi Afoniki might see you as a threat."

"Why—" Because she was the granddaughter of two wise geezers? She briefly considered the notion, but she wasn't any more suited to be a wise person than her parents.

"Phin thought Aleksi was the one who—" she stopped. "It was never proved."

She did not know wise guys needed proof. Was it a Hatfields and McCoys deal? He might not have liked the two families joining DNA, leaving him standing alone, but it didn't happen.

So, what, revenge visited on the next generation? It was not a happy thought. When mafia types got you in the crosshairs, they didn't tend to back off. She was a bit hazy on the conditions of Witness Protection, but it seemed logical to assume that she'd need something to trade for protection. So far, all she had was a ring she couldn't admit she had. And DNA she didn't want. Annoyed did a spike. "Why are you here?"

Her brows arched. "You're my granddaughter."

Nell did skeptical. Grannie not-dearest looked away. Then Nell got it. This visit wasn't about her. It was about Dad. Her son. That she hadn't seen for thirty-plus years. Who she'd never see again. Was it longing she sensed beneath the anger? Or the old lady could be trying to play her, find out what she knew.

"Did he make music boxes...before?" Nell asked.

That put some surprise on her face. "No..." She blinked. "He...no."

"Oh." Nell hesitated. "Maybe it was his way to sing without singing." Or a way to distract himself from missing what he'd left behind? "He was terrible. When he wanted to make us laugh, he'd do this lounge singer routine—" Nell stopped as the surprise grew, removing some of the scary matriarch vibes. "Did he sing a lot when he was little?"

A pause. "I suppose he might have in school."

Where did he come from, she wanted to ask? Instead she tried again. "He fixed cars."

"He always liked cars." For a second the old lady almost looked relieved.

She hesitated, but decided Dad would want her to know. "They were happy. Everyone said so at," she took a steadying breath, "the funeral."

The dark gaze had gone back to giving nothing away. Nell didn't know if this mattered to grandma not-dearest, but she felt the need to say it.

"They said it was fast. They didn't suffer." Nell looked away, staring at the dust motes drifting in a tiny ray of light that had snuck past the drapes. She remembered laying on the rug next to her dad while he spun her a tale about the mote fairies. It was as bad as his singing. She'd edited it as he told it.

Her fingers tried to break out of fists as images began to take shape in the sunbeam. She'd need to sketch another mental dump and soon.

The chair creaked as the old lady shifted position, scattering the images into the shadows again. The silence drew out, but not as uncomfortable. Nell stole a look. Not much had changed in how she looked, but...

"Can I ask you something?"

The old lady stiffened some. She didn't answer, but she didn't say no.

"Do you have any pictures of him? When he was young?"

The slow turn of her head toward Nell was interesting, though Nell wasn't sure why. A slight nod.

"I'll arrange something." She paused. "I don't have any of...your mother."

Not exactly a shock. Or maybe she did have one but she had used it for dart practice. "Would you like a photo of—"

A pause, followed by a slow, an almost imperceptible, somewhat grudging nod. This time the silence wasn't as comfortable, though not in a bad way. Just kind of itchy. She wished she knew how to end the meeting. She was sure there wouldn't be any hugging. Probably no "call me" or a "let's do lunch." The dark gaze, not quite so chilly, studied her for what felt like a long time.

"You're very like your mother."

Oddly enough, it didn't sound like an insult. Though it probably was.

∾

IT WASN'T MUCH, Alex thought, looking at the meager
pile that—other than a daughter and a butt load of questions—was all that remained of Nell's parents. Very few
papers. The letters were from Nell. Either no one else
wrote them, or they didn't keep anything but her letters.
Their wills. Some photo albums, a Wal-Mart apron, a
wrench, a goofy Halloween tie.

"Is this all—everything?" Ben asked.

"There's the music box," Sarah said, giving her a grin.

The two men looked at Nell. "It was my dad's not-so-
secret vice."

"Not a vice, Nell," Sarah protested, "more like an
endearing quirk. And he got quite good at the carving. It
was just—" She stopped with an impish look.

"What?" Alex asked, suspiciously.

Nell grinned. "His music choices were so cliché. It
was—"

"Cute," Sarah insisted. "I gave his Christmas tree box
to my Aunt Carol Sueanne a few years ago. It still works
great."

"*O Christmas Tree?*" Ben guessed.

"At least that player doesn't make your teeth hurt."
Nell looked rueful. "Mine is his first. It's just awful, but,"
she looked from one to the other of them. "I had to keep it.
No one else would love it. He called it Old Bertha. Mom
called it The Horror."

"Where is it?" Alex asked.

Nell said a bit guiltily, "It started in the office, but
clients would lift the lid."

"We were trying to build the business, not drive clients away," Sarah put in with a grin. "Their eyes would twitch and then get a little wild, because it doesn't stop until it played a complete refrain."

"So we moved it to a place of honor in the sitting room," Nell finished.

Sarah stiffened. "Did the old lady notice it? Say anything?"

Nell shook her head. "I guess Dad started making them after the flit."

Alex exchanged a look with Ben.

"Mind if I grab it?" Ben asked. "I promise not to lift the lid."

Nell shrugged and nodded but warned, "It's heavy."

Alex sorted the papers into types. He was relieved to turn his attention to the music box when Ben lugged it in. Though Alex was no expert on music boxes, this one did seem to be a bit unusual by any standards.

For one thing, it was big. And square. The craftsmanship was rough. Not that he was an expert in woodworking, but it looked rustic. Almost crude. He wouldn't call it a horror, but it wasn't pretty.

Nell traced one line of the minimal scroll work etched into the top. "Dad said it relaxed him to make them. Mom had a kind of love-hate thing going for them. Some days she was happy to send him off to tinker, others she wanted to hit him with one."

If they were all as big, that was a serious threat.

He and Ben studied it, taking care not to lift the lid,

but there wasn't much to learn from its exterior. It was roughhewn, but tight. No warping at the seams. With an apologetic look, he lifted the lid and peered inside, releasing a painfully tinny rendition of *Memories*. Not just a cliché, but a bad cliché.

There was not much space under the lid, maybe a couple of inches of nothing. The base seemed solidly fitted in there, too. Again, no warping, suspicious or otherwise. He felt all the way around the interior. He'd opened it and he needed to look like he had a reason for causing them pain. All he got was a sliver for his trouble. He shut the lid and let it finish the refrain, then tipped it gently one way, then the other. No sound of anything shifting. He looked at Ben and shrugged.

"I'll put it back."

Nell touched the top of the box, then sat back as Ben returned it to the sitting room, a worried crease between her brows.

How would he feel if he found out his dad wasn't who he thought he was? It sometimes boggled him to think about who his dad actually was. Being part of his Baker's dozen had not exactly been a cake walk through the years. Thanks to his friends he'd found out where babies came from too soon for comfort.

When Ben returned, they went through the papers. It didn't take long. Alex lingered a bit over the photos, looking—he told himself—for clues or cues. She had been a cute kid.

In the end, they both leaned back, defeated by how

innocuous and ordinary it all was. If they'd brought anything but Nell from their previous lives, it wasn't obvious. If it was hard for him to connect them with the wise kids, how much harder must it be for Nell?

Ben rubbed his face. Alex wanted to. Ben hefted the wrench and arched a brow.

"I sold all his tools, but I wanted something—" A smile wavered on her mouth. "I needed to travel light. Who knew it was a family tradition?"

"We need the police file," Alex said finally, reluctantly.

How much risk was there in trying to get into the files? They needed more than the file, though. Who had died in that car bomb? Who had faked the identification of the bodies? Why had someone tried to kill two wise kids? Who had financed their escape? They'd have needed help to get away so clean, wouldn't they? Had her parents killed two kids so they could escape?

"Grannie not-dearest said she tried to help them," Nell said, as if he'd spoken out loud. "She did not seem that fond of my Mom. Or her mom."

"We need our old man," Ben said, without enthusiasm.

Sharing his lack of enthusiasm, Alex still nodded agreement. It was Dad or Curly, and Alex didn't trust Curly. "I'll go talk to him after I shower."

SOMETIMES THE MOUNTAIN *must come to the man.*

Bettino Calvino didn't like it, but he didn't have to like

something to do it. It felt necessary. He studied the narrow, shabby street through the tinted protective glass of his Humvee.

Calvino wasn't prescient. He did not have to be to know he might be in trouble. He'd felt the chill of danger down his back, the sense that change was coming even before Phin's elimination from play. Was it personal or part of something larger?

Just because he was paranoid, that didn't mean someone wasn't out to get him. A lot of someones had motive, he thought with an almost smile. Most of them did not have means or opportunity. He'd have bet the house that Phin was as paranoid or more so. And he'd have lost.

They'd been a triangle of power, precariously balanced on that old pact. Twice it had been tested. Twice it had survived. Who had gotten to Phin?

A new player?

Or an old one wakened from a long sleep?

A bear? Did Russian bears hibernate? If Aleksi died next, he'd know.

When they'd been waiting on Zafiro to die, he'd wondered why the old man didn't beg for the bullet. Now he knew why Zafiro had clung so long to his empire. At the time he'd considered it a mercy killing, or that's what they'd told themselves. Not that they'd needed a lot of convincing. They'd all wanted to live. It was them or Zafiro. Easy choice.

Calvino didn't feel old, though his body surprised him at times by reacting old. But inside, where it counted, he didn't feel different. His mind was sharp, maybe sharper than when he'd been the young wolf. He'd taken his hits, had stood fast when everything almost came apart. He'd had the hard surf of that pound him into iron.

He thought he'd buried the past and all the people who'd betrayed him. Thirty years. Was it unreasonable to expect the dead to stay dead? Thirty years and he was in, almost, the same place. Almost, he could hear Ellie's mocking laugh as he reached for the door handle.

Both bodyguards scrambled out, flanking him protectively as Calvino emerged into the spring heat. He stood for a moment regarding the modest dwelling, before striding to the rear door. At his nod, one of the men rapped sharply on the wood. After a long pause, the door opened, revealing a severely battered kitchen. And Zach Baker.

Calvino did not expect surprise and he was not disappointed. One gray brow rose in a query. Calvino matched his brow with the rise of both of his.

After a long pause, Baker stood back and gestured for him to enter, though he held up a hand when his bodyguards tried to follow.

"If he doesn't come out, you can shoot me," Baker offered, then closed the doors in their faces.

ALEX GRIPPED the steering wheel of Ben's SUV, his gaze tracking Calvino's return to his Humvee, the two bodyguards covering his retreat. When the Humvee pulled away, when it had passed him, Alex pulled into the spot they'd left.

He wasn't too shocked to pass up a prime parking spot.

He got out, but instead of going inside, he headed down the block. If he faced his dad now, he'd know...what would his dad know? What would Zach see in Alex's face? Alex sure as hell didn't know what he felt, what he thought.

He was a guy. They hated feelings. Except being pissed. Okay, so he was pissed. He turned the corner, relieved to be out of sight of the house. He should be pissed. His dad had—what? Alex stopped, looked back the way he came. What had his dad done? Just the facts.

Calvino had come to their house.

Calvino had left their house.

He didn't *know* he'd been inside.

He didn't know he hadn't.

Why would Calvino seek out his dad? He half reached for his cell. Stopped. He started walking again.

He reached the next corner and turned back in the direction of the house. They were grown-ups. He'd ask the question. He'd go inside and say, "You'll never guess who I saw walking away from our back door."

Then his dad would shake his head and say the one thing that would ease the hard knot in Alex's chest. He was his Dad, so he'd make it...better.

Alex turned the last corner and strode toward home. He slowed as he reached the rutted driveway with the cement that needed to be broken out and replaced. He knew where to step, where to avoid. He reached the back door. It opened, framing his dad in the opening.

"Alex? Was just heading your way. Good, you can give me a ride." Zach pulled the door shut, locked it. "You didn't need anything in there, did you?"

Alex shook his head, turned to follow his dad back to Ben's car, without speaking. He couldn't with the question —and the knot—stuck in his throat.

THANKFULLY FOR NELL's sore tush, they'd moved to the smaller living room and softer seating for the next round of discussions.

This room was where she and Sarah lived when they weren't in the kitchen. It had the same, battered comfort of home, unlike some of the more formal rooms left over from the reign of Sarah's parents.

Nell shifted a clutter of pillows to one side and settled in. Despite the gravity of the situation, she didn't dare look at Sarah when Alex's dad joined their confab.

Last night she'd noted that Alex looked a lot like his dad and then tried not to think about him in relation to his dad because, wow, thirteen kids. And yeah, she was back in shallow, but it felt okay. It kept her head above water. Or the illusion that her head was above water. For all she knew, she was about to go down for the third time. And that might be the good news.

Ben had departed to try and discreetly round up files.

It was probably her imagination he wanted to be gone when the dad arrived. She had the odd feeling Alex would have gone, too, if he could have come up with a good excuse. She caught him giving his dad an odd look, a look that vanished when Zach looked at him. Maybe it was a son/dad thing?

Zach asked for something to drink, a slight frown between his bushy, gray brows. Alex started to get up, but Sarah stopped him with a gesture.

"I'll get it."

Left with the dad and the son, her sense that things were tense ramped up. Had they disagreed about something? Her? Was she inflating her importance? More than likely, she decided.

Sarah returned with drinks and a tray of snacks, and then they all settled in for some serious information exchanging. As Zach began to talk, Nell wondered, was it interesting or creepy that the three wise geezers had started out as friends, or as much friends as bad guys could be, all three young goons for this Zafiro organization? Both, she decided. And a bit unreal. She had no way to connect the dots between them and her parents, even with the pictorial evidence.

"They competed in everything. It was assumed that the final competition would be for total control," Zach said, "but when Zafiro died...and it was all kind of—"

"Friendly?" Alex asked with skepticism he did not try to hide. An edge in his voice earned him a hard look from his dad, a look he deflected with an overly bland expression.

Zach half shrugged. "It was an...orderly transfer of power that law enforcement had not expected. No one was happy it turned into three organizations, but they were glad it didn't turn into a blood bath. It would have if Zafiro had lived. He liked the violence, the fight." He hesitated. "Instead, it was...almost civilized. Oh, there was a bit of jockeying, some head bumping, but it was—"

"What?" Sarah said, curiously.

"At the time, everyone wondered if it was for show. If they'd come to some private agreement to share power. They still saw each other socially and—" He stopped, his gaze tracking to Nell.

She didn't know why, so she arched her brows.

"Your grandmother." He stopped again, his look one of a man ordering his thoughts, followed by a look that indicated he wasn't happy with the order of them. "It was the three of them and Helenne—"

"Helenne?" Nell interrupted. "But—"

"She was a beautiful woman." No hint of admiration in Zach's voice, however. "Classy, but—"

When he didn't go on, Nell said, "If you're worried about my feelings, don't be."

His gaze, so like Alex's, studied her for several seconds, something easing in there. He nodded.

"Fair enough. She wasn't straight, honest. She knew who and what they were, and she liked it. Liked the fight, too. Thought she could have her pick of them. Had probably planned to have the one who got it all. But they didn't fight."

"You...didn't know her?" Surely he was too young?

"She was five years older than me. Ellie, your grandmother, Eleanor, was a year younger than Helenne."

Ellie? Nell blinked, exchanged a look with Sarah.

"Did you know...Ellie?" Sarah asked.

This time Zach looked at Alex. "She dated my brother in high school."

Alex frowned. "Who? Which one?"

"Charlie."

"But—" Alex stopped. His lips compressed.

"He had a fight with my dad and disappeared right after he graduated high school," Zach said. He didn't look like he wanted to continue. His tone was on the dogged side. "Ellie married Calvino six months later."

"What was she like?" Nell asked, finding it even harder to find dots to connect between them. "Was she like —" Helenne was what Nell couldn't bring herself to say.

He shook his head. "She was nothing like Helenne."

Nell took a cracker and some cheese from the tray and nibbled it. It gave her fingers something to do, while her thoughts spun with questions and images.

"No one quite got why Helenne took Ellie up as a friend out of high school."

If Ellie really had looked like Nell, well, she knew. "She wanted a friend who was no competition with the guys, someone who made her look good, someone she could pretend was a friend."

For about two minutes, Nell had wondered if this was why Sarah had picked her as a friend, but Nell had always had a good bitch-o-meter. Grandma not-dearest had definitely set it off. Which didn't explain how Ellie had ended up married to one of the bad guys.

"Well, if that's why, it backfired on her in a big way," Zach said, grimly. "The story is that they all wanted Ellie."

"Sounds more like a fairy tale," Alex said, his tone amused, his gaze not so much. "They wanted her because the others did."

"Could be, though I wondered..." Zach trailed off, his gaze distant.

"What?" Nell prompted, curious about this woman she shared a face with.

"She was good." Zach half shrugged. "They weren't good, they aren't good, but they are superstitious."

That didn't seem to add up to three wise guys and a wedding, did it?

He looked at Nell, sadness in his eyes now. "She was too nice to be mixed up with any of them, but too innocent to realize it until—"

"So she chose...Calvino?" Nell asked.

"That's the story," Zach's voice went flatter than Kansas.

"Story?" Alex asked sharply.

Zach shrugged again. "I was a freshman in high school, more worried about making the team."

Four years at that age was like a different lifetime. Had

his brother left because of Ellie? Who had broken up with whom?

"Helenne married St. Cyr the same year, but she had Phil before Toni was born. About four months too soon."

"She got pregnant to get him," Sarah guessed.

"Could be."

"But which one did she want?" Nell wondered aloud. Who'd had the most power? That's the one the old lady would have wanted. But according to Zach, they'd shared the power equally. The question really came down to who would have won if they had duked it out?

And why would that guy have settled for less than all of it? Unless—would Calvino have bargained for Ellie? *I'll share power but I get the girl?* Surely not? And yet, her dad had given up everything for Mom and she had the same face as Ellie. But her dad wasn't a bad guy looking for redemption. He was a good guy who'd escaped hell.

"Calvino was the front runner," Zach admitted.

"She wouldn't have liked settling," Nell said. Zach looked a bit surprised, so she added, "She stopped by today."

Zach's gaze arrowed to his son, who went on the defensive.

"I was going to tell you. There's been a lot going on. And not all of it is need-to-know. You are retired."

Nell exchanged a look with Sarah while the two men tested who had the strongest will. It didn't feel like a concession when Zach said, "So I am."

He turned his attention back to Nell. "I graduated,

went to college, met Zach's mother and joined the force. I used to see Ellie around when my beat brought me into her neighborhood. Toni was maybe, ten or so?"

He paused to eat a cracker, but Nell had a feeling it was a stall while he decided something. He drank some water and sighed.

"The thing is, Charlie told me Ellie dumped him. Says she told him she was in love with someone else. When he took off, well, I had no reason to feel...kindly toward her. But I started to notice she wasn't happy. Now that might be because she discovered she'd given her life and heart to a scumbag, but I got called to an accident between her car and another. And she," Zach paused again, his gaze looking into the past once more, "brought the conversation around to Charlie. Something about the way she looked, the way she asked, well, it got me thinking."

Nell felt her body turn to ice. "Calvino...coerced her into giving Charlie up?"

"I don't know what he said or did, but I drove away thinking it stank." His smile was on the grim side. "If he did, I don't think it did Calvino much good. He'd started messing around before Toni was born."

And Curly? How did he fit into the story? He was the one carrying around a picture of her mom. "I wonder where that Afoniki guy fits in?" she asked, since Zach and Curly were friends.

"Afoniki never married."

Nell blinked. If the old man was anything like the

nephew, she couldn't imagine him nursing a broken heart. A vengeful one? Yeah, she could imagine that.

"So what happened to Ellie?" Sarah wanted to know.

"She's dead," Nell said.

"How do you know that?" Zach asked, his tone suddenly hard.

"Grandma not-dearest told me. Why? Isn't she?"

"She disappeared around the same time as Toni and Phil." He hesitated. "It was generally assumed that she ran off with a lover. Whether they made it..."

Did one want to know one's grandma had had a lover? No, one did not. If Calvino had coerced her, then one did not blame her for bolting. If she'd bolted. That would make a good cover story for a creep like Calvino. He'd ruined more than Ellie's life.

"Did you ever hear from your brother?" Nell asked.

Did it seem that Zach hesitated, before he shook his head? Could his brother have come back for Ellie? If life were a gothic romance novel, maybe.

Zach shifted again, as if his chair wasn't as comfy as Nell knew it was. "What?"

"When your dad...when Phil was—" He stopped and rubbed his face again.

Nell shot a look at Alex and found him once again giving his dad an odd, hard stare, with worry mixed in there. Fear did a complicated dance down her spine as the hesitation grew into a long pause.

"What?" Nell said again. It was becoming second nature to brace for incoming.

"Around the time it all went pear shaped, there was a goon, name of Dunstead. Roger Dunstead. He—" Zach paused as if unsure what to say next, "—worked freelance, did stuff for all three of them."

"Freelance?" Sarah asked.

"Stuff?" Nell added.

"Protection, payment collection, the odd hit." A pause, then he said, "He worked for Zafiro before he died."

That felt kind of random, but Zach's face didn't look random. "How did Zafiro die?" she asked.

"Heart attack."

"I didn't think wise guys died of natural causes," Sarah said, a bit ironically.

"Let's just say the jury is still out on what caused the heart attack," Zach said.

It wasn't like she didn't know both grandfathers were major creeps, but she still winced a bit. "You think they did more than amicably agree to split up the business?"

"There was no evidence against any of the three, at least none available to law enforcement," Zach said. "And no one looked too hard because—"

"—they weren't shooting at each other," Alex finished.

And back then, some money probably exchanged hands. The NOPD of the past wasn't exactly known for being squeaky clean.

Alex frowned. "They wouldn't have used Dunstead and let him live."

"I wasn't deep enough in to know much. Just that

Dunstead contacted the feds and claimed he knew something that could bring all three of them down."

"Something?" Nell frowned.

"Something big." Zach leaned back, took another sip of the water she'd brought him. "Lots of rumors, wild stories before, during, and after it went wrong."

Of course it had gone wrong, since the three men had survived and apparently thrived.

It seemed that Alex had gone tense. Nell gave him a worried look.

Zach couldn't be involved. He was just a street cop, not in on the big investigation. Except, he could have been first on the scene...all of a sudden Nell wished she hadn't read so many mysteries. It turned you into a nasty, suspicious person.

"I presume whatever he knew died with him?" Sarah leaned forward to take a drink.

Her thoughts didn't look like they were going the same direction as Nell's, but with Sarah, one didn't always know.

Zach looked almost wry. "It's kind of legend among those who were there. Some think that it's still out there, like Lafitte's gold. Most think it was destroyed. Or maybe they just hope it was." This time he made a point of not looking at Nell. "Would have been a nice insurance policy for someone."

"You think my—Phil killed him."

Now he looked at her, met her gaze without flinching. In fact, he looked sorry. "Phil was eighteen. He hadn't been blooded. There were rumors, he hadn't...embraced the family business...that...pressure was being applied. He was questioned about it, but then he died. And the case was filed away as cold."

Maybe some of them were happy to have it go away, afraid of what too much digging would unearth? If... people...thought Phil had had that "something" on the wise guys, but thought he was dead, and then found out he'd survived?

What would they think, what would they fear from his daughter? She could kind of see why her presence could make them uneasy, especially a bunch of people who lived at the corner of uneasy and suspicious.

St. Cyr had tried to coerce his son into the family business. Was that why he'd given her the ring? The man she'd sketched might think that was a way to get back at the son who'd rejected him. She sighed. There was no way for her to ever know what St. Cyr had thought that day, so she moved on to the other two.

Even if she worried them, she couldn't see them panicking and ordering a hit. If she'd come to town to exact revenge, she wouldn't have waited two years. Even they could figure that out. Obviously at least Afoniki had been curious enough to send his nephew to take a look at her.

With this hindsight came clarity. It hadn't been her imagination that he'd been creepy and a bit weird during the brief meeting. It sort of explained the *'til we meet again* comment, though—no—not really. Unless he was just trying to keep his options open.

All this assumed that her dad had killed Dunstead and that he had left with evidence, this so-called insurance policy.

She didn't believe it of the dad who had raised her...but—pressure? Could he have done it for Mom? And if they'd known a baby was incoming? Pressure plus.

She had no doubt her dad would have killed to protect them, but, if he had the information as protection, why hadn't anyone tried to find it after he died? Why hadn't he warned her at some point? It all made her head hurt. She'd never know why they'd done what they did either. They were also gone and couldn't tell her their plans, past or future.

"Dunstead could have given it to someone for safe-keeping. Someone who was afraid to use it," Sarah pointed out.

"Or someone who is using it now," Nell said, thought-fully. Long-term blackmail? It was possible.

Zach looked at her like a man who had tried to consider everything. "Not a lot of friends when you're a mob enforcer. His wife died within a year. He had a kid who went into foster care."

"How did she die?"

Zach shook his head. "If she was murdered, it was covered up better than usual," he hesitated. "Back then, the cases that were—there was a smell about them. I don't recall anything like that. But it has been over thirty years and it wasn't my beat."

Did he remember so much about it because of Ellie or his brother? Nell's gaze rested thoughtfully on Alex again.

If a woman were not happy in her marriage and there was a sort of friend from high school around, one you felt you could trust, a man who had been your true love's younger brother...

"Your friend, Curly something, was he in the same high school with the rest of you?" He was older than Zach, possibly closer to Ellie's age?

Zach's gaze narrowed a bit, but he nodded. "He was a year older than Ellie. But if you're thinking—Ellie never dated Curly."

That he knew, Nell amended. "So why did he have my —Toni's picture?"

"He wouldn't have been stupid enough to mess with Calvino's wom—with Ellie. Even if Calvino had moved on."

He sounded a bit too defensive, though he had a point. "Then who was her," Nell choked a bit on the word, "the lover she was supposed to have run off with?"

Zach blinked, as if she'd finally asked a question he hadn't prepared for. "I don't know. Not sure anyone knew."

"But," Sarah protested, "someone must have gone missing at the same time. Some guy that was around and then wasn't?"

"I never heard a name," Zach said, a hint of mulish to his tone.

What if Charlie had come back and Zach knew?

Suspected? Helped them get away...? He'd have needed to be very careful not to put his family at risk.

"Maybe it's in one of the files," Alex said. "If Ben can spring them, or get a look..."

Instead of worried, Zach said, "It's possible."

So he wasn't worried. She caught Zach looking at her, that slight frown back between his brows. She felt a little lame saying, "What?" again, but didn't know what else to say.

"You look so much like her, like them, it's a bit..." he shrugged.

Nell stared at him for a few seconds, before saying slowly, "I have their face, but I'm just me."

Ordinary when they'd been extraordinary. The most she could hope for was to be as brave as they'd been.

CHAPTER NINE

She is no one.

Aleksi had lied. Dimitri knew this. The woman had mattered, did matter, but he hadn't known how much. He'd thought—he did not know what he'd thought. But this. It took all his self-control not to lash out at this messenger. If one killed one's snitches, then information dried up. This one had not wanted to talk, had wanted to hold this last card. It wasn't a sure thing. Sometimes knowing was not power.

His uncle should have told him. Oh, he knew why the old man hadn't. It was not the thin edge of a wedge. It was a hammer at the old man's head. At them? He wondered. So much depended on what the woman had on him. If it was solely about the pact his uncle had made with Calvino and St. Cyr, then that was his uncle's problem. Unless— would his uncle flip? He might if he thought his nephew was not being sufficiently helpful. He was that vindictive.

And the woman?

He'd underestimated her importance. It was not like him. Though he could not see why she hadn't acted already. Two years. What had she hoped to accomplish by waiting? What pieces had she hoped to get in place? Was St. Cyr's removal part of her plan? He suspected she had not planned on anyone shooting back. If the shooting had been directed at the woman.

He frowned and the snitch at his feet trembled. He signaled for him to be released. Alive.

His frown deepened. The shots could have been meant for the cop. It might have had nothing to do with her. He'd not had dealings with Alex Baker, but he had encountered a couple of his siblings. Everyone on his side of the law knew what it meant to be "Baked."

But it had taken place outside her residence. He recalled his uncle's belief that Helenne St. Cyr had tried to kill her own son. She might be behind the hit. If she hated the woman's grandmother as much as his uncle believed...

What was she like?

The only question his uncle had asked. It didn't give him a lot of insight into the problem. Would his uncle tell him what he needed to know? He knew the answer even as he asked the question. Not a chance. And if he did, could he trust what he was told? Never. He paused.

Was there a kernel of truth in the old story?

Even a slight possibility Aleksi Afoniki had harbored feelings for any woman for over thirty years? No...he could believe many things, but not that. But if the woman carried the blood of a Calvino and a St. Cyr—did his uncle hope to bring Zafiro's organization back together? Had he hoped the granddaughter was like the grandmother? That she would capture his interest?

Alone with his thoughts, inside his own head, he might concede that the woman had been more interesting than expected. That she could be heir to two organizations made her almost irresistible.

They needed to talk, but Baker had her locked down— his phone shrilled.

It was the man he'd asked to monitor the situation with the woman. Dimitri listened to what he had to report, snapped some orders and cut the connection.

So, she'd emerged from seclusion. What a clever girl.

"Bring my car around," he ordered.

"You—" Ben stopped, then finished, "they shouldn't have gone—"

"To a cemetery when someone wants one of them dead?" Sarah finished for him, not without mild sympathy and, regrettably, some amusement.

He was annoyed, but a cute annoyed. Funny how two brothers could be so alike and yet so different. She'd been mildly piqued when Alex hadn't seemed interested at that first meeting, until she saw who did interest him. He had good taste and more sense than most of the men she met. She smiled at Ben, saw his annoyance lose traction and broadened the smile. He really was cute. And if a smile helped ease his pain...

"You could have talked her out of it," Ben pointed out, not weakly, because he wasn't a weak man, but with less force than the last comment.

Would he, could he understand the rules between two women who were the best of friends? Could he know that when you trusted someone the way she and Nell trusted each other, there was power that must be wielded with care?

Most likely she could have convinced Nell not to go, but—and this was the deep bond part—Nell knew that there might be danger and had still felt a need to go. And she'd always supported Sarah when she felt compelled to follow her instincts, even when it involved bad karaoke or passing out canapés.

Who would expect her to go to a cemetery? And she was with a cop. Whoever had shot at them yesterday had to know that now, even if they hadn't known it before. It was not a good plan to shoot at cops. And a really bad idea to shoot at one as connected as Alex.

"Nell needed to go," she compromised. Sarah didn't know why Nell felt this need to visit a grave where her parents weren't buried. She did know Nell had taken some hard knocks in the last twenty-four hours.

"It's complicated," she added. Nell was a complicated person. She looked like this sweet, absent-minded librarian and she was, but—underestimate her at your own peril.

Was it the wise family roots? It still kind of boggled,

even factoring in what Sarah did know about her friend. One would have to work hard to find a person more solidly in the straight and narrow column. The friend least likely to shoot you. Or at you. She would shoot for you, in defense of you. Because she did know how to shoot. Her daddy had made sure of that. He'd taught Sarah, too, on those visits that never got reciprocated for reasons that were now very clear but weren't back then.

"Obviously," Ben said a bit dryly. Or that might have been wryly.

He did have six sisters. He might have more of a clue about women than most men. And he might even have the sense to know when not to say something to a woman.

"What do you think your dad expects to find that we didn't?"

He'd gone into the kitchen not long after Nell and Alex left, looking even more not happy than both his sons. He'd probably had more practice at it.

Ben grinned. "He did have a knack for seeing what was right under our noses. When he was home."

A cop with thirteen kids probably couldn't afford to be home much. Second oldest, Ben might remember his mom. He would have had to help out after she died.

"Do you think there's anything to find?"

He sighed. "No." A pause. "But someone does."

"Lots of someones," Sarah felt impelled to point out with a slight grin tacked on. She was from New Orleans, so she knew about parades. Seemed like Nell was getting her own second line going here. She frowned, as a thought occurred to her. "Doesn't it make more sense to wait until Nell makes her move?"

"Maybe they think she is making her move? Or they want her to move faster?" Ben said.

Sarah nodded doubtfully, but she didn't say anything. Reading a few mysteries did not an expert make.

"Pissing off the mob is a bad idea, but if you got someone else to do it for you..." Ben went on, almost to himself.

"Oh wow, that is devious and..." Bad for Nell, if the mob had decided she was the one doing it. "Will anyone help Nell if—" She stopped, not sure how to ask the question.

"We'll do our best." For a moment he looked very *Dudley Do-Right.* "There are Bakers everywhere in law enforcement. And Alex and I have something on all of them. One of the rare times it's good to be older."

She had to smile then. She'd always had a soft spot for *Dudley.* "Do you think he'd mind if we watched?"

"Dad's used to an audience," he said, with a rather wry grin.

They headed into the hall, turning toward the kitchen. He pushed open the swing door for her. Sarah was halfway in before she realized Zach already had an audience.

The scary Widow St. Cyr had returned, trailing a couple of goons and a pissy expression.

~

FOR THE FIRST time in thirty years, Calvino extracted the photograph from the locked drawer. Let himself look at them, let the memories out, too.

He'd been mad, he knew now, almost blind with it. Had they planned it that way? Played him so he'd agree to take one third when he could have had it all? Had he really thought that having Ellie made up for getting one third? He'd wondered so many times after the madness faded, and he was left looking into Ellie's eyes and seeing...nothing.

He'd known she didn't love him when he made her marry him. He'd thought it wouldn't matter. That getting her, possessing her would be enough. It wasn't. He hadn't known someone could hide so deep inside themselves that no one could find them. He didn't know how she did it, just that she had. She'd managed to deny him so well, getting her had been dust and ashes.

He'd tried to make her jealous. That didn't work. So he left her alone. No one else could have her. That had to be enough.

At least there was Toni.

His little girl had loved him as her mother wouldn't.

His little Toni. He touched the cold, flat surface. Remembered the warm curve of her small cheek when she smiled at him. When he was daddy and still her hero. Before...

He should never have left her to Ellie, but raising a child was woman's work. She'd gotten her revenge, oh, how she'd gotten it. He'd thought Toni would never—

His shoulders rose and then fell in a heavy sigh. He'd been wrong about her, too. This time he would not be wrong. He could not afford to be wrong. The choice was clear. He could let it happen. Or he could fight.

It surprised him to feel fight surge up out of his gut. Age, it seemed, had not made him resigned to fate. He could not roll over. He could not give in. He sure as hell wouldn't sit here and take it like Phin.

A soft tap and his PA looked in. "It's here, sir," he said with his usual lack of inflection.

Calvino nodded, agreement and dismissal in it. The PA retreated, closing the door as softly as he'd opened it.

Calvino replaced the frame in the drawer, pushing the faces slowly out of sight. He locked it, tucked the key back in his pocket.

He opened another drawer and extracted the handgun. He checked the magazine, then slotted it back in place. He slid it in its holster, strapped across his chest under his suit jacket. He rose and straightened his tie, then headed for the door.

It was past time he met this child of his Toni's, past time to find out who she belonged to, where her loyalties lay. And if he could use her to save himself. Perhaps, in the process, he could lay the ghosts that had haunted him for too long...

∾

"IT'S QUIET."

It was the first time Alex had said anything since he pulled his brother's car into the somewhat dubious parking spot on one corner of the cemetery block. It was another reason she was happy to pedal around the city on her bike. The parking issues and the fact that she was truly dangerous behind the wheel of a car.

They'd walked in silence along the long white wall, cracked in spots, with weeds sprouting up from those cracks. She noticed it changed heights for some reason on the other side of the narrow entrance. It was an odd place for a cemetery, surrounded as it was by city, but it wasn't the cemetery's fault the city had grown out to it, and then beyond.

A green neutral ground ran down the middle of the street, separating this side of the cemetery from some houses and possibly a gas station partly hidden by some trees. It felt as if the street weren't sure whether to swing residential or commercial. It was a common problem she'd noticed in her peddling, her gaze caught by a church-like spire peeking over the top of a house of some sort. The quirky image made her wish she'd brought her portfolio.

"Too quiet?" he muttered.

Nell had the feeling the question wasn't for her. He surveyed their surroundings like a cop looking for threats.

"Do you think we were followed?" She didn't remember anyone behind them when they'd circled the block twice before settling for the dubious parking space.

"This is a bad idea." He frowned at the less than salubrious cemetery interior.

Nell turned to join him in his contemplation. It might not be the best idea ever, but bad seemed a little harsh. She'd followed her instincts, but if his cop instincts were twitching—a burst of chatter broke the local silence and a gaggle of tourists were herded out of the dead space by a guide. He directed them across the street and out of sight, letting silence settle in once more.

Dead space. The nickname suited these cemeteries.

Alex shifted from one foot to the other and hunched his shoulders. Was it her imagination that his cop instincts settled? His last survey seemed a little less intent, falling more in the annoyed range. He wanted to ask her why. She felt that to her toes.

Perhaps if she knew why...but she didn't. Nell couldn't explain why she'd felt a need to look at the place where her parents weren't buried. Maybe she just wanted to get out of the house. Sitting anywhere, being watched like she was about to break out in wise-kid-ness made her want to crawl up the wall. Or out of her new wise-skin.

Sarah was only one who hadn't acted shocked when she said she'd like to do this, though she was hard to shock. It was one of things that made her so great. And so terrifying. It was why Nell joined the band, did bad karaoke with her, even when she'd rather poke out her own eye.

"You don't even know where—"

"I know." This wasn't her first visit to a cemetery, though the Metairie cemetery was more upscale than this one. Were cemeteries upscale? Calling a burial up felt wrong, though most people weren't buried here. They were interred, so it was kind of a lateral move.

This particular "little city of the dead," had a high sinister vibe and a low maintenance look with lots of mildew creeping up the sides of the crypts, rusting mini fences and crumbling stone. The signs of life, the city sights and sounds around them should have reduced the creep factor but somehow didn't. It really did look like a creepy little city.

"Why do you suppose they put them here?" She'd read in the paper that St. Cyr would be interred in the Metairie cemetery in the family crypt. Why hadn't his son been put in the family crypt? It was possible it hadn't been available at the time. Tombs couldn't be opened for a year and a day after use. But it had been thirty years and several days. Was this the wise guy version of being banished?

"They aren't buried here," he reminded her with a touch of impatience.

"I know, but supposedly they didn't know." Who were the crypt surrogates for her parents? Dead body doubles? This place was so different from where they were actually buried. Flat, green, tastefully sprinkled with graceful trees. Neat rows of headstones between narrow, paved lanes. Well-kept versus unkempt. The artist found the contrast intriguing. The daughter—not so much.

"We don't even know which part of the cemetery the crypts are in," Alex said, eying the cemetery entrance without enthusiasm.

Was this the cemetery with the voodoo queen's tomb?

The silence felt intense, despite the sounds of a busy city all around them. She'd mostly gotten used to city noise. The sirens, the horns honking, the clamor of engines revving and brakes being applied, but for some reason this place made it all feel both more and less. Like they were in a dead bubble, not really part of the city but too alive to be part of the cemetery. Some of the dead might rest easy in this place, but not all of them. If you'd been buried under the wrong name, did that make you one of the uneasy?

"Wouldn't you rather—"

She didn't get a chance to hear the rest of the question. A bulky Humvee rumbled down the street and, without even a pretense of trying to park, stopped in one of the three traffic lanes on their side of the neutral ground. Even before doors opened, Alex turned as stony as the angels on the tombs.

A dark-suited guy emerged from the front and opened a rear door. Another dark-suited guy emerged, then another one. The last one to emerge was an old man wearing—in a departure from the black theme—an elegant, gray suit that was wholly unable to mute the thug vibes.

"Calvino." There was a lot of not happy in the single word.

Nell studied this sort of grandfather, curious on so many levels. Well, maybe not that many. Mostly she kept waiting to feel some kind of genetic connection with one of them. A call of shared family blood. This was the husband of her mom's mother. The father of her mom. Part of her DNA string. The thug who may have blackmailed Ellie into marriage. Yeah, her DNA was probably thinking, "I do not know this man, girl, and I do not want to."

He was broad at the shoulders and across his beam. His hair was iron gray, and his eyes were dark and chill. The skin around the eyes, in fact his whole face, had aged pretty well. The lines cutting through kind of reminded her of an evil Tony Bennett. If he had a heart, he didn't wear it on his sleeve. He might not even have it on him. It was a bad time to remember both his wife and daughter had runaway from him.

He stopped about a yard from them, giving her a broad smile that didn't dent the lethal in his eyes, revealing teeth so white and so even they had to be caps. It was a good thing she hadn't expected a happy family moment.

Alex took a half step forward, not interposing himself between them, but kind of implying it. At least somebody liked her.

The silence started to get uncomfortable as Calvino's gaze assessed her face. The eyes narrowed and he uttered a soft, vulgar expletive.

"—you look like—"

"I know." Nell cut him off, tired of everyone looking at her and seeing someone else.

Gray brows arched some and his scary smile got scarier. Then his gaze shifted past her, to the cemetery, and the humor faded. What? Was it a hostile act to visit her parents' not graves? One gray brow arched, as if asking her why? She arched both brows back. It was not his business.

"Visiting Toni's tomb, Calvino?" Alex asked.

Calvino's attention shifted toward him, the smile doing a fast fade. "A Baker." The smile returned, with tiger overtones to it. "Which one are you? There are so many of you, I lose track."

"Do you?" A scary pause, then, "I'm the one with her."

That was one for Charlie, Nell decided, shifting closer to him in mute support. Did his arrival mean someone had been following them or was it a weird coincidence?

Before Calvino could react, another vehicle rumbled down the street. This time it was a long limo. It also scorned actual parking, choosing to stop in the lane next to the Humvee. She guessed that traffic laws were small beans to wise guys, but it still seemed brassy to turn two of three lanes of traffic into personal parking...

More doors opened. More bodyguards emerged. More bodyguards than Calvino had. Then Dimitri Afoniki emerged. One wise guy could, maybe, be a coincidence, but two? All they needed now was grandma not-dearest to take that last lane.

Nell gave Alex a bemused look, but he didn't see it. His glare had expanded to include the new wise guy and his wing men. Flanked and outnumbered, but he still didn't look intimidated. He'd managed to pull his piece without her noticing.

She mentally backed up. His weapon. She wasn't a wise girl and didn't plan to start thinking like one. Besides, she didn't know what wise guys called their armament these days.

Dimitri arched a brow. Was it a required skill for wise

guys? His amused gaze swept past Calvino before settling on Nell. His thin mouth curved into a smile that should have looked good on a face that pretty. And now that she knew why he was interested in her, she liked him even less than before—if that was possible.

"An odd place for a meeting." His gaze took a little trip between her and Calvino again. He ignored Alex as if he were invisible.

Nell sensed some puffing, some ruffled feathers. Lots of alpha-vying-for-dominance, which the already thick air did not need.

It so reminded her of rival boys meeting at the checkout desk. She couldn't help it when librarian dropped on like a shroud—like a coat. *Like a coat.* She needed to better edit her analogies. She gave both men her boosted, stern librarian look, the one heavy with "not in my library you don't."

To her amazement, they looked a bit abashed. A couple of the goons even shuffled their feet. She caught a small twitch of Alex's lips and felt a hint of warm ease the chest tightness she hadn't realized she had.

It wasn't silent, because, hello, city all around, but the street looked and felt quiet, like they were in one of those westerns where all the normal people took cover before the shoot out.

Not a happy thought, but Nell felt the urge to sketch as everyone stared at everyone else, though not all at once, since no one had more than two eyeballs for the job.

It didn't stop them all from trying, which made

everyone but Alex look a bit twitchy. He managed to look both cute and menacing, but she might be a bit prejudiced. One sensed the shadowy presence of all of his siblings and his dad at his back. It more than trumped the plethora of wise guys and goons.

Had she interrupted their meeting or had they come here because of her?

No one wanted to be the one to ask the first question. And there was so much she didn't know it was almost impossible to know where to start her asking. Or to figure out if she really wanted to know.

If they were here because of her, she could figure out why the two wise guys and their respective entourages were interested in a chat with her. They were both afraid she'd come to make a deal with the other. She could tell them she didn't have it—whatever it was—didn't know where it was, couldn't make a deal with Alex Trebek, but why would they believe her?

They most likely didn't believe anything ever. These were two men with major trust issues, weapons, and goons with weapons.

She tried to think of something she could say that someone would believe. The weather wasn't bad, but she didn't think they'd care.

With the weather off the conversational menu, what was left. Religion? Politics? Good places to eat? She sucked at small talk without the cemetery, goons and guns.

The silence was trending toward deafening again when Calvino broke it.

"How do you like the Big Easy?"

Nell blinked. No argument that she'd enjoyed the city more the day before yesterday, but it wasn't New Orleans' fault things had gone uneasy overnight.

"It's—" whatever she'd planned to say, got lost in a squeal of tires. Two squeals, she realized.

Two SUV's swung around the corner.

Both vehicles raced toward their position.

They had to swerve, single file, round the parked wise-vehicles.

There were shrieks as brakes were applied and tires tried to grip pavement.

Both veered toward the line of parked cars but managed to skid to stops that blocked the limo and the Humvee.

And the rest of the street.

Windows slid down.

Muzzles began to slide out.

Alex grabbed her arm and pulled her back toward the cemetery entrance.

The tough guys signaled an intent to fight, until they saw the level of the opposition.

Tough guys turned into Keystone crooks as they scrambled for the only available cover inside the cemetery.

The melee pushed Alex and Nell apart.

Nell landed on her stomach just inside the wall, the breath knocked out of her in a rush. Stars did a spin around her head.

Bullets whistled over her head and dug into the walls and crypts closest to her.

Lots and lots of bullets.

A cacophony that increased as the small missiles hit stone and ricocheted every possible direction.

CHAPTER TEN

It would have been funny if it weren't so damn dangerous.

The brief struggle to get inside the cemetery.

Bullets and bodies going in every direction.

Alex lost his grip on Nell, tried to get to her but had to dive for cover when the bullets tracked his way.

Through the press of scrambling bad guys, and as he skidded behind a crypt, he caught a glimpse of her hitting the ground on the other side of the alley.

He grabbed a rusted fence to keep from skidding back into the line of fire.

He saw one of the goons slam into the ground the next crypt over. Good thing there was plenty of them to go around. No sign the shooters were skimping on bullets.

Alex almost felt sorry for them as two more went down, tripping a third. One scrambled, crab-like, behind a low wall and looked around. Maybe to check on his boss.

Maybe not. Hard to tell if the bodyguards were guarding or dodging.

One guy started to shoot back. Then another. Alex planned to shoot back, too, but not while the shooters were being so generous with the return fire.

Nell had moved on, he noted. Good thing. The attackers lined up like they wanted to come inside and play.

Alex retreated left, heading for a break in the line of crypts, cursed when the ground cover changed to crushed shells. Good thing there was lots of noise cover—the shooting stopped as abruptly as it started. Alex froze, grabbing a fence to keep from falling, the shift of shells underfoot seemed loud in the sudden silence.

A movement to the right drew a short, sharp burst of fire. Someone got dropped.

A hand fell into view, the gun sliding Alex's direction. He stared at it, tempted by the extra fire power. He eased forward. The shells shifted a bit, and then he was back on asphalt.

The gun seemed to be out of sight of the shooters but probably wasn't. He couldn't be that lucky. He eyed a scraggly bush, broke off a section as quietly as he could, and inched it toward the weapon.

He hooked the trigger guard. Tugged. Bullets kicked up dirt all around it, then one hit the handle. It spun toward him. *Thanks, asshole.*

He didn't waste time checking it, not when someone

had made his position. He waited for the fire to kick up again and darted down the alley.

He made it to better cover before they stopped shooting. He crouched by a crypt, trying to slow his breathing.

He needed a plan. And he needed to find Nell. Had they been separated by accident or design? No way to know, so he didn't waste more than a brief thought on it.

The best way to find her was get more help. No sound of sirens yet. Didn't the neighbors care? He pulled out his cell. Too quiet to call, but a text should start something.

He made sure it was on silent, and opened a text window. It felt kind of like trying to drive and text. He had to keep watching—damn spell check.

He wasn't at the secretary, he was at the cemetery. Maybe Ben could figure it out.

Because he could tell he needed to move again.

NELL DID NOT EXPECT to feel homesick with all the bullets flying around, so it caught her by surprise. Her dad had loved the shooting range. Was it genetic?

Not a good time to be the only one not packing—carrying. *Not carrying.* Was it proximity with the goons that was messing with her vocabulary? She hadn't learned to think goon at home, that was for sure.

One of the goons staggered back, falling on his back almost under her nose. He blinked, his stone face breaking into surprise. Surely he knew that being shot was one of the risks of being a goon?

He looked at her looking at him and surprise gave way for something else. Something that prompted her to lean forward. His hand grasped her arm between the wrist and the elbow, the grip on the feeble side.

"Take it."

She started to ask what, but then saw the hand loosely clasping his handgun shift a bit. She felt a bit guilty that the universe had delivered her firepower at this cost, but also grateful. She hadn't made him be a goon.

She leaned forward, gripped the stock, her fingers meshing with his for a couple of creepy seconds. She eased the gun away, feeling a commensurate rise in confidence in her ability to survive. He tugged her arm again, the now free hand inching inside his jacket.

"Magazines—"

She had to admire a goon who could focus on the details like that. Nell reached inside and found three. She also found his wound, blood smearing along the back of her hand as she abstracted the magazines. She stowed them in pockets, one magazine to each, hoping she wouldn't need them. She needed to move but—

"Why?" She wasn't sure he heard her at first.

"Knew your grandma—" His gaze caught hers. "Nice to me when I was a kid..."

"Thanks." It was all she could think to say.

"Go." His head moved in a parody of a jerk, the light in his eyes fading fast.

Before she could, a gunman stepped into sight. The rifle on his shoulder firing almost without a break, he began to pivot her direction.

Range training kicked in.

She lifted the gun and fired. He staggered. She fired again, then jumped and, at a half crouch because the height of the crypts varied without warning, ran for it.

She felt panic rise when she realized the line of crypts were set too close together for her to get through. Her only hope was the alley that looked like it cut across at the end. If she made it that far. And it did cut across.

She didn't dare look back. She knew that would slow her down.

It might cost her the seconds she needed to survive, but her imagination did a great job of bringing another shooter into play, looking for who'd downed his buddy. His rifle lifting, aiming at her back—

Bullets tracked after her, hitting the crypt near her face as she rounded the sort of corner.

Bits of stone rained on her as she skidded sideways, bounced off a metal fence, righted herself and pushed forward, heading for the next turn and then the next. She dodged left, then right—froze when the shooting stopped as abruptly as it began. Flight paused, leaving fright to take its place.

The pungent bite of mildew mingled with the stink of cordite, making her throat and eyes sting. Because she wasn't crying over a goon that used to know her grandma—

She saw a sort of shabby pantheon-like crypt, with

steps and chipped columns. The steps were slightly less gnarly looking than the ground. She sank down on them, avoiding eye contact with the hanging spider webs.

She noticed she still had blood on the back of her hand and tried to scrub it off on her jeans.

Her panicked breathing began to slow. It wasn't silent, but it felt quiet, an intense quiet that magnified the sounds of flight and pursuit.

Everyone seemed to be either listening or—Nell heard a scuffle of sound that was quickly followed by some shots. Was someone actually trying to kill her? Or had the wise guy entourage dragged them into a fire fight?

The last seemed more logical. It didn't take that many shooters to take out a librarian. That she'd dragged Alex into it sucked, even though he'd insisted on coming here with her when he couldn't talk her out of it.

She hadn't really believed anyone wanted to kill her, she realized now, though this didn't feel like it was about her. But she'd been glad Alex came along because she liked being with him, not because she was afraid.

She closed her eyes, took a couple more breaths. Last time she'd seen him he'd been all right. He was smart and tough.

And she'd just shot a man. Her hand shook and she realized she hadn't secured her weapon, which was currently pointed at her calf.

Great. She secured it, checked the magazine. Five shots left. One chambered. Okay. She waited for a burst of fire to cover the sound before shoving the magazine back in place. The stock sat snugly in her palm, the feel of it comforting. It wasn't about the wise DNA, but about her dad. He felt close. She hoped it wasn't because she was about to join him in the afterlife.

He always said where there was life there was hope. Okay, he tended to live in cliché-ville, but he always managed to make even the most tired cliché seem reasonable. And he'd know, wouldn't he?

That she felt sort of safe was an illusion. Something tickled her neck and she turned the shriek into a gasp. She managed not to use the hand holding the gun to swat at whatever had decided to crawl on her neck. If she was going to be chased through a cemetery by bad guys, she shouldn't have to deal with bugs, too.

Was that movement she heard? She strained to hear, her gaze passing over crypts that had little fences around them, creating not just dead spaces, but tight spaces.

She felt caught between the need to get away and a realization that she didn't know where "away" might be. Cowering and hiding seemed indicated, but she also needed to retreat. Where to go was an open question. Not in the direction of the shooting seemed like a good choice. She wished she could figure out where that was. What with the shooting at, and the shooting back, how was a girl to know—

She'd been staring at the crypt across from her without seeing it, straining to hear, but suddenly she *saw*. Her mom's not-grave. She'd managed to find her mom's not-grave by not looking.

Antonia Calvino. 1963-1980

That was all. No *beloved daughter of* or a *rest in peace.*

She checked both sides, not really expecting to see Phil's not-grave close by. Why would their families care that they'd wanted to be together?

Like the tombs around it, it looked neglected, though someone had left a posy of forget-me-nots at the base. No more recent interment dates on the slab. Did that mean the tomb hadn't been opened since her mom's not-burial?

And just like that she knew why she'd wanted to see this. This wasn't the place where her parents had died. It was where they'd been born.

Later, if she lived, she'd feel guilt for undoing what they'd done. But just for this moment all she could feel was grateful to them both for what they'd given up for her. And she knew, because she knew them, that she had been the driving force, the reason they'd fought to live, had built that ordinary life in Wyoming. They'd managed to survive. Could she do less?

It might feel safer here by her mom's not-grave, but it wasn't. In the distance, she heard the sound she'd been waiting for: sirens. At what point would everyone quit shooting at each other and flee before the cops? How long had there been shooting?

She looked at her watch, but she hadn't looked at it when it started, so it didn't help. It probably not been as long as it felt. The cops couldn't take forever to get here, could they?

It seemed she had two choices. She could try to find a

place to hide. Or try to get out. Only way out, that she was aware of, was the way she'd come in. Either way, she should probably move—

She started to lean forward, when she heard a slight sound. She shrank back as a shadow grew long on the narrow path between two crypts to the left of her mom's not grave.

ALEX STOPPED and considered his current location, trying to fit perp movement to his memory of the cemetery layout. It felt like they were being herded. He hated that almost as much as he hated getting shot at. Seemed like if they wanted him going one way, he ought not go that way.

He crouched in the shadow of a tall crypt, wondering why the sirens wailed in the distance without seeming to get any closer.

The silence wasn't a good one. It felt weighted by the menace stalking the many alleys. Other than the usual city sounds, it had gone quiet again. Like everyone was listening. Or thinking.

Thinking seemed like a good idea. Felt like the shooters were trying to herd them away from the gate they'd come in, so that's where he'd go. If backup hadn't arrived, he could remove any roadblocks to getting the hell out and brief the first cops on the scene when they did arrive.

He'd resisted thinking about Nell. He couldn't help

her. She'd surprised him before, though. He hoped she'd surprise him again. That's all he could do for her right now, just hope.

He worked his way toward the outer edge, aided by the occasional outburst of fire. He noticed it seemed to be moving away from him. He made almost no sound. Who knew those nights trying to sneak out of the house would work for him now?

AS QUIETLY AS SHE COULD, she drew her legs up, so that she was crosswise on the steps, as much in the shadow of the crypt front door as she could manage. Suddenly cozy with the spiders didn't seem that bad. They were almost her best friends right now.

It wasn't going to be enough if someone was really looking, but if she made a run for it, well, hard to outrun a bullet. Her heart pounded so loud she didn't know how it couldn't be heard several tombs away.

Everything seemed more. The dead smells. The stealthy sounds. The silence between the sounds. And the shots. A soft sound from the other direction made the one shadow stop. Then another shadow slowly grew on the path on her other side.

Her heart, her breathing either stopped or got too slow to feel or count.

The sense of being in *that* nightmare, the one where

someone looked for her, the struggle to wake up and not being able to...

She shrank back into the moldy stone, aware of the hot, damp smell of rotting things and oddly cold stone through her thin shirt...

The shadow on the right appeared to reach out for the next crypt. The limbs and body distorted, but despite that, she could tell he held at least one weapon.

The other shadow appeared frozen in place.

Sirens filtered in, though they still seemed too far away.

Off in the distance a horn honked.

Both shadows jerked, as if startled, their images wavering on the ground.

A long pause...

Right shadow moved again.

Her brave plan to live for her parents seemed like wishful thinking now...

Left shadow decided to move now, too.

Right reached the point of exposure first.

Dimitri Afoniki. His attention was directed away from her first, then his head began to track her direction. He stopped. He stared at her, weapons ready.

She stared at him. Pretty sure she couldn't get hers up in time—

It seemed like he'd started to lower his, when he spotted the left shadow.

Even if he didn't shoot her, he could shoot her in the crossfire.

Left shadow paused at exposure point, then stepped into view.

Calvino.

He stared at her. Then at Afoniki, then back at her.

If moments froze, then this one did, despite the heat. Nell felt the chill of death reaching out of the crypt at her back. Felt it laughing...

Like weird mimics, both men lifted fingers to lips, paused, then gestured for her to join them. What a choice. And how did a girl choose either without getting shot by the one she didn't choose? Not that she wanted either one.

Before she could figure it out, a scrabble of sound had both men darting forward out of sight.

My heroes.

Before Nell could find a new spot, too, the scuffle of sound came closer, and she spotted yet another shadow. Now she had time to ready her weapon.

A man stepped into view one crypt down from where Afoniki had been.

She knew he was one of the shooters because he held a rifle, auto or semi, she couldn't tell which. And he had a nylon stocking over his face.

Time slowed. His head was turned away from her and angled for listening.

He started a turn toward her. He'd see her. He couldn't help but see her—she sighted her weapon on him—

A sound, a shift of footsteps on gravel in the direction of Afoniki's heroic retreat.

The shooter hunched, hesitated, and then headed toward the sound.

Nell made herself count to ten, then lowered her weapon, sweat beading along her upper lip and running down her back.

Time to move. She wasn't good enough to go ghost, like the military guys liked to call it, but she felt like a ghost. She bet she was pale enough to pass as one. She wished she was as invisible as one and hoped not to be dead as one...

She shook her head—and her thoughts—told herself to get moving.

She worked her way back along the crooked line, changing alleys, trending toward the entrance as sirens continued to wail, though she'd lost the ability to tell if they were getting closer.

A flurry of shots broke the long silence. An exchange, she decided. Rifle fire and handgun fire. Was that a shot across the alley? She couldn't tell, but it seemed closer. Maybe she should find a place to sit tight and wait—

"Someone flanked us! Johns and Stevens, get back and cover the exit," a harsh voice ordered. "Don't want no one getting out of here alive."

ALEX KNEW it was a risk dropping the shooter watching the bad guys backs, but he'd had to take his shot. No way to make a quiet approach. He cussed at the shouted order and made his run for the street. He paused by the wall and did a quick check. No sign of anyone, but they could be hiding, waiting for him to pop out.

Heard footsteps pounding toward him.

Make his move or fall back—

He dodged out into the street, weapon ready and headed toward the car, zigging and zagging, using the line of parked cars for cover as soon as he could dart between a couple.

When no shots took him down, he dug in his pocket for his keys. He came around the driver's side, shoved the key in the lock, and turned it savagely. He yanked the door open—a shift in the heavy air was his only warning before the blow...

NELL HEARD the pounding of footsteps coming down the main alley and heard others—they seemed like they were outside the wall? She angled her head. It sounded like it.

Lots of confused sounds, mixed with confused shooting. She used the confusion to make a short dash that took her within sight of the cemetery gate.

She crouched down, aware her position wasn't great if the ordered-back shooters swept the area as they came by. She readied her weapon, though she was less certain of her ability to hit a moving target.

And then they were there, running in a weaving pattern down the center alley, weapons pointed back the way they'd come. The two paused twice to let off a couple of rounds and then they crouched once and fired a sustained burst at someone.

She heard a car engine start. That got their attention. They jumped up, picked up the pace, their attention directed toward the street now.

The two shooters ran past her position, as she pressed against yet another damp and web-infested crypt, tracking their progress with her gun. Once they had passed by, Nell eased up, ready to duck down if they looked back her way. They reached the gate and stopped, starting a right-to-left sweep—

The shots caught first one, then the other, sending both staggering back a few steps before they dropped, first to their knees, then they both fell forward onto their faces.

A car came into view on the street, backing toward the snarl created by all the wise rides.

Ben's car.

Alex. It had to be Alex.

Nell cast a careful look back along the alley. She didn't see anything. She un-chambered the bullet, tucked the gun into her jean's waistband, then jumped up and ran, passing between the two walls.

She made the turn that put the wall between her and the cemetery's interior with a lot of relief and a renewed burst of energy. An arm waved from the driver's window, then disappeared. Seemed like Alex wanted her to drive. So he could shoot, she guessed. He didn't know she was a crappy driver or that she had a gun. No time to tell him she should be shooting, not driving—

She scooted between two parked cars and grabbed the handle, scrambling behind the wheel and pulled the door closed with a hearty slam. She fumbled with the controls a bit, managed to get the car in gear and started down the street with only one wobble. Only after correcting that did she glance toward Alex—

Only it wasn't Alex.

It was that bald Curly guy.

And he had a gun pointed at her. As Ben's car rolled toward the corner, she noticed something lying on the ground between two, parked cars. No, not something.

Alex...

CHAPTER ELEVEN

Nell didn't have to tell bald Curly that she hadn't driven for a while and no, driving wasn't like riding a bike. She kind of sucked at that, too, with or without the gun pointed at her.

She'd never been that great at self-propulsion. And it was hard to get better at it in a city with a million-plus pot holes. Just saying. Okay, just thinking, because even talking was outside her skill set at the moment.

"Do you have a driver's license?"

The question sounded like it emerged from between gritted teeth.

She did not have time to verify that. Steering an unfamiliar car down narrow, rutted streets with other cars playing chicken required all her attention—well, the parts left over from worrying about Curly and that gun she assumed was still pointed at her.

"Wyoming one." Barely. She'd passed her driving test

because it was late in the day, and he only made her drive around the block. A very quiet block.

"You've lived here two damn years!"

There was a kind of yelpish wail to that last word, as Nell narrowly missed the streetcar, which seemed to think it had the right of way. She didn't have time to wonder if it did. There were more obstacles to dodge. People to not hit.

"Been on a bike for all of them." Unless Sarah drove, which she always did. Sarah knew all about Nell's lack of driving skills.

A light went from green to yellow. She hit the brakes and heard a screech of tires behind her. She made the mistake of looking in the rearview mirror.

She closed her eyes and braced for the hit. It didn't come. She wasn't sure if she was glad or sad about that.

Bald Curly let loose a string of swear words, ending with, "You don't never brake at a yellow light!"

"But I wouldn't have made it through before the red," she felt compelled to point out. Was the bad cop really criticizing her for a legal stop at a light? If her eyes weren't scared open, they'd have twitched. With extreme reluctance, she looked at him. It had to be asked. "Which...where..."

"I need what your Ma and Pa left you."

It wasn't a huge shock, though it was a relief he didn't seem to know about St. Cyr's ring. She bit back a "get in line" snark. She didn't want to make him any more pissed off than he already was. She'd always hated line jumpers.

And bad cops. She didn't mind guns but didn't like them pointed at her. She licked dry lips.

"Only things that I have left from my *mom and dad* are back at Sarah's."

"Then that's where we're going."

Nell noticed the green light for the other direction was going yellow. "I don't actually know how to get there from here." This statement was so true, she almost winced.

"You don't know how to get home?"

"When I know where I am, I can get home just fine. But I'm not really sure where I am." She'd spent most of the drive watching Alex drive, rather than watching where Alex drove. Obviously she had not expected to have to drive home. Her gut clenched at the thought of Alex, of how still he'd looked laying there. "Did you kill—"

"Didn't have to. He didn't see me."

It was not comfortable feeling relief and panic at the same time. She was glad for Alex. Sorry for herself since she was looking Curly in the eyes. She didn't like Curly. She hadn't liked him from the moment she met him.

The light changed.

"Get this bucket moving," he ordered, moving the gun in a threatening manner.

Not the brightest bad cop around, if he wanted her to keep driving. On the one hand, moving was good. He couldn't shoot her. But there were cars and people all around. And he was an old dude. How fast could he flee a scene? And why should she do what he said when—

"You're just going to kill me. I think I'd like to get it

over with." She lifted her hands from the wheel and folded them across her chest. She didn't look at him as she said this.

She didn't actually want to get it over with and he might notice that. But she didn't see why she should have to drive herself to her own death. Which probably wouldn't go well. The driving and for sure the dying.

Horns started to honk.

"I'm not—"

"I've seen you. I'm not stupid." Interesting how people equated smarts with driving skill. She had a high IQ. And was easily distracted. Not ADD, her mom used to joke, but definitely DD, a daydreamer, she'd explain to the various teachers when they became baffled enough for a parent-teacher conference.

The level of honking increased. Some shouts joined the complaint parade.

"I won't have to kill you," he said, with a thread of desperation, he cast a look out the window, then kind of ducked his chin as pedestrians started to stare. No crowd yet, but give it some time and maybe the Lucky Dog cart would show up. "I promise I won't kill you," he added in what he probably thought was a sincere tone. "I wouldn't—"

Nell gave him a skeptical look.

"You won't talk cause of what I know about your Pa."

Did he really think she'd care enough about what people thought about her dead father to keep her mouth shut about him? Because she was dang sure her dad wouldn't care. Or was he hoping she'd be stupid enough to believe him?

Probably that last one.

"And—" The hesitation was long enough for Nell to give him a reluctant look. It might have been what he'd wanted. He gave her this ghastly grimace that was probably meant to be a smile. "Calvino ain't your grandpa—"

"I don't want to hear it." Nell jerked her head away from the sight of his attempted paternal-ness.

"But—"

"Don't say it or I swear I'll crash this car." Actually... she eased up on the brake, though not a lot. She'd never been that good at thinking and driving. She made it through the light before it changed, but she left some unhappy people behind who didn't.

She took it slow enough to get caught by the next light. *I don't believe him.* That goon had called Ellie a nice lady. If she hadn't wanted the rich bad guy, she sure as shooting wouldn't have had an affair with the dirty cop. And there was Charlie Baker. Nell didn't know him, but she had a feeling that once a girl fell for a Baker...look at Zach. He'd got two women to have a bunch of kids with him.

For some reason, this focused her thoughts. Her head felt clearer than it had since she rode into Alex's car jacking.

The photo. Something about it had bothered her at the time—had it been just last night? With a sort of awful clarity—admittedly culled from watching television—she realized that it might be the kind of photo someone gave a hit man.

Had he been the one hired to kill her parents? Had he dug through old photos, or weird trophies, for the photo, so he could pretend he'd loved Nell's mom?

Was she supposed to believe that he'd have been stupid or reckless enough to have an affair with a wise guy's wife? Or that her grandmother had an affair with him? Forever no. Did. Not. Believe. Him.

She gave him a surreptitious look out of the corner of her eye. He didn't look happy. This helped ease some of her unhappy, though not all of it, since he still had the gun. There were a lot of stoplights between here and home—at least she assumed there were, since she wasn't sure where home was from here. How fast could she get out—

"Do up your seatbelt." He gave her a bland look. "Wouldn't like you to get hurt if someone rear ends us at the next yellow light."

Okay, he wasn't stupid, just because he looked and sounded stupid. She pulled the belt across her chest and snapped it in place. She noticed he hadn't done his up.

Apparently he wasn't worried about getting hurt despite having seen her driving. Her escape thoughts quit circling. Landed even. Yeah, it was time for a crash. It would probably happen whether she planned it or not.

The light changed. This time she punched it. The force of it slammed her against the seat back. She may have half closed her eyes. She'd never felt the need for speed.

And this was more speed than she'd ever wanted or needed.

Curly squealed in terror.

Nell peeked.

She yelled.

She spun the wheel.

Managed to swerve around a car.

And into oncoming traffic. She almost swerved back.

But the sounds of Bald Curly's pig-like squeals were kind of music to her ears.

And it wasn't as easy to swerve back as it looked in the movies. Not pelting along a seriously rutted road.

He shouted something she couldn't hear. She probably didn't want to hear. He couldn't shoot her until she stopped, so she probably shouldn't stop...

Cars came at them, swerved away with squeals and honks. Lots of honking. One car swung to the side, narrowly missing a parked car, revealing another car behind it, one that didn't have as much time to react to her bad driving. Off to the side, she saw a free section of curb. It looked like a great parking spot.

Though for her, it would more likely be a great crashing spot.

She hit the brakes and cranked the wheel. Too hard.

The car spun in a complete circle, but did skid toward the curb. And that sweet parking spot.

Going to miss it—

The incoming car clipped the fender, altering their trajectory just enough.

Though it didn't slow the sideways skid—

The curb was high enough for the hit to jolt her to the roots of her teeth.

The crunch of metal to cement was loud. Horrifying, yet kind of satisfying.

Even belted, her head made painful contact with the steering wheel.

She might have heard Curly's head slam into something.

His whine cut off, but any silence got swallowed up in the sound of multiple vehicles crashing into each other. Tires squealed from brakes applied by other drivers.

She heard a crash louder than the others and saw a truck sliding right at her...

WITH AN ICE PACK held against his aching head, Alex morosely scanned the chaotic scene.

The attack squad, well, what was left of it, was face down on the street, their hands cuffed. Looking a bit surprised they weren't cuffed, were the wise guys—what was left of them—making two uneasy huddles off to one side.

A pity both Afoniki and Calvino had managed to come out alive. It looked like someone had winged Afoniki.

The cops that weren't watching bad guys and wise guys were searching the cemetery. Shouts hadn't brought Nell out of hiding. Some cops were searching the surrounding area, but what if whoever had clocked him and taken Ben's car had also taken Nell? If she saw the car, she might think it represented safety.

One of the searchers came out, a cop name of Higgins. When he caught Alex looking, he shook his head.

Alex didn't sigh or look relieved. He was a cop with a bunch of cops. Higgins gave him the guy version of a worried look.

"You look like you could use an ambulance—"

"I need a car." Alex cut him off. If she was in Ben's car, if she was still alive, it was because someone still hoped she had useful information. Or they'd guessed she had the ring? And the only place where she had anything was back at the house. "Put out a BOLO on my brother's car."

He gave them the deets and Higgins fed the info into the radio. Should he send people to the house? Ben was there, but he hadn't answered his cell. Alex tried him again. He frowned as the call once again rolled over to his voicemail. It didn't have to mean something bad. Just because nothing had been good for two damn days—

While he waited, he considered what he knew. It wasn't much, but he'd guess that no one would go to this much trouble to take out the former librarian. According to the first arrivals on the scene, someone had logged a bunch of fake 911 calls that had sent the first responders scrambling and had resulted in their late arrival here.

"Um, Baker?"

"What?" Alex spun around, his frustrated pacing cut short.

"We have a hit on that plate. Accident about three blocks from here—"

"Take me there, Higgins. Now."

IN TYPICAL NEW ORLEANS FASHION, the traffic snarl quickly out distanced the main crash site. Their progress stalled at least a block away. Alex shoved open the car door.

"I'll walk the rest of the way." He looked around. "Get more people here, Higgins."

He had to jog for over a block, then turn a corner—there it was. Ben's car. It looked like it was parked against the curb. Not a bad job except for the truck embedded in the back half. He rubbed his aching head, which jogging had not helped.

A Lucky Dog cart hovered near the outer edge of the melee. He shook his head. He'd seen them beat the cops to an accident scene more than once, but it still surprised him.

Speaking of which, the crowd looked unruly, angry—except for those buying dogs—and the center of angry was a big guy yelling and gesticulating to someone inside Ben's car. Driver's side. Sirens in the distance. One of them an ambulance.

He started forward, used his badge to shift people out of the way. He felt a need to get to the car quickly—while reluctant to see what was inside. Who was inside. Some uniforms arrived from the other direction, also on course for the heart of the accident. He sorted through the jumble, saw five cars in addition to Ben's, either smashed together or damaged.

Alex reached the big mad guy and tapped him on the shoulder. When he didn't turn fast enough, he spun him around. And saw—*Nell*. He shoved the bully to the side and bent to look inside.

She gripped the steering wheel, staring out the windshield, beads of sweat turning her hair damp around her face. She was pale and had blood trickling down the visible side of her face, but she was alive. Relief almost took out his knees.

Beyond her, on the passenger side was—his brain almost froze. Curly? He tapped on the window when he wanted to smash it. "Nell?"

After what felt like a long pause, she turned and looked at him, relief breaking over her face like a wave. She fumbled with the door, got it open, tried to scramble out and couldn't. She looked surprised by that.

"You're still buckled."

"Oh. Right." She looked down like she didn't know how to unbuckle. Maybe she didn't.

Alex reached in and released her seatbelt. She fell forward into his arms. Heat from the car came out with her. Lots of nasty, but not enough to make him move. He hugged her tight. Muttered soothing crap. It seemed to help. Her trembling began to ease.

"Are you all right?" he asked at the same time she asked him the same question.

A spurt of laughter shook her, or maybe it was tears. She scrubbed her face with one hand, glanced a bit uncertainly around.

"He...I thought...I saw you..." She buried her face in his shoulder again.

"It's okay. I'm fine." He had to add, "Nice parking spot."

A muffled chuckle. Then a sigh. "Your brother won't think so."

Another pause, but Alex couldn't disagree with her, so he just grunted comfortingly.

"His gun is under my seat. I took it from him after—"

She shuddered and he patted her some more. Then Curly gave a groan. Alex knew he probably had at least one more weapon unaccounted for, maybe two, if he'd brought his own with him. Which he should have.

"Can you stand?"

"I think I'd rather sit." She shifted to the side, sinking onto the street with her back against the car and she used her sleeve to wipe her face.

Still no color. A bruise formed around the swelling on her forehead. Bleeding looked to have slowed some, though. They both owed Curly one. He crawled in and did a swift search, extracted two more weapons. Handed two of them off to a hovering uniform and stowed his back where it belonged. Then he crouched down by Nell and waited for Curly to notice him. He groaned a few times, finally turning his head and meeting Alex's hard gaze.

He blinked, puzzled at first. He glanced around. Alex saw the moment when memory dots connected. There was a mix of defiance and shame in his eyes.

"Alex—"

"Save it for your lawyer."

Nell watched as the EMTs extracted Curly from Ben's car and settled him on a stretcher. Curly kept his eyes closed. Perhaps he sensed Alex's stony glare following him, until he'd been stowed in the ambulance. Behind the fury, Nell sensed pain. He'd been a family friend. His dad's friend and partner. That was a worry. Nell had no frame of reference for judging Zach, except by his kids. Until the swamp of her parents' past has oozed up into her life, Nell would have taken that as proof Zach was clean. Now....

Without comment Nell submitted to her own period of assessment while Alex strode around securing the crime scene and looking tough and yes, tragic. He had this wrinkle between his brows that made her knees go weak. She needed to quit mooning and start thinking about how to survive. It was more important than how to get the cop to kiss her again. Though if she was going to die—

She shifted, trying to ease the stabbing pain in her side.

"Something hurting you?" The EMT asked.

Nell put her hand to her side and realized she still had

a handgun stowed there. She'd shot someone and then left the scene. Was that going to be a problem? She didn't think it would be a good idea to produce it in such a cop-intensive environment.

They were all peeved at her, even though it was Curly who was dirtier than the gutters. Would that make them trigger happy? She did not want to find out. So she smiled a bit stiffly at the EMT and said, "Everything hurts right now, but not—"

He seemed satisfied by her answer. He got up and handed her an ice pack. Nell must have looked confused.

"For your black eye."

"I have a black eye?" Great. She applied the pack to the indicated eye.

"You probably ought to have your head examined."

Not good to have someone say that to her two days in a row.

"Can I get my head examined later or do I have to do it now?"

The EMT shone a light in one eye, then the other. He considered it for several seconds. "You can go, but you need to follow up with your own doctor."

He was in Wyoming, but Nell didn't mention that. She nodded. If she didn't figure things out, her next doctor's visit was likely to be with a coroner anyway.

Now there was a happy thought to add to all the rest. She gave herself a mental shake. Doing it for real would hurt like a son of a gun.

She was a librarian for Pete's sake, not a quitter or a

whiner or—a wise kid. She didn't have time to wait for the headache to clear. Suck it up time, as her dad used to say. That was one advantage she had.

She didn't know this—didn't know their past. She didn't know the wise family, didn't know who they'd been, but she knew *them*. She knew her parents, obviously not as much as she'd thought, but they'd raised her. They might have tried to keep this from her, but they had to know that could change. They had to know the past could come back to bite them—or Nell—on the butt.

Her best friend lived in New Orleans. They couldn't have kept her away forever, despite the spirited attempts to do just that. That must have caused them some heart burnings, but they knew Nell, too. They'd raised her so—

They'd prepared her. Her dad prepared for everything. He'd been a walking plan. She needed to sort through the past, through the homilies and lessons and things that didn't look like lessons then, but probably were lessons seen in hindsight. So all she had to do was figure out which ones applied to this. She blinked. It hurt, but she persisted.

Okay, the teaching her to shoot was obvious. Those hours at the shooting range, balanced against the family budget? Yeah, that was one of the lessons. It hadn't seemed like it at the time. Most everyone in the state shot at something at least once. But what else?

Have a plan.

Suck it up.

If you're not dead, then you're all right.

Yeah, those were part of it. So what had been their

plan for this? For the big reveal? There had to be something in the stuff she had—unless she'd given it away—no, she decided. They knew her. They would have made sure she didn't give away the farm—and just like that she knew. She *knew*.

CHAPTER TWELVE

Alex was relieved to drive away from the crash site, even if it was in a rental car. He was surprised he'd managed to get one, though his insurance company probably hadn't had time to black ball him yet. It had barely been twenty-four hours since his truck went down.

He glanced at Nell. She stared out her window, as if the street were more interesting than it actually was. She had her elbow propped on the edge of the window so she could hold the ice pack over her eye.

He cleared his throat. "How—are you all right?"

She looked at him with her uncovered eye. "My mom used to tell me, if you're alive, then you're all right." A pause. "Lessons from the former wise kids. Kinda gives it a new twist or something knowing that..."

Her grin was crooked. Her tone was wry. Her sigh made his chest tighten. He felt an all too familiar sense of not knowing what to do. With six sisters, it was almost a constant. "They were kids."

"Yeah. It's kind of hard to imagine your parents as kids and then..." She adjusted the pack and sighed again. Silence reigned for a couple of blocks.

"I saw it, well, one of them."

"Saw what?" It felt like he missed a beat. This was also a familiar feeling.

"Toni's tomb. The place where my mom isn't buried."

"Oh." Was that good? Bad? No clue.

"Someone had left forget-me-nots there. They were pretty."

Most flowers were, weren't they? Did he know what forget-me-nots looked like?

"I wondered if someone didn't want to be forgotten? Or they didn't want to forget?" She looked at him. "It's kind of sweet."

Women always thought flowers were sweet.

He cleared his throat. "Did it...help...with your...problem?" He'd like to know he got shot at and allowed his brother's car to be tanked.

"Oddly enough, it did."

He did not know what to ask.

"It's like, I've been trying to connect the dots between then and now and—"

When the silence drew long, he reluctantly prompted, "And did you?"

He had to admit, he'd never tried to connect his dad to anything. He wasn't big on connecting dots if there weren't bodies involved. He kind of winced, since this one did involve bodies. Lots of them.

"Yes and no." Her smile was wry, a bit sad. "I'll probably never be able to wrap my head around my parents being those two kids."

"I don't suppose anyone can with their parents." Of course he'd seen pictures of his dad, of his mom, when they were young, but they didn't look like his parents. Not even slightly.

"They were just kids," he said, surprised when he shouldn't be, he supposed. He'd known, but he hadn't *known* it. At eighteen he'd headed for college, not into hiding—well, it was a kind of hiding. He glanced at Nell. "What were you doing at seventeen?"

The hand holding the ice pack lowered, as if she'd forgotten it, allowing both eyes to widen, then narrow in thought. She looked pretty cute with a shiner.

She'd surprised him again, crashing the car and disabling Curly. Not to mention walking out of that cemetery alive. Her mom and dad would be proud of her. They should be proud of themselves, too.

In some weird way, they'd managed to prepare her for this, while totally not preparing her for this. His temple throbbed a bit. His brain didn't like this kind of non-crime-solving thinking. It never had.

"Seventeen. Oh wow." She half sighed. "Semi-painful. Graduating, not top of class, but not bottom." A slight smile curved her mouth. "So excited to be going somewhere, I didn't mind—" She stopped.

"Mind?"

"My parents talking me into becoming a librarian."

"Instead of art?" he guessed.

She nodded. "They were big on practical. I guess pregnant at seventeen and fleeing for your lives does that to parents."

"Would do that to most people," he agreed, using the pause for a light to study her. He wondered why he felt uneasy. There was a slight frown between her brows. Combined with the swelling, it gave her a puckish look. "You didn't mind leaving your high school sweetheart behind?"

It was the fishing kind of question he usually only used in interrogations, but since he couldn't call it back...

She looked down, tracing the printing on the ice pack. "I didn't have a boyfriend, though I had a serious crush on Luke Skywalker."

"Luke? I thought all the girls went for Han Solo."

"I was a geek. He didn't have a girl. I didn't have a guy. I felt a bond." Her grin was cute and it chased some of the shadows from her eyes. "What about you?"

"Me? I was desperate to leave." He would have crawled on his hands and knees to get away. "School dorm was a fortress of solitude compared to home."

"Wow? Seriously?" He nodded. "It freaked me out for about five minutes. There were probably more people in the one building than my whole town. And then Sarah—"

"—formed the band?"

She chuckled. "That came later. She came in and

looked at me for what seemed a long time. She was beautiful, confident—everything I wasn't—and I was sure she was disappointed in her roommate, because girls totally daydream about that stuff at seventeen. And then she... smiled and I knew it was going to be fine. Great even. We stayed roomies for the whole four. Are friends forever."

"Must have freaked your folks for you to get a New Orleans roommate. Did they seem upset when you visited?"

Nell looked rueful. "I never did. They were good. I never suspected a plot. Bright bulb, aye?"

"Parents know what buttons to push," Alex said, with a touch of bitterness. Look at him, living with his dad again. And wondering what Calvino had to say to him. Afraid to ask.

His hands gripped the steering wheel. It was one thing to wonder if Curly was a bit crooked. But knowing his dad had been his partner—he'd never wondered before. Until Calvino. He wished he'd punched the guy.

"That they do." Nell sounded more resigned than bitter. "I'm still trying to wrap my brain around a grandmother who was wooed by three bad dudes and then fled with her lover into the night. Not the grandma you dream about." She hesitated, as if considering a tough question. "Do you think she really is dead?"

"Legally she is." Could she have hidden like her daughter? Still be out there somewhere? Maybe with a life insurance policy? She'd have needed something to elude

Calvino. The case against her was as compelling as the one against Nell's parents.

Curly had implied he'd known Nell's mom survived, that he'd helped her, but now Alex wondered. He'd been pretty shook up for someone in the know. It didn't matter now. Grabbing Nell had sealed his deal, of course, but it did make a cop think. And wonder....

"It's kind of funny, in a way."

"What is?" He blinked, impressed she'd found anything funny in the situation.

"You know too much about your family. And I know too little." Her grin was brave, a bit ragged around the edges. She looked good with the shiner.

But she was wrong. He didn't know enough about his dad. Not nearly enough.

THEY WERE ALMOST to the house and Nell still hadn't found a way to tell Alex about the guy she'd shot.

Oh, by the way, I popped a guy in the cemetery.

So there was this guy with a gun and I had to shoot him...

No matter how many different ways Nell tried, it just sounded...creepy. Wise kid-ish.

Were there right words for admitting you'd shot some-one? All those years of movies, TV and books and nothing to help with the problem. How sad was that? With confession time running out, Nell let her thoughts edge up to the actual shooting. It had surprised her how easy it was. That she hadn't hesitated.

Was it the wise DNA? Or her training?

Whatever the reason, it had probably saved her life, but still, didn't one pause and reflect or something? Have that split second moment where you made a conscious choice?

Even now she felt worse about the goon who'd given her his gun than the guy she shot. Maybe if she had to look at him on a slab. Or in the eyes. Maybe the reaction came later? Post traumatic something or other? Not a lot of catch-your-breath time yet. And she'd about ran out of confessing time.

She still hadn't figured out how to tell the cop she'd shot someone. Shot sounded better than, *I killed a guy*. She didn't know he was dead. He probably was. She might not drive straight, but her shooting...

Maybe if she'd been raised wise—no. That wouldn't have helped. They never confessed. They called lawyers.

She glanced at Alex, caught him glancing at her. He looked puzzled, possibly a bit worried. Of course he was worried. And more than a bit. He had to face his dad, tell him about Curly, and then tell Ben about his car. All of which had happened because she drove her bike into his carjacking.

"I am so sorry." She could tell him about the shooting, hand over the gun later. It wasn't cowardice. It was kindness. Okay, so it was cowardice *and* kindness. Whatever.

No need to pile on the bad news until it was time to pile it on.

Nell showed Alex how to get into the driveway that snaked between the back of the house and what used to be the carriage house in the old days. He pulled to a stop behind his dad's car and turned off the ignition but didn't reach for the door handle.

"I should be the one to tell your brother about his car," Nell muttered. "It's all my fault."

"You didn't hire the shooters."

"Definitely not in my budget." She frowned. "I wonder who did hire them? And who they were hired to—" She stopped.

She didn't really wonder that, at least, not now. They had to have been after Calvino and Afoniki. It was the only thing that made sense—if anything could. At the moment, all she wanted was to go into the house and not leave until the shooting stopped. She needed a bathroom, too.

"Time to face the music."

Nell grinned. "Air guitar or drums?"

Alex grinned back, shoved open the door and came around to open hers. She couldn't hide a grimace as her body protested movement.

"Are you sure you shouldn't be in an ER?"

Oh temptation. "If this goes badly, we'll both need an ER," Nell said, a bit wryly.

Alex didn't disagree, which told her more than she

wanted to know about how things would probably go down.

Alex pulled out his phone and activated the screen. He frowned. "Still nothing from Ben. He might have been called into work."

Nell didn't know if she should be worried or grateful. She didn't feel like the same gal who'd thrown her leg over her bike yesterday morning and ridden off into the rising sun, or possibly away from it.

She let her gaze trail over him as he started to put his cell away. He was a good man. Some women liked bad boys, thought good was boring. Now, more than ever, Nell was grateful he was good. He wasn't at all boring.

He looked good, kissed better—was she bad to be thinking this stuff right now? Last time she'd asked—but last time she'd been Nell, the wait/author/librarian. She'd added quite a few more tags to her identity in the last two days. Would it come out who she was? If it did—like she'd had a shot at him anyway.

He'd kissed her like she had a shot.

He was divorced, probably had baggage left over from that. Everyone seemed to, if one believed the talk shows and reality television.

He didn't like kids and she seemed to attract them like flypaper. Three strikes, actually probably more than three. She was too tired to add them all up. It was easier to just accept that she was out. What was it about her grandmother, and to some extent her mom, that had attracted guys? And why hadn't they passed any of it on to her?

Before Alex could stow the cell, it vibrated insistently. He looked at the number. "It's Frank. I'd better take it."

Nell couldn't remember where Frank fit in, though she was sort of sure he was a sib.

She nodded, then pulled the door open and slipped inside. Maybe if she confessed before Alex came in, Ben would be mostly over it. Or not blame Alex for it.

She headed down the long hall that had been the servants' entrance back in the day, reaching what was now the mudroom. She stopped in surprise at the sight of the goon waiting there.

He looked at her.

She looked at him.

He'd been with old lady St. Cyr, she realized. Why had she come back?

Nell wasn't sure she cared, except for being too tired to deal with formidable right now. She blinked and realized the goon's mouth had curved up into a sort of smile. He wasn't good at it, but perhaps goons didn't get a lot of opportunities to smile.

She tipped up the edges of her mouth, all she felt capable of. "Hi."

His smile widened, though it still kind of sucked as a smile. "Yo."

She blinked, wondering why she was surprised to hear him speak. Of course goons had voices, even if they didn't use them a lot around the boss.

She searched for something else to say. She didn't find anything. She wished Alex would hurry. She felt uneasy, with no discernible reason why. Well, except for the goon part. She studied him almost absently.

She wondered where his partner was, while glad he wasn't here staring at her, too. The artist in her took note that he looked older than...what?

Guess she'd always thought, in a vague sort of way, that goons were on the young side. That they had a prime, like guys in sports. He wasn't bad looking. Blonde. Cold gray eyes. A Bad boy, but not a sexy one. Just a creepy, middle aged one.

"That's some shiner."

Nell touched her eye. She'd left or lost her ice pack. She couldn't remember where. "Banged it on the steering wheel."

He frowned. "You were in an accident?"

Technically it wasn't an accident when she'd made it happen, but it was too complicated to explain—not that she wanted to explain to him, so she gave a tiny, noncommittal shrug.

She wished she knew a way to retreat. And she wondered why she felt she couldn't? She didn't feel like she could go forward either. She didn't want to get close to him or turn her back on him. Her bump throbbed.

"I need some ibuprofen." That meant she had to go toward him. Get past him and everything would be all right, right? She sucked it up and took a step toward him, then another. There was no upstream at sea level, but it felt like trying to swim up something.

He stepped to the side, as if to let her pass, but the next

step brought her in line with the laundry room door. It wasn't usually standing open. Something caught her eye, and she looked, even though there was a distant, gut twitch against it.

The second goon lay sprawled in front of the washer. And the dryer. He was long. And limp. "Does...he need help?"

"No. Not anymore."

"Oh." Nell blinked a couple of times. "Did he try to—" —kill you, she'd meant to ask, but he cut in.

"He got in my way."

"Oh." Nell edged back, lest she too get in his way.

"I'm Roger Dunstead," he said, then added, "Junior."

"Of course." Without the clarification, she'd have surely thought he was his dead father. Okay, with all the people turning out to not be dead, maybe she did need the clarification. "Do they call you Junior?" Oh crap. What were goons called? "Or Mr. Dunstead?"

She attempted a bright, clueless look, as if the name meant nothing to her. She didn't want to be disrespectful to the guy who probably had a gun—oh yeah, there it was. Not quite pointed at her, but definitely deployed. Suppressor, too.

"I can shoot Baker when he comes in," he said, his tone calm and cool. "Or you can step in there. Stay real quiet until he's passed by."

Nell didn't hesitate. Alex wasn't expecting a problem. She couldn't, she wouldn't let him be gunned down. She also couldn't let herself think about the others who must be somewhere in the house...couldn't worry right now about whether they were dead or alive...

She stepped carefully over the dead guy, trying not to look too closely at him, while somehow managing to see the bullet hole—she wrenched her gaze away and leaned against the dryer.

Her knees had lost structural integrity again. She had a gun, but it was stuck in her pants and she was pretty sure Junior would notice if she tried to get at it.

He followed her in, shifted the downed goon's legs out of the way, turned on the light—there was no window— and shut the door.

He did it matter-of-factly, efficiently even, without taking his eyes, or his gun, off her. Not sure why this seemed odd. Goons would need to be efficient, or they wouldn't last long.

It was bad enough to smell the dead guy's nasty after-shave, but the close quarters also brought to the forefront her own need for a bath after her adventures in the ceme-tery and car crashing.

She took a cautious sniff—no reason to give him more reasons to shoot her—and regretted it. Oh yeah, she needed a shower and clothes change. Her gaze seemed unable to stay off the body, so she turned it to the shelf of laundry-type stuff. They were almost out of laundry soap...needed to get it on the list...

She knew her thoughts were trivial. Trivial helped keep the scream down in her chest. It kept trying to crawl up her throat and if she screamed, Alex would come running—

The creak of the door opening made her jump. She heard footsteps coming down the hall. She tensed, wondering if he'd shoot Alex anyway? Why should she believe him?

ALEX STOWED his cell and walked up to the door, his steps as slow as his thoughts. The word about Curly was spreading through the family. Frank was worried about Zach. So was Alex. Everyone wanted Alex to talk to Zach. He wanted to talk to his dad, too, once he figured out what to say to him, what to ask him...his frown deepened.

It was a strange thing to realize your dad had lived a life you knew little about. That he had secrets. Why hadn't his dad mentioned Charlie's connection to Ellie Calvino that night? Or, if he didn't want to do it in front of Curly, why not later? He frowned.

He knew the names of his dad's siblings, for the most part, but Charlie's name hadn't come up much. He'd thought he was dead, not missing. Was he presumed dead? Did it matter now? It felt like it did, though logic said it was more of a footnote than a clue to anything.

Alex rubbed his face, leaned his back against the closed door, just for a minute. Or four. His head hurt. Pretty much every part of his body hurt. And tired? He'd passed tired sometime in the night. He was now deep in the sleep deprived zone. On the fast track to zombie. He wanted to go lie down somewhere dark and sleep until he couldn't sleep anymore. Then he wanted to sort the mess into something less messy.

Then he could, maybe, talk to his dad. And face his siblings. Face Ben and tell him he was without wheels, too.

Two days.

Had it only been two days since Nell rode into his carjacking and upended his life? Forty freaking eight hours? What would she do with three? If she had just minded her own business—

His thoughts ground to a painful halt, because, yeah, his brain hurt, too.

If Nell hadn't ridden into his life, she'd be dead.

Oh, there was still some doubt who had been the target of the first shooting, but his gut had no doubts. Alex might have a cavalcade of perps who hated him, but most of them were too smart to shoot a cop. They didn't like the heat.

All three wise guys had a next-in-line who wouldn't like an heir to two of the organizations popping up. The only one who might benefit if she lived was Afoniki. It gave him a shot at bringing it all back together. Alex had a feeling the slime ball had figured it out, too. He'd tried to be suave before the shooting started.

Calvino had shown up without his heir apparent, who might feel threatened enough by Nell's existence to try to take her out.

And the old lady? According to Nell, that meeting had been chilly. In fact, Nell had yet to have a happy family moment. His family might make him crazy, but as far as he knew, none of them had tried to kill him—at least intentionally.

He rubbed his face again. It didn't help. Time to face the music and he hoped to hell it didn't involve air guitar. Almost reluctantly, he smiled. Nell did play some mean fake drums. Okay, maybe he wasn't completely sorry she'd ridden into his life.

He opened the door and stepped inside.

Now, when it was too late, Nell wondered why she'd believed Dunstead when he said he wouldn't hurt Alex. Didn't Miss Marple advise against believing what people said? And this was a bad guy who probably hadn't been on speaking terms with the truth for years.

As if he heard her thoughts, or suspected a revolt incoming, he murmured, "You kill a cop, you get more heat."

Not a stupid man, despite making his stand in the laundry room. Nell tried not to be offended by the notion that her death wouldn't result in "heat." She did have other things to think about. If this was a kidnapping, then what happened next?

It seemed to take a long time for the steps to pass the door and continue on. She exhaled a tiny sigh of relief. The air was too nasty for a big sigh. Damn, she could taste it in her mouth.

After another long pause for Alex to get down another long hall, she heard the distant murmur of voices that seemed to say that Alex had reached the kitchen safely. And that someone was alive in there to talk to him. She gripped the edge of the dryer and tried to figure out what to do next.

Funny how strong the will to survive was. For the first time, she felt a connection to those two wise kids.

"So, now what?" She kept her voice low. At the moment this was between her and Junior. She didn't have much time. It wouldn't take Alex long to smell a rat. He was a smart guy. And there was a lot of rat to smell.

"I want the proof," he said, turning so his back was against the door.

"The—" She didn't have to pretend to be puzzled.

"She told me you had it. The proof your father killed mine."

"She..." It wasn't really a question. He worked for grandma. But there was something else in his voice. "My... grandmother told you that?"

He stiffened. "I'm more kin to Mrs. St. Cyr than you are. I've been here for her when no one else was."

Yeah, between kin it was all formal names and all. Not that grannie had asked Nell to call her anything family-like. But it did seem that Grandma had wound him up real good, like she'd tried to do with Nell, she realized. Had she pointed him at St. Cyr, too?

"She tried to kill my father." Nell didn't actually know this, but it felt true and might be a way to mess with his head, particularly if Dunstead thought the old lady had material instincts. "Her own son. You really think she'll be loyal to you?"

"Phil betrayed her. She told me all about it. I would never do that to her. I'm better than a son. I've helped her for years, and I gave her something Phil couldn't. I gave her the secret."

"The secret?" His dad's secret?

He half frowned. "I didn't know I had it or I would have told her sooner. But she understood. I was just a kid. When my dad told me, I didn't know what it meant. And when he died, people hounded my mom about it, but they never asked me."

"How old were you?" Nell asked. It seemed like keeping him talking was a good plan until she figured out a better one. "When your dad told you the secret."

"I was twelve."

"And she...helped you?"

"She gave me a job when I left—when I turned eighteen."

She didn't help him a whole lot. More like she helped herself to a useful tool, one with mama and papa issues.

"But you didn't tell her the secret until recently." Zach had said the feds thought Dunstead had the dirt on all three men. Could he really have told his twelve-year-old son where it was?

"He told me not to tell."

"And the—Mrs. St. Cyr never asked you about it?"

He shifted uncomfortably. "She did a couple of times, but I didn't know, I didn't realize she was okay."

That must have pissed grandma off. All those years and he had it. Dunstead didn't know it, but grandma would make him pay for that—when she didn't need him anymore.

"She told me about how she and my dad were supposed to be partners, but the old man told Phil to take him out. So then I knew it was okay, that she was the one I needed to tell. When we get the proof, I'll be her right-hand man and we'll run it all together."

How would the proof that her dead dad had killed his dad thirty years ago help them "get it all?" And why would Phil have kept information that incriminated him? It made no sense. But if it incriminated Grandma—had her Dad known? Had he been kinder to his mother than she'd been to him?

Or—had he known that to use it was to let her know he wasn't dead? Had he protected his family by keeping her secret, but kept whatever it was because he could never be completely sure his mama wouldn't find him?

"I'll need the ring, too." He half smiled. "I saw the old man slip it into your case. I was watching it all go down. For her. I set it all up for her, and she asked me to be her eyes and ears for the hit."

Poor Phil. Poor Dad. And poor me, stuck in a laundry room with a crazy guy and a black widow outside waiting for this tool to deliver her the goods. "Does...she know I have the ring?"

"I wanted to surprise her with it. She thinks the cops have it." His smile turned down. "Binx was supposed to get it after he popped the old man. He claimed he did get it but wanted more money, so he pretended he'd hand it over. He shouldn't have lied."

Memo to self, don't lie to the crazy guy. Not that she'd planned to. She sucked at lying. She studied him thoughtfully, anxious to postpone the truth-telling moment. If he was the old lady's go-to guy...

"I suppose you're the one who shot at us," Nell said.

He grinned. "She doesn't like you."

"She hadn't even met me," Nell pointed out.

"You were surplus to requirements."

That sounded like a direct quote.

"And now?" Nell shouldn't have asked it. She knew the answer.

"You have something we want."

And then she'd be surplus again.

ALEX STOPPED in the kitchen doorway, his gaze sweeping the room. His dad, the scary widow, Sarah and his brother. No one looked happy. At least he wouldn't be bringing the mood down. "Where's Nell?"

"What do you mean? I thought she was with you." Sarah looked alarmed.

"I had to take a call." He didn't think he was outside

that long. Had she slipped past this room? Was she worried about facing Ben? That didn't seem like her.

"Perhaps she wished to refresh herself before joining us," Mrs. St. Cyr said.

They both needed to freshen up a lot, Alex conceded, but something in the old lady's eyes bothered him. Her lashes swept down, as if she sensed his interest and just like that his brain went from fuzzy to clear.

He knew the power of a stare. He was a cop, so he deployed it. She held it pretty well for maybe a minute, but finally lifted her brows, a shade of annoyed creeping in.

He kept the pressure on, while he mulled what she might be up to. Was she making a move? The old lady shifted, a small one, but a shift. Oh yeah, she was. But what was the end game? They couldn't get Nell out of the house without—chaos and confusion.

They thought—or were afraid—Nell had something. He didn't need to look at the two boxes they'd left stacked by the door, waiting to be ferried back upstairs. They even had her name written on the side with markers. Old lady didn't know she had her hopes pinned on nothing.

Big house. The three men couldn't cover every exit and search for Nell. A little divide and conquer on the menu? Take them out one at a time? If that was the plan, it was a bold move for the old lady. Did she really think her bodyguards would take the fall for her?

But how had someone got Nell past this door? There was nowhere in the short hall from back door to kitchen where someone could hide—wait. There was a door. He'd seen it, without seeing it. A coat closet maybe?

"What's behind that door back there? Between here and the back door?" he asked, without taking his gaze off the old lady. Her lashes flickered at the question. Score.

"The laundry room?" Sarah asked, puzzled and worried in her voice.

There'd been something about the door. Something he'd noticed when he walked by...

"Where are your bodyguards, ma'am?" Alex asked. Light. There'd been a thin line of light showing in the dim hall. Not a lot. It wasn't that dark in that very long hall. It could have been natural light.

"I sent them on an errand."

"I'll bet you did." Alex smiled grimly. "Does the laundry room have a window?"

"No." Sarah's voice was harder now, too.

"You think they are holding her in the laundry room?" Ben asked the question. He was up and around the table before he finished. He hooked a hip on the table edge by the old lady and pulled out his weapon, not pointing it at her, not yet.

The old lady answered his question with an involuntary tightening of her lips.

"That's crazy," Sarah said. "What's the point?"

"In confusion, there is opportunity," Zach said, a weapon appearing in his hand, too.

For a fraction of a second, Alex wondered—his dad looked at him.

"You got a plan, son?"

Alex grinned. "If they want confusion, then maybe we should give them some."

～

"Taking them a while to miss you."

Nell made a sort of face. "I've always kind of blended into the woodwork." Until New Orleans. Wearing the face of a wise wife had popped her out of the background.

"Nell!" It was Sarah. A pause, then she said quite clearly, "She could have gone up to her room. Let me check."

She gave Junior a "see, people do miss me" look. Sarah's footsteps pounding up the stairs seemed a little louder than usual...

"Time to start talking." Junior pulled out his cell phone and waved it at her. "I text Mrs. St. Cyr with the location of the proof and we leave. No one gets hurt."

It seemed unlike Grandma Not-Dearest to put herself at risk like this. A chill shot down her back as she realized that none of them were supposed to walk out of this house alive. The others would live just long enough for her to talk and then...

"I don't think I trust her to keep her word," Nell said. It was them against Grandma and Junior, but only she knew it. If she was going to make her move, she needed to come up with one sooner rather than later.

Her gaze bounced around the small space. All the toxic

liquids had stinking child-proof caps. She had trouble with them when she wasn't under threat of death.

Her gaze went past the mops and brooms. Tracked back. No child locks on a broom. Granted she'd never jousted but she had seen *A Knight's Tale*. Surely that counted for something. And if the hit was good and solid, it might give her the time she needed to get the gun out.

Nell shifted, grimacing as if she hurt. It was easy to do, since she did.

With her right hand, she rubbed her back, as if trying to ease the pain, but using it to get closer to the broom. Or the mop. Either one would do. Which would be easier to deploy? Neither had what she'd call great balance. She needed the pointy end, so thinking the mop. The broom had that big, straw end. Mentally she planned her grip, her moves.

"I wonder if she went back outside? I meant to bring her cell in, but I forgot." It was Alex's voice.

Junior went on full alert, his gun leveling on her. Nell tried not to frown. Alex knew she didn't have a cell—was it a message? Did he suspect they were in here? It was possible.

Hope poked a little sprout up out of the dark determination. If he knew—but what did he want her to do—cell? She looked at Junior's cell.

Junior frowned, waved the gun and mouthed, "Back."

Nell pointed at the back wall and he nodded. She did it with meek obedience. It put her right where she wanted to be. The sound of footsteps drew Junior's attention back to the door. Nell used the moment to check out the clutter. Yeah, for sure the mop.

His cell phone vibrated. The sound oddly loud in the small space. His gaze jerked down.

Nell grabbed the mop. Swung it up and around.

She lunged forward.

She almost tripped on the dead guy.

She staggered a bit, but momentum carried her forward despite the stagger.

His gun started to come up.

"Now!" she yelled.

The point caught him in the solar plexus. She knew that because she was a librarian. She even knew how it was spelled.

The jolt of the hit reverberated through all her sore places. And knocked the mop from her grasp. His gun went flying. Her foot landed on a dead guy body part.

She jumped back.

She managed to get the gun out of her pants, but she had no time to chamber a round.

The door flew open, possibly from a well placed kick. It hit him in the back.

He staggered toward her. Gasping like a landed fish. He tripped over the dead guy. He tried to grab the dryer.

She just had time to apply the butt to the temple he presented so invitingly.

He dropped like a stone onto the dead guy.

And then Alex and Ben were in the room, making it very crowded, but in a good way.

CHAPTER THIRTEEN

While Ben called in the troops, Alex followed Nell to the kitchen. Zach had the old lady covered, which widened Nell's eyes a bit until Sarah grabbed her and hugged her.

Alex met his dad's worried look with a slight, reassuring nod. The only one who didn't look happy was the old lady, but she'd probably forgotten how years ago. He didn't know if they'd be able to bring it home to her. Dunstead had started to unravel as soon as the cuff's snapped around his wrists. His elevator had probably quit going to the top a long time ago. But he'd damn well try.

Nell, her lop-sided gaze sober but steady, watched the old lady call her lawyer, then get escorted out by a couple of uniforms.

"Are you all right?" Sarah asked, bringing her a glass of water and a couple of tablets of something.

"It's a bit weird to see your grandmother get hauled out

in cuffs. I suppose, if my parents hadn't run away and had managed to not get killed, I'd have grown up used to that." She blinked, then smiled ruefully. She looked at Alex. "She was in on it, though Junior is so whacked, I wonder if she'll managed to wiggle out of it."

"In on what?" Alex asked, making the automatic switch to cop. It was easier and more comfortable.

She'd hugged him after Curly, but this time there'd been too many bodies between them for hugging. He liked her, maybe more than he realized before the near-death experiences.

She was funny, cute, he was impressed she managed to arm herself in the cemetery, and she could handle a mop.

His dad had stowed his weapon and pulled back from this scene. Now he watched Nell with a slight frown between his old man brows. Was he remembering Charlie? No question they all needed some thinking time—which wouldn't happen until Alex got some sleep.

"She told him I had proof that my—that Phil killed his father."

Alex tried to process this, but it made no sense.

"Why would Phil—" Zach started to ask, then stopped. "Can't fix stupid."

"She played him pretty good," Nell said, propping an elbow on the table and resting her cheek on her hand. She looked like she needed the help keeping her chin up.

"You're pretty whacked," Alex said. "Why don't you give me the short version and when you're rested, we can get your official statement?"

Nell blinked, covered a yawn with her hand and nodded. "Short version. Right." She added the other hand to the chin prop. "Junior hired the guy who popped St. Cyr on the old lady's orders. Then he killed that guy. He is also the one who shot at us and killed your truck. Oh, and he told her the secret that his dad told him." She paused, as if replaying things. "And he knows about the ring. He was watching the whole thing." Another pause. "I think that's the big stuff." She frowned, rubbed her face.

"You're done," Alex said. "Do you need help up...?"

"I'll go with her," Sarah said, her eyes worried, despite the smile.

Nell stood up like everything hurt, which it probably did. She started to leave, but stopped, her gaze moving between him and his dad. "Thanks."

For a minute, it seemed she wanted to say more, but exhaustion defeated her. Alex didn't mind. He wasn't ready for more. He turned back and found his dad watching him, but he wasn't ready to talk to him yet either.

"I need to help Ben," he said and walked out before Zach could play the dad card.

NELL SANK onto her bed and looked at Sarah, seated at her desk.

"So." Sarah sat relaxed, her fingers tapping the desk-top. "You're not dead."

"I'm a little surprised about that," Nell admitted. Maybe three times really was the charm? She needed to shower, but the climb had sapped her. It had been forty-eight hours that would live in infamy, not to mention memory. If not for the kiss, she'd have tried to scrub them out.

Sarah made a scoffing sound. "Your DNA has to be loaded with survivor instincts. Look at your parents."

Nell had been trying to see her parents for two days. "I saw Toni's grave."

"You mean her not-grave."

Nell's smile felt wan, she looked up, found Sarah's eyes full of compassion. "In a way, it really is Toni's grave." Nell gave her friend a wry smile. "It's like they both did die here, were buried here, because they stopped being those two kids and became my parents."

Sarah sighed. "It's still hard to believe."

"I know." She made a face. "I'm so over cemeteries for the time being." She gave her the short version of her adventures in bad guy dodging.

"You wield a mean mop." Sarah shook her head. "Girl, you could write a book."

"That has its big finish in a laundry room?"

"Saved by the broom." Sarah chuckled.

Nell made a face, which made her shiner hurt. "Kind of embarrassing." Should she have told Alex about the music box?

"What's wrong?" Sarah tipped her head. "Besides the obvious."

Nell managed a wry grin, but it faded fast. "I think I know where it is."

"It? The proof?" Sarah straightened.

"The something."

"But we looked through everything—" she stopped. "We didn't look inside the insides of the music box."

"It's probably the only thing my dad would know for sure I wouldn't get rid of."

NELL WOKE to sunshine and the knowledge that while there was still crime scene tape across the laundry room, all the cops were outside the house, not inside anymore. Ben had explained that, until they had a better idea of the wise guys' intentions, there would be surveillance on the house.

Nell wandered around and eventually found Sarah on the phone. When she hung up, Nell asked, "Please tell me everyone isn't canceling their bookings?"

"Quite the contrary. We've just about doubled our bookings," Sarah glanced at her watch, "in the last two hours."

"How many of them are my scary relatives?"

Sarah laughed. "I haven't had time to Google all of them yet, but they seem to be the normal rich people who can afford us."

Nell sank back in the chair. "Wow." The relief was, well, there was a lot of it.

"I'd still have preferred that the business got toasted instead of you."

"You—"

Sarah held up a finger. "Don't say it. We're sisters from different mothers, though I have to say, I thought I was the one with the *motha*."

Nell laughed then and it felt good, even though the question felt like it hung in the air between them. It for sure was in Sarah's eyes. She rubbed her face, then sighed.

"I think I have to open it, even though I don't want to." If there was something in there, then the last, faint hope that this was all some weird mistake would be gone forever. Okay, it was gone now, but forever was still in play. Or at least denial was still sort of possible.

"I kind of figured you'd say that." Sarah stood up, bent and lifted the music box onto her desk. Then she slid a flathead screwdriver and a hammer into view. "Oh, almost forgot." She pulled out some duct tape. "For the lid."

That made Nell laugh again. For sure she did not need *Memories* playing as she dived into the murky past. "Right."

They taped the lid shut, then tipped the box, so that one seam of the base was exposed. It might have been hard, but she was her father's daughter. She didn't work a lot in wood, but she'd helped him whenever she needed to talk to him, or he needed to talk to her.

She gently worked the flathead into the seam, then tapped it until a gap appeared. She took her time, working her way around the base. When it was ready to lift clear, she looked at Sarah and got a thumbs up.

"Right." She lifted the base up and off and set it on the desktop. Sarah hooked a hip on her side of the desk and leaned close, though she waited for Nell to take the first look. She leaned over. "There is something."

Plastic wrapped, it seemed to fill the space until she lifted it clear. There was a compartment, a fairly substantial one. The base of what she guessed were the music box workings appeared to start about halfway to the lid.

Nell studied the package. She found the edge of the plastic and pulled at the seal. There were several layers of fabric, possibly to mute any rattling if someone shook the box, as Alex had done. Nell peeled back each layer of stiff, faded cloth until finally—

"It's a letter, addressed to me." The paper had yellowed, the sealed edge no longer perfect. Nell slid a finger in and the flap lifted. She pulled out a couple of folded sheets and spread them out on the desktop, so Sarah could see. She did it without pausing, because if she stopped to think about it...

"Do you want me to—"

"No. Sisters remember?"

So, shoulders almost touching, they bent over the faded, but familiar script.

OUR DEAREST DAUGHTER,

We are both so very, very sorry. We hoped and prayed

that this moment would never come. That you would never need to see this letter. At first we thought we'd never tell you. Why should anyone ever connect you with the kids that we were? But every day you grow more and more like me in looks. And your drawing shows such promise. Who is to say that some day you won't be famous? It is my hope that when that day comes, that we are here to tell you our story. But even normal life is full of uncertainty and risk. We could not leave you ill-prepared if some mischance should bring you in contact with either of our families.

THE STORY WAS, for most part, what Nell had heard. There were a few details that weren't known.

MY MOM TOLD *me that Dad and Phil's father had plotted and planned for us to get married, but that we wouldn't be allowed to choose what kind of life we wanted to have. I was seventeen and I learned that my dad had forced my mom to marry him, that he would only love me if I did what he wanted. And then I found out I was pregnant. If I lived long enough to have you, would they let me live to raise you? Your dad and I didn't think so and neither did my mom.*

"SO ELLIE DID HELP THEM ESCAPE," Nell murmured. "I wondered." She scanned the sheets. "But they don't seem to know what happened to her either."

"No mention of anyone else helping them," Sarah said. "I wonder how old they were when they wrote this and sealed it up?"

Nell shook her head as she re-read the final paragraph once more.

TAKE THIS PACKAGE, *leave it sealed, please, and give it to the proper authorities.*

"You shall know the truth and the truth shall make you free."

Don't fear it or forget it, our darling daughter. And please know that we loved you more than anything or anyone. Love, your mom.

"THE PROPER AUTHORITIES?" Nell looked at Sarah.

Before she could answer, her phone shrilled. After a short conversation, she hung up, looking a bit bemused.

"That was Frank Baker, the one who is with the FBI. He wants to come and get your statement." She grinned. "If he looks proper, I say we hand this hot potato off to him."

"Works for me," Nell said, her gaze once more on her parents' last message.

~

ALEX SLEPT deep and he slept long. He woke feeling like he'd had a few dreams, but he didn't remember them and wasn't sorry about it.

Nell did her mental dumps by sketching. For Alex, he did his mental dumping in his dreams. This morning, he didn't want to know what worried him. He checked the time on his cell and amended that to afternoon.

It had been late when they finally cleared the crime scene. He'd been relieved his dad didn't wait up for him. Would he be that lucky now?

He swung his legs over the side of the bed, rested his forearms on his knees and put his head in his hands. It still ached, along with most of his muscles. He needed to think. He hated to think. He preferred doing, but he didn't know what to do without thinking. Crap. He'd shower. For some reason, thinking was easier in the shower.

But it wasn't. Oh, the water helped ease the aches and pains. But his thoughts cycled uneasily between his dad and Nell.

How did you ask the dad—who could still kick your ass, by the way—what had really happened thirty years ago? And why had Calvino been to see him? And oh, by the way, would it bother you if I went on a few dates with the wise guys' granddaughter?

He shouldn't see her again. He didn't have to if he let Frank and Ben take over. He wasn't actually official anyway.

But he wanted to see her again.

He was a cop.

Even if she wasn't a crook, she was related to a bunch of them. It could hurt his career. Or it might help it. You never knew for sure what would help or hurt in the Big Easy. But he should probably put it in the negative column, just to be on the safe side, right under "she attracts kids like honey attracts flies" and before "would probably piss off his dad."

The reasons to see her were not compelling. She was cute. She had guts. She made him laugh. She'd gotten him up a tree. It had been nice up the tree. He liked kissing her. A lot. He would like to do it again. He could probably find someone else to kiss, but he'd learned that if you wanted to kiss one girl, kissing a different one didn't help all that much.

Dating, even kissing a girl, wasn't like marrying her. They could go out, be friends, couldn't they? He didn't like admitting it, didn't plan to admit it ever again if he could help it, but he wasn't sure he could stay away.

He dressed and headed into the kitchen, hoping that— hope died.

Zach sat at the table, sipping his coffee like a man who had years to sip and wait.

"Sit down, son," he said, pushing a chair back with his foot.

He didn't have to. He was forty years old and he could damn well—his legs kind of went wobbly and his butt hit the chair. Okay, the old man wanted to talk, they'd talk. He looked at his dad, opened his mouth to ask about Calvino, but what came out was, "I like her."

His eyes widened in horror, not helped by his defensive tone or his dad's grin.

"She's more like Ellie than she knows," Zach said. His grin faded. "And she's got some of the same problems."

Alex considered this, considered several responses before saying, "I'm not going away, Dad."

Zach studied him for as long as Alex had pondered. Then he smiled, a bit wryly. "I'm glad to hear it, bubba." He pushed back his chair. "I've gotta meet Leslie, and Frank wants you to call."

Alex opened his mouth to ask—but he closed it. He still wasn't sure, though he did know one thing. His dad was a good man.

CHAPTER FOURTEEN

*ne week later*

NELL STARED AT HER SKETCHBOOK. Between giving statements to Ben and Frank, Nell had sketch-dumped everything she could onto page after page of multiple sketchbooks.

Alex had come by a couple of times, but he'd been a cop both times. She'd seen him make the switch after the shooting, so it wasn't a shock. She might have been a little disappointed, but she sensed he was clearing decks, too, just in a different way.

It didn't mean he'd come back as a friend. Her relatives had to be a problem for him, or his career anyway, even if he might kind of like her personally. A little. He'd kissed her like he liked her.

She tried not to think about the kiss. It made her swing between hope and despair. It had been a great kiss and it would suck to never do it again. Most of the time she managed not to think about it, though it was harder at night. And when she was tired. And when Alex was around and not kissing her.

No one told her what had been in the sealed bundle she'd given to Frank, and she didn't ask. After he left, she'd carefully closed the case up again and returned it to its place in the sitting room.

She'd even lifted the lid and remembered her parents through one, still painful refrain. Then she decided she could remember her mom and dad without the tinny music and went to find Sarah.

About halfway through the week, Alex's baby sister, Maddy, showed up and told her she was going to represent Nell's interests. She also explained what it meant to be "Baked."

Nell had no comment to make on being Baked but had felt a need to point out that, "I can't actually afford a lawyer."

"Oh don't worry about it. I need the practice and I like the view."

Nell wasn't sure what this meant until Alex arrived. There was obviously some sibling-type, ongoing joke between them. They may enjoy it for different reasons, but Nell also liked the view when Alex was around.

Nell wasn't sure it was Maddy or the wise families that killed any mention of her from the news stories about the shootings.

From Maddy she learned that Curly had had a heart attack and probably wouldn't live long enough to go to trial.

Information about Junior and Grandma Not-Dearest was also hard to come by.

Maddy said she might beat the rap. She was a "canny old bird."

It was also Maddy who told her they would be exhuming the bodies from the not-her-parents'-crypts tombs.

"ID is going to be a bitch, if they can even get one."

"Because it's been so long?" Nell asked.

"That and, you know, they remove the bodies from the coffins after a year or so and deposit them in a lower part of the tomb, so that the crypt can be reused. All the remains will be mixed together. And then there's the heat issue. Chances of any DNA being left is slim and then matching it to anyone thirty years ago? Doubtful."

Nell nodded. "Why bother then?"

"My sister, Hannah, loves a challenge. And you never know. They matched that king that was in the parking lot."

Nell blinked. She did recall reading that story, but who was Hannah—

"Hannah's a forensic pathologist."

"Wow. Your family really does have all the bases covered." They were steeped in law enforcement. A totally law-abiding family. And she was steeped in what? Her genetics were hip deep in crime, in crime families, but her nurture had percolated resolutely through dull. Ordinary. It was an uneasy combination. And amazing. In a very dull way. So dull, she'd almost died in a laundry room. Which made it both dull and ironic.

Afoniki-the-younger had cancelled the dinner party, and paid the fee without a single threat. No one but Sarah knew Afoniki-the-older had invited Nell to dinner. It was a couple of weeks out and who knew, maybe he'd die before she had to figure out what to do about it.

There'd been no further contact from either branch of her newly discovered relatives. When things calmed down, she would like to research Ellie's family. She figured that had to be the line where her honest genes came from. Perhaps some research would turn up the honest DNA in her dad's family, too. Though she wasn't too eager to dig into that murky pool. For some weird reason, she was a bit miffed the Families seemed to be ignoring her. It was illogical and a bit crazy.

Sarah must have sensed her feelings. "It's better not to have expectations about family or—"

—anyone else, she didn't say. She knew that Nell knew all about not having expectations about guys.

"I just wanted to reject them first," Nell admitted with a wry grin. "I guess I should have expected the bad guys to be better and faster at it than me."

Each time Alex came as a cop, and left as cop, Nell's hopes sank a little lower. She'd liked him and had thought he liked her. Could they be "just friends?" Okay, probably not, unless it was friends with kissing and what guy could handle that?

But she needed to apologize to him. She'd apologized to Ben about his car.

Zach had looked a bit bewildered by her apology to him. She couldn't explain to him she was sorry about wanting to draw him as a zucchini and the whole blushing around him deal.

Laura got one, too. Nell still hadn't got her head examined. Weird how the first apology, one that was oddly cathartic, had led to more and more until she'd had to stop herself from writing apology notes to her grandparents.

Nell hadn't left the house—or gone up the tree—since Grandma got arrested, but she knew they were still under surveillance. One of the cars occupied a really sweet parking space out front. The other made their back parking challenging. She wasn't sure if they actually needed protection, or the cops couldn't bring themselves to give up the prime real estate.

It had been a couple of days since any Baker had been by. It was a pity. The black eye was nearly gone, and she could almost walk without wincing—not that she jumped up when the sonorous front bell clanged—though she did jump.

She heard Sarah tap down the hall toward it and turned her attention back to her sketch, tweaking one of the images that wasn't quite right...

"Hi." Alex leaned against the jamb and grinned at her. "You look...better."

She was mostly more rested, though she did have intermittent trouble sleeping.

"Thanks." He looked better, too.

And she noted with a tiny flicker of something that might be hope that he looked less cop. In fact, he looked very relaxed. Cheerful even.

She felt the edges of her mouth curl up and her insides relax. *Oh crap. I like him.* Her heart wasn't on the line. She'd known him for nine days, but there might be bruising in her heart's future, if she weren't careful.

He straightened, took the two strides—my his legs were long—and sank down next to her. Not quite touching, but close enough that she could smell him. Dang, the boy smelled good.

"Is Maddy helping you okay? She's new at the lawyer crap."

Nell's brows arched. "You sent her?"

He grinned. "She wouldn't have come if she thought I sent her here. Let's just say I...wound her up and aimed her. But I'll deny it if you tell her."

Nell chuckled. "I like her." *I like you. Dang it.* Now that he'd relaxed, she realized how tense and grim he'd been during their two days in wise-hell. Even when he'd come up her tree, he hadn't been this easy going.

"Something's happened?" Changed for the better?

"That is the general trend according to my brothers."

He frowned, but it wasn't a grouchy frown. More a thinking frown. But different from the cop thinking frown.

You've known him nine days, girl. You don't know him well enough to know his frowns. Chill.

"And to what do they think things are trending?" That sounded so librarian. She almost winced, except he smiled and turned on the couch, lifting an arm to rest along the couch behind her.

Maybe there'd been a hint of sexy librarian in there? A girl could hope.

"According to Frank, the families have issued a hands-off order on you."

She felt the warmth of his arm along her back, though it wasn't quite touching her.

"So that's a good thing?" Unless it meant Alex couldn't touch her. If he wanted to—

He grinned. "Very good."

What could have made them care, she wondered. "Because I don't have any information anymore?"

"And," he shifted a bit, his grin turning a bit devilish, "the various Bakers might have let it be known our family has an interest in your well-being."

"Oh, Alex." Nell didn't know what to say. "After everything that happened, all that's gone wrong since I rode into your carjacking? You all should have signed a petition or chipped in on a hit to take me out..." She looked into his oh-so-blue eyes. "Thank you."

He shifted now, looking uncomfortable. "It's our job, in one way or another."

"So does that mean the guys out front are leaving?" And you, she wanted to ask? Is this the last time you'll be by? She could get clingy if she weren't careful.

"If we can get them to give up the parking spot, they should be gone by tonight."

"So much good news, is there any bad?"

"Actually, after a week-long battle with the insurance company, I am mobile once more."

"Congratulations." Nell smiled.

"Yeah, they get the first born I'll never have, and I get to pay my arms and legs in insurance premiums. But I'm rolling again." He gave her a look that had a touch of hopeful in it. "So, we both have something to celebrate"

"We do?" Nell gave him a suspicious look. Was the comment about the first born a warning? Or just a joke?

"I have wheels and you don't have to go into Wit-Sec."

She hadn't thought about Witness Protection. Since Junior might end up there, Nell did not mind missing it. She'd have missed Sarah, too.

She was tempted to suggest picking air instruments, but she didn't think she had the nerve. She could ram a goon with a broom, but—what?

She couldn't ask him to kiss her again. Been there done that. Doing it again would sound needy. He liked coffee. She could offer him coffee. She sniffed cautiously. Maybe not. She didn't know how to make it. She had never learned to manage Sarah's pot.

"That is good news," she said. She hadn't felt this awkward up the tree with him. Maybe she could ask him—

oh my gosh. She was not asking him up a tree again. She swallowed dryly. Did a brief, frantic search for something else... "How is your dad?"

Alex kind of grimaced. "He's got a girlfriend."

"Really? I mean, how nice. Is it...nice?"

"I don't mind. At least...he's been alone a long time."

Thirteen kids would tend to isolate a guy. Maybe as much as not wanting any kids? Nell still wasn't sure how she felt about Alex's anti-kid ban, but did not feel it a ban to further kissing. Nor was it her business. Apparently.

"He wanted to set me up." Threads of horror filtered into his tone.

"Ouch."

"He acts like I can't find my own dates."

"You must meet—" Nell stopped when he gave her a look. "Homicide. Yeah, probably not a place to meet—but your sisters. They must know..." Was she really advising him on how to get dates? She wasn't sure who she was more annoyed with.

"I don't need their help either." He scowled a bit. "I met you without their help, didn't I?"

At a crime scene, but—did that mean he saw her as a potential date?

She realized his gaze was kind of fixed on her and sort of shifted in a way that could be taken as agreement without committing to it if she were wrong about what he meant.

She felt a weird need for him to show her she was more than a witness, slash, victim to him.

She studied him through veiled lashes. Maybe he was as nervous as she was? He didn't look nervous. *You probably don't look nervous either.*

"So," he rubbed his face, "now that I'm rolling again, well, you know."

Nell knew. Or did she? She wasn't sure, but she was willing to look sure while he looked at her like that. She tipped her head, studying his eyes.

Yeah, she liked that look, though describing it was beyond her mental capabilities at the moment. He leaned in, the arm on the couch back shifting down until there was contact. Not like arm-around-her contact yet but touching.

His other hand shifted closer, too, just shy of touching. Close enough for her heart to speed up. She hadn't meant to smile yet, but her lips slipped the leash and curved.

He smiled back. Leaned in some more and covered her hand with his. Comfort and something not comfortable flowed up her arm.

"It's very brave of you to be rolling again," Nell said, her eyes going wide for some reason. "With all those potholes and bad drivers."

He was tempted. She saw it in his eyes for a second, but he didn't say it. Besides, she wasn't driving anywhere, not even on her bike. She had a thought, as both warm and friendly amped up in his gaze.

"If you have wheels, that means—you parked out there?"

His grin widened. "I did. Not as good a spot as the last one, but decent."

"Well, considering how that awesome one turned out, decent is probably better." It seemed like he'd gotten even closer. Only polite to lean a bit, too. The hand he wasn't holding began twisting a lock of hair around her finger.

"That's what I thought."

"Should we gather the band to celebrate?" Her grin might have turned a little evil. For just a minute she had him, then he laughed. That made her toes curl in her boots.

"I have a better idea. I think we could manage to make it to *The Italian Pie* without getting shot at this time, though I make no promises, you understand."

He'd definitely angled his head closer to hers. Nell met his angle by tilting her head the other way.

"I still like pie. Enough to risk it." She couldn't help the quick glance toward his mouth. It was as nice as his eyes. She liked the bit of tip to the edges.

When she lifted her gaze to his again, there were little flames in the eyes. Holy cow. They had to be for her. There was no one else in the room.

"Then it's a date?" He moved in as he asked the question, a very tiny gap between her mouth and his that made thinking and talking a challenge.

"Totally." The word was more sigh than anything and about all she could manage. He halved the gap to minis-cule. "See, you were right."

"I was? About what?" He paused, just shy of contact,

looking a bit puzzled, but not so much it mitigated the flames any.

"You can get your own date." She grinned, though it felt a bit shaky around the edges. She had a date with a cute cop and if she wasn't wrong, he was just about to kiss her—

Oh yeah, he was...

∾

THANK you for reading *Relatively Risky*! I hope you enjoyed it! The next book in the series is *Dead Spaces!*

I hope you'll check out some of my backlist books by visiting my website!

To find out about all my releases, be sure to sign up for my New Release eZine and get a free eBook by visiting my website.

If you enjoyed this book, I hope you'll consider leaving a review. It's not just because I'm needy (even though I try not to be!). Reviews help other readers decide which books to buy. :-)

∾

BONUS: FAMILY TREED

"Family Treed" is 1.5 in my Big Uneasy series. This short story is my amuse bouche, because it is a taste, a quick bite for my readers, a chance to check in on Nell and Alex (from *Relatively Risky*).

Nell's not sure why the mob wants to have dinner with her. She is sure she wants a cop at her side.

Alex wouldn't let Nell dine with the mob without him, despite much unease from his many siblings.

But when Nell's newly found relatives start making threatening noises, Nell wonders if she's putting Alex's life in danger.

Can they survive dinner with the killing cousins?

It was a dark and stormy night.

A shot hadn't rung out.

Yet.

She was having dinner with the mob.

Nell Whitby didn't want to have dinner with Aleksi Afoniki and his creepy nephew, Dimitri. She didn't want to have anything to do with any of them.

Miss Manners had been no help with an invite minus an RSVP.

So here she was. About to drive into the den of the Russian Wolf and his, um, evil cub.

The invite had been directed to her and her best friend, Sarah, but Nell hadn't told her. She hadn't planned to tell Alex either. You didn't spit into the wind or expose your friends to the mob, even if one of the friends was a big tough cop.

Nell stole a peek at the big tough cop. Alex Baker had been showing up, off and mostly on, since her world spun off its axis into weird mob-relatives-ness.

The on times had gotten more frequent, but there was a part of Nell that expected him to bolt at some point.

He was a cop, the son of a cop, the sibling of legal types up the whazoo.

She was related to two mob families and had been insistently invited to dinner with a third mob family.

If that weren't enough of a kiss of death for the relationship, Alex, the oldest of thirteen, had a serious kid phobia going.

And she attracted kids like honey attracted ants.

It was a hookup made in hell.

He'd probably break her heart.

She kept telling herself to tell him no when he called. So far she'd not listened to herself. She hadn't had a lot of cute guy in her life up to now, and he was the poster guy for cute. Dark hair. Tall, with broad shoulders and narrow hips. His eyes were an amazing blue and he had a stubborn, needs-a-shave jaw.

He had tough guy down pat, but not bad boy. He wasn't bad. He was good. He couldn't leap tall buildings, stop bullets, or outrun locomotives. But he'd saved her life once or twice, made her heart skip with a look, and kissed her like he didn't want to stop.

How did a girl say no to that?

He looked at her and grinned, and yup, her heart skipped. Despite the skipping, she noticed that he didn't look worried enough for a guy about to drive into the Wolf's den.

"You're not wearing a wire, are you?" Did she hope he was? The idea his many law-minded siblings might be listening in was a bit comforting, but not if it got them killed. Bullets did move faster than cars. It was the kind of physics even a former librarian could do.

He grinned. "Afoniki'd expect that."

Not exactly a no. "But you're carrying?"

It didn't like a good idea to go in without one of them armed and dangerous.

She might be a bit wistful that she wasn't the one. It's not that she wanted to shoot someone again—she mentally winced over that memory—but it felt wrong to be the unarmed lamb among the Russian wolves.

His grin widened. Armed, dangerous and cute enough to kiss. She half sighed.

"You nervous?" Alex slowed his truck and gave her a concerned look.

Lightning flashed against thick dark clouds, fitfully illuminating the brooding outlines of the mob mansion. It was such a cliché. How had they managed it? Did they have something on Mother Nature, too?

She studied the appropriately sinister gates, their widening gap a bit too canine. The heavy rain made them almost foam. A cliché on steroids.

"I'm scared almost out of my mind," she said lightly, as if joking, even though it was the truth. When his look of concern deepened, she summoned up a smile, though it had some wry to it. "If the old man is half as creepy as the nephew..."

She'd met Dimitri Afoniki about the same time the past bitch-slapped her. She hadn't liked him before she found out he was a wise guy.

"We can leave," Alex offered.

"And drive straight to Wit-Sec?" Just how offended would the wise geezer be if she stood him up? Did she want to find out?

Alex considered the question, then shrugged. "Maybe the food will be good?"

As if they'd sensed her desire to flee while she could, the gates snapped closed behind them with an ominous clang. Okay, maybe ominous was a bit dramatic. A lot of people knew where they were going, most of them related to Alex and packing weapons.

If they disappeared, there'd be a lot of heat on the Afonikis. Of course, the fact that they lived in New Orleans seemed to indicate they could handle the heat.

Alex steered his truck along the drive that curved toward the house. It passed under a portico, then turned back toward the gate. Every light in every room of the house appeared to be on but it still managed to be unwelcoming.

Some goons waited under the portico, and one of them stepped forward to open her door. The other goon opened Alex's door and indicated his intention to park the truck for him. Or drive it off for stripping and shipping to Mexico.

She should probably set her expectations low when breaking bread with a wise geezer.

At least she wasn't related to Afoniki.

She hoped. Were there still secrets waiting to ooze up out of the past? Was that why he'd summoned her to meet some of her mob cousins in this so-called neutral territory?

The ornate entry was about as welcoming as a funeral parlor. Nell looked around. No, that was unfair to funeral parlors. They were definitely more welcoming. Though this place smelled better. Maybe the food would be good.

There was a brief transition from damp warm outside into headache-inducing cold inside, then the large doors closed them in the wise dwelling and there was no more warm. Just cold.

Another goon, who bore a faint resemblance to a butler, indicated her sweater with a brusque, "Take that?"

Nell clutched the edges and shook her head. Maybe her host had cranked down the A/C to enhance the house's "Return of the Czars" theme. Too bad she'd left her white fur coat in the store. With the new dress she also couldn't afford.

When she and Alex stopped at the doorway of an obscenely ornate room, occupied by a small cluster of possible cousins and Dimitri, Nell realized she was not the only one to go with the basic little black dress.

And that not all little black dresses were created equal.

There was a blonde whose little black dress took the room prize for littlest little black dress. The fabric to skin ratio was interesting even for New Orleans.

The brunette had more dress but she had more to cover. They'd also donned some serious snooty to go with their blingy bling. If their noses elevated any more, they'd fall on their backs.

With some reluctance Nell considered Dimitri, their host's bad boy cub—a host who did not appear to have made an appearance at his own dinner party. There was no sign of a geezer-like dude from their vantage point. The cub flanked the girls on one side.

Opposite Dimitri was a guy who was as pretty as the two women, only with more clothes. His perfectly tailored suit probably cost more than she'd make the rest of her life.

It took Dimitri a moment to realize they were there—or he'd pretended to take a moment—before he turned, starting with considerable charm. Nell would have liked to know how he managed that. Making rude seem charming would be a useful skill for this new reality of hers.

Her chin lifted as the chilly gazes of both women swept down Nell's dress—which hit modestly at her knees—to the black flats. Sarah would have lent her some killer heels, but Nell had thought wearing anything killer would send the wrong message.

Dimitri surged her way, lightly clasping Nell's shoulders. When he leaned in to kiss her on one cheek, then the other, Nell quelled a totally natural desire to knee him in the groin. Luckily he didn't cling, so quelling was possible.

Nell wished she dared edge closer to Alex. She didn't like feeling pinned in place. "You remember Alex, don't you, Mr. Afoniki?"

The look in his eyes told her that, yes, he remembered Alex and wasn't happy she'd swapped him for Sarah. Nell had sensed a little something from Dimitri for Sarah, which is why she hadn't told Sarah she'd been invited. Not the way a friend thanked their bestie for pulling one out of the pit of despair. Not to mention giving her a place to live and a job.

The charm of his smile lessened, though he nodded politely enough at Alex. Perhaps he thought the DBYOC —Don't Bring Your Own Cop—was so obvious it didn't need to be added to the invite. Too bad there wasn't a Wiki on how to deal with these people. And how sad was it that she'd looked?

He ramped the charm up again and deployed a smile. "I thought I asked you to call me Dimitri?"

To mute her deer-in-the-headlights, yeah-that's-never-going-to-happen look, Nell deployed her fake smile, then shifted her gaze to his companions and lifted her brows in what she hoped was polite inquiry.

"I'm sure you're anxious to meet your cousins." He stepped back, widening their little circle.

She wasn't, but there was no escape.

The other guy reached her side first. "I'm your second cousin, Guido Calvino."

He took her hand, lifting it to his mouth. His lips lingered way too long. Why did he feel a need to be a second cousin? Or a cousin at all? She'd kind of expected her wise cousins to disavow her. Or shoot her. That had been grandma not dearest's choice.

"It's," Nell hesitated, but there really wasn't a polite alternative, "nice to meet you."

Her fake smile was getting a serious workout and they were only minutes into the evening. Nell got her hand back and looked toward the two women, deciding that laugh lines would never be a problem for either of them. Okay, that was a bit bitchy. Usually she tried not to be.

"Mirabelle St. Cyr," Dimitri said.

Nell would have known she was a St. Cyr without the intro. This cousin was a feminine version of their recently deceased grandfather, Phineas St. Cyr. She certainly had his dissecting gaze. If looks could kill—

"And this is our cousin, Cinzia," Guido said, positioning himself on Nell's other side while gesturing toward the voluptuous brunette, who did not look at all like their still living grandfather, Antonio Calvino. Both she and Guido must take after their mamas.

Cinzia va-va-voomed her way into their little circle, managing to brush against Dimitri before she got all her assets stopped on the other side of Alex.

She gave Nell a token smile, then ramped it up for Alex.

Mirabelle had seemed content to stop next to Dimitri and subside into sulky sexy, but perhaps her competitive instincts were roused.

Whatever the reason, she insinuated herself between Nell and Alex, forcing Nell closer to Guido. As if Nell had done it on purpose, Guido looked delighted.

He took her arm and led her toward a flash bar setup off to one side of the room. Digging in her heels didn't help. Her flats didn't have heels. Dimitri closed on her other side, then passed them so he could play bartender.

"What would you like, Nell?" The question was innocuous, the tone too friendly. There was no reason she could think of for him to be friendly to her.

What did she want? To flee into the night like a gothic heroine? "Just some water, thanks."

Behind her, the deep rumble of Alex's voice was broken by feminine laughter of the flirtatious kind. Nell didn't look at them, though it wasn't easy. And it kind of was easy. Was she afraid of what she'd see?

Both women were more everything than she was. She halfway expected to other two men to head back to the fun group, but they didn't. Guido leaned against the bar. No question he made the bar look better. Was he a bad guy? She honestly couldn't tell. If he was playing nice, he was very good at it.

"Flat or sparkling?" Dimitri held up one of each.

"Flat is fine." Maybe she should have chosen sparkling. Flat felt too much like a metaphor.

As if Guido sensed her need for flight, he began a funny—and oddly soothing—story involving sparking water and a politician. Though not good at small talk, Nell had a good handle on no talk, being a former librarian and all.

Imperceptibly she felt her insides begin to relax, and even managed to chuckle once.

Dimitri kept the conversational ball rolling. When she finally found something to say, she looked at Dimitri and caught him looking at her with a weird look in his eyes. He masked it quickly, but it was too late. A prickle of unease ran down her back like a targeting dot. It was totally the moment for that shot to ring out.

Instead of a shot, there was the ping of an elevator arriving.

She started and turned toward the sound, just in time to see an ornate wall out in the hallway turn into an elevator door. Inside was a shriveled figure in a wheel chair, a creepy crowish shape that had to be the wise geezer, Aleksi Afoniki.

He rolled forward like a small but deadly storm cloud.

She'd met the other two wise geezers, so a comparison was possible.

St. Cyr had papered over creepy with some charm the one time she'd met him. Her other grandfather, Antonio Calvino, had tried to be the hearty hail-granddaughter-well-met bad guy, which had been a different kind of creepy.

This man made no effort to be anything but evil.

Dimitri came out from behind the bar, but stopped next to Nell, waiting as his uncle rolled toward them, their gazes clashing.

No lightning flashes, but there should have been. It was that intense. It not only stripped away the charm of the younger man, it exposed his dark heart, showing what he was eager to have, what he was willing to become to get it.

Instead of angry at this challenge from the young cub, Afoniki smiled grimly at his nephew before his gaze tracked to Nell.

The smile changed to something harder to parse. Nell's chin lifted again. She might not have grown up "wise," but she was her father's daughter. And her mom's.

She knew what he saw when he looked at her. She'd been told often enough that she looked like her mom, had learned she also looked like her grandmother, Ellie Calvino—a woman the three wise geezers had apparently vied for way back when. A woman who had chosen someone else.

Afoniki didn't look like the type to hold a grudge. Why waste time on grudges when you could hire a hit man? Is that what he'd done?

Ellie Calvino was missing, presumed dead, and had been for a very long time.

His skeletal hands clenched the arms of his wheelchair drawing her attention to the huge, emerald stone of his ring —the ring of his wise guy power. All three wise geezers had had one, though with different gem stones. She'd seen St. Cyr's. He'd managed to dump it on Nell just before he died.

Did Afoniki wear it all the time or had he brought it out for her to see?

The crash of thunder that came next was disturbingly apt.

Alex's dad had raised him to respect old dudes, but this was one bad, old dude.

All he felt was a strong desire to punch the guy out.

It was gonna to be a long night. And that was if things went well.

The air was so thick with something, his gut was ready to light the bat signal.

His sibs had been vocal about this dinner and about the wisdom of dating Nell. They all agreed she seemed okay, but—fill in the blank with twelve varieties of this is bad for your career.

And when that didn't work they reminded him he could end up dead or missing like Uncle Charlie. Uncle Charlie who had made the mistake of falling for Ellie Calvino. Had Afoniki played a part in removing him from the competition for Ellie's hand?

Only his dad hadn't said much about Nell. Alex had thought that was good. Now he wasn't so sure. His family had long experience with bad dudes. He got it. They were worried. Only they didn't know Nell.

Neither do you.

Okay, so he didn't know her know her, but she'd grown up in Wyoming, not a Mafia princess. And they weren't engaged or anything. He liked her. Liked spending time with her. Liked kissing her. He wasn't ready for more.

What if she wants more?

He mentally shrugged that question away.

What if you want more?

That was harder to shrug away. The way she attracted kids was a bit crazy, but seeing each other was a long way from having kids together, something he'd managed to avoid with his first wife.

No question her relatives were a big tick in the negative column, but other than trying to kill her a couple of times, they'd not seemed that interested in her.

Was this dinner a sign that change was coming? And if it was, why? Curiosity or something more?

He glanced over at Nell, wondering how she felt about

it. But she had her back to him, her head tilted back a bit as she listened to Calvino flap his jaws. She'd said she didn't need family bad enough to get mixed up with Family. But it must be a little tempting. Since her parents' death, all she'd had was Sarah.

Family. He knew all about family. He had a big one. They annoyed him, but he'd give his life for any of them.

Commit a crime for them?

That question was harder to answer. He'd have thought—no. But he'd learned some things since Nell exploded into his life. His family had a few secrets that Alex had realized he didn't want to examine too closely. Granted Nell didn't have the history with this bunch that he did with his family. Did she have the need? Stupid question. Of course she did. Who didn't need family?

She shifted, giving him a look at her profile. She'd managed to get up to speed on her poker face in a short time.

Maybe it came natural.

"That's some seriously bad blood," his siblings had all managed to say or imply about Nell. The blood might be bad, but the packaging was nice. He'd thought her ordinary the first time they met. Until she smiled. Maybe that's when he stopped thinking. Or he'd matured. He found her quiet charm, the hint of mischief in her eyes, and her sense of humor a real turn on. Maybe he had matured.

There was another reason she was hard to walk away from. If he left, this bunch would eat Nell alive. The lamb among the wolves. Silent, subdued by their surroundings and the bad guys, she looked like glass about to shatter.

You've underestimated her before.

She was a lot tougher than she looked.

What else did she hide that well?

He knew the facts of her life. His family had made sure of that. It all appeared straightforward, but what if it wasn't? Just how far could he trust her? He knew he couldn't trust them.

Her family had already cost his family Uncle Charlie. How far was he willing to go for Nell? How much was he willing to risk for a woman he'd known for a couple of months? It wasn't like he was in love with her or anything. He liked her, that was all.

You sure about that?

"You look like—" the old geezer's voice was thin and cold, his accent heavier than Junior's.

"My grandmother," Nell cut in, her voice polite, but chilly. "I've heard it mentioned a few times."

Aleksi smiled with what might be real amusement. "You must forgive an old man for seeing ghosts."

There were more than ghosts thickening the atmosphere. Nell smiled politely at the old man, but she didn't look that forgiving.

Alex knew how warm her smile could be, so this one chilled him. It gave him a picture into what she could have been had she been raised a Mafia princess.

What she was now?

Aleksi's gaze traveled to Nell's hands, lingered there for too long. Did the old goat know she had St. Cyr's ring?

The old man finally broke the tense silence. "Dimitri, you have not offered our other guest a drink."

Apparently this was permission for the groups to merge. Normally he wouldn't have minded the attention from two beautiful women.

His life hadn't been normal since Nell knocked him down.

Dimitri arched a brow at Alex when he was close enough. "What can I get for you?"

Evidence that will stand up in court? "Same as Nell, thanks."

"Religious scruples?" Mirabelle asked it lightly. "Or are you afraid to drink with us, cousin?"

"My parents were killed by a drunk driver." Nell's tone was carefully cleansed of emotion and tone, but her gaze held Mirabelle's for at least a twenty count. Mirabelle looked away first.

Score one for the ex-librarian. Or mafia princess wannabe?

The wise geezer's gaze shifted Alex's direction. "You're—"

"Alex Baker," he said, bracing for some kind of reaction. Was that the real reason he'd come? As a stand in for Uncle Charlie? Was that why his dad had given him the, "I hope you know what you're doing" look?

The old man's mouth widened in what might have been a smile. Alex took the chilled bottle of water from

Dimitri, glad the top was still sealed. Almost his lips twitched as he recalled meeting his ex's family for the first time. Seemed it was always a risky business. Not that he was meeting this family for the same reason.

Nell's gaze started to track his way.

"Do you like my house?"

She blinked, then looked at the old man. A short pause, then said politely, "It's very grand."

"I heard you grew up in a log cabin or something." Mirabelle gave her a bright, fake smile.

Nell took her time responding. She'd have been good in an interrogation room. Or running a crime empire?

"Or something."

The old man snorted. Bitchy exchanges were probably his mother's milk. A hint of color warmed the sharp, cold lines of Mirabelle's cheekbones.

Before the silence could turn even more uncomfortable, a burly guy in an ill-fitting white jacket and a loosened tie appeared at the other end of the room and cleared his throat. "It's ready, boss."

Alex hoped the food tasted less fancy than it smelled. And that his siblings didn't turn out to be right. He hated it when they were right.

The dining room was like something out of a bad comedy —without the funny part. Nell sensed there'd been some reshuffling in the seating. Even if Sarah had come, it wouldn't have been boy-girl-boy-girl unless another guy had been expected.

Nell didn't feel bad at upsetting the seating. Sarah wouldn't have liked the girl cousins and wouldn't have been afraid to show it. The cousins probably had a hitman on speed dial.

The two Afoniki's, not unnaturally, sat at the head and foot. Nell expected to be seated next to the old man, or away from both of them, but that's not where Dimitri steered her before taking his own seat. Instead she found herself across from Cinzia and to the right of Dimitri.

Alex got the seat next to the old man, but he didn't feel close to her, even though he was on her side of the table. Was the distance physical or something more?

The look in his eyes when he'd met the old man made her wonder why he'd really come here tonight. Was this more about Uncle Charlie than her? They hadn't been dating long enough to know.

Unbidden words from her dad bubbled up from the past, the most cynical words she'd ever heard him utter. "Everyone has an agenda, sweetie. Not a big deal, unless their agenda rolls over yours."

When she'd been separated from Alex, when they'd steered to the bar, she'd felt adrift in a cold sea and had had to resist mentally latching onto Guido.

It didn't seem smart to trust him without knowing his agenda. But—did she convict them all of being bad? Her dad and mom had been raised knee deep in crime and had managed to be honest citizens.

Other than lying about who they were for thirty years. Sharp longing for what she'd had made her heart clench. Sarah was great, but she missed family, missed belonging, missed the innocence of not knowing her parents had been wise kids. Finding out all the crap had felt like she lost them again. Was it possible to find—not that because it was gone forever, but a sense of family again?

She'd looked into Ellie's family, hoping for normal there. Not a huge shock that her grandma's parents had died about six months before she disappeared. Had the noxious Antonio held her family hostage to keep her from bolting?

Probably.

Was she here because she couldn't figure out how to say no? Or because she'd hoped against hope that she'd find family again?

Maybe.

What was her agenda? She heard her dad ask the question inside her head, followed by silence because she didn't know. Between the Family and Alex—who was rich in family—Nell felt more alone than she had when looking down at her parents' graves.

Trying to escape her tangled emotions, Nell looked around. It was kind of apt that Cinzia and Mirabelle were each framed by tall, narrow windows. The heavy drapes were held back by gold cord with thick tassels. Rain blurred the glass, and turned the irregular, but insistent flashes of lightning into changing art pieces.

The room was big, chilly, and as overdone as the rest of

the rooms she'd seen. Matching dining chairs lined the walls, in between all sorts of fancy crap, like pedestals with urns and busts of no one she recognized. A pristine white tablecloth covered the table top. It was littered with china and crystal and gold-plated utensils.

She noticed Guido watching her. He grinned and winked, as if he shared her feeling that it was all a bit much.

"It's very grand, isn't it?" Mirabelle's voice was kindly, patronizing. She flicked a glance at each of the men, as if seeking their approval for her fake kindness. The kitten look wasn't bad, but the back of her eyes were soulless.

"Very." Nell held that dead gaze as long as she needed to. But...she shouldn't have come. These people had different rules than hers. Like alternate reality different.

"What did your parents do while they were...away?" Cinzia asked delicately, before lifting an exquisitely cut crystal glass to her blood red lips.

If she was pretending to care, she was better than Mirabelle, not as good as Guido.

"Mom was a Wal-Mart checker and dad fixed cars." Did they think she'd be embarrassed by their honest labor? They'd walked—well, run—away from their families, from all of this. Had chosen ordinary over crime-fueled money. As far as Nell could tell, they'd never looked back.

"How...enterprising..." Cinzia finally managed.

"It was better than being dead, which seems to have been their only other option," Nell pointed out, a bit dryly. Someone—possibly someone in this room—had tried to kill them. That someone had believed they had killed them until Nell made the mistake of moving to New Orleans sporting a familiar face.

The old man, still in his wheelchair, crouched at his end of the table, a faint gleam in his old eyes from, Nell presumed, the undercurrent of contention. His happy place was probably everyone else's crap zone. He waited for the first course to be served before speaking.

"So. Claude." He played with his bad guy ring, turning it so that the green stone caught the light from the massive chandelier. He looked up, his dark gaze first meeting Nell's, then moving to spear Mirabelle. "I had hoped he'd make our little dinner."

"Claude?" Nell wasn't happy to realize she'd said this out loud. Did the old man know Nell had the St. Cyr ring? He could. Bad guys always knew things they shouldn't.

Into a small silence no one seemed to want to break, Alex said, "Claude St. Cyr. The heir."

"Oh." At least she wasn't the only one to mess up the seating.

Nell had sort of expected someone—or someone's lawyer—to show up demanding the ring. Only no one had. Surely this Claude wasn't afraid she'd declare herself the evil overlord of the St. Cyr crime empire? He couldn't think the ring totally trumped the legal crap could he? She stared hard at her plate, pushing food she didn't recognize from one side to the other.

"He wanted to come," Mirabelle said, a thread of iron in her voice. "But business is business."

Had any of them really wanted to come? It all felt wrong and so not neutral ground. More like sticking your head into the Wolf's maw.

"What troubles you, little cousin?" Guido asked

Nell smoothed the frown and decided to overlook "little." The accent helped it not sound totally condescending.

"I just thought it would all be more—" Nell had meant to say Sopranos, but Alex coughed, covering his mouth with his hand. So they were all pretending they weren't a bunch of bad-a crooks? Okay. "....there would be more rivalry between you all. Competing business interests and all," she finished, a bit lamely.

"We all run in the same social circles," Mirabelle said. "And we've known each other for forever." She gave Dimitri a special smile that seemed to indicate the knowing had gone pretty far. Or she hoped it would. "I'm a bit surprised you haven't popped up in our circle, cousin? Now that you know."

Nell could arch her Botox-free brows and did. "I was at the Children's Center fund raiser last Friday night." Nell's smile was fake guileless. "I thought the food was particularly good. They should always use that caterer."

Mirabelle blinked a bit. Not that Nell was surprised she didn't know Nell had worked the event as a wait for Sarah's company.

Dimitri grinned, looking almost human. "The food was especially good that night."

"How odd to think we were all there and didn't know

each other." Cinzia fluttered her lashes at Dimitri. "So kind of you and Aleksi to bring us together like this."

Clever. Not everyone could use the high ground to look better—and down on—someone. Mirabelle's fingers curled into claws. Good thing they were on the other side of the table. If a cat fight broke out, Nell did not want to be between them.

"It was our pleasure," Dimitri said, like he meant it.

Pleasure? They were enjoying this? Because destroying lives and amassing ill-gotten wealth wasn't enough of a buzz?

"Family is important," Guido said. He smiled at her and for a second she forgot he might be a bad guy and returned the smile. His lids drooped a bit, as if to mask a sudden gleam of satisfaction.

So he was pretending to like her, but why? She had nothing they could possibly want.

"Family is everything," the old man said flatly.

Okay. Nell addressed her attention to her food as little murmurs of assent rippled around the table.

"We're all hoping this won't be our only meeting, Nell. May I call you Nell?" Cinzia asked, like she really wanted to know. Mirabelle gave a slight, very slight snort.

"Of course." Nell didn't mind, though she'd prefer they didn't call her ever.

Dimitri appeared delighted, giving each woman a look of approval. The two women basked in their turn, then engaged in some polite staring when his attention moved on. Did they have hopes for a dynastic marriage with him?

"We're so looking forward to introducing you to our friends, Nell," Guido said, his amused glance seeming to read her thoughts and confirm them.

Dimitri lifted his glass. "To Nell. She was lost, but now is found."

Not exactly something to celebrate. A month ago, she would have hated the attention. Okay, she still hated it, but she hid it better. She hoped.

Alex lifted his water bottle, a bit ironically, it seemed. Her gal cousins didn't look thrilled at the toast. Of the two, Mirabelle had the harder time hiding her discontent, but at what? They were actual mafia princesses. Nell wasn't even a wannabe.

Nell stole a peek at the old man. Afoniki looked like a shriveled slug sitting there watching them. His pale eyes gleamed with what might be pleasure, but why? What was it that tickled his evil fancy? Why had he invited her here? He'd have a reason, even if it was a crazy old, bad guy reason.

"Thanks," Nell muttered, then looked down at her plate. "This is delicious." She hadn't actually tasted it yet, so she shoved a small bite between tense lips, so it wouldn't be a lie—and the thin edge of the wedge.

When the silence had turned a bit tense, Dimitri broke it. "Since our last meeting, I found time to read your book."

Was she supposed to be impressed he'd managed to work his way through a children's book in just under a month?

Nell had learned not to ask, "Did you like it," but

hadn't come up with an alternative yet. It was Mirabelle who saved her, though Nell was pretty sure she hadn't meant to.

"You wrote a book?"

There was polite disbelief Nell had managed to write a book and the implication that only one book was not something to brag about.

"She writes children's books," Guido said, trying out another intimate smile on Nell, "about an artichoke."

A pregnant pause while they processed this. Another while they tried to figure out what to say about it.

"Do you write under your own name?" Cinzia asked, managing to be bitchy without sounding bitchy.

"Just my last name," Nell said. Mirabelle opened her mouth but Nell forestalled her. "Whitby."

Nell had chosen to use her last name as a sort of homage to her parents. Of course, when she did it, she didn't know the name was as fictional as her artichoke.

Her world shifted under her feet. It had done that a lot lately. She took a drink of her water to hide it. Don't let them see you sweat, her dad used to tell her. If she sweated now, it would form icicles on her skin and they'd for sure see it.

"You could take the family name," Guido said.

"That would pop you out of the pack," Cinzia added.

Which family name? And how flattering they thought she needed popping out.

"Or you could marry," Dimitri put in smoothly.

In the suddenly weighted silence, the lights flickered

ominously and the explosion of thunder rattled the chandelier and table glassware.

It really was a dark and stormy night.

Nell knew Dimitri watched her, but she didn't know why. Was he mocking her because her parents' marriage probably hadn't been legal? That the name she used wasn't hers either?

"Perhaps," the old man said, "history will repeat itself."

"Jeez Louise," Nell said involuntarily, thinking of her parents who'd almost been blown up, and the whole teenage pregnancy thing. Not that she could have a teen pregnancy at thirty-two but... "I hope not."

"I'm sure you will make a better choice than your grandmother." The old man's words fell into the gap between another round of thunder.

For some reason, the storm seemed louder all the sudden, as if it wanted the party over, too. Nell could think of several responses to this—none of them polite. Finally Nell met his gaze with as much firm as she could muster. "I will."

Alex shifted, as if he wanted to say something, but was restraining himself. She'd liked to have looked at him. She could have used one of his reassuring smiles right now, but she seemed to have lost the ability to look at him. Or she was afraid to? Was she afraid of what she'd see in his face?

As if he knew, the old man looked at Alex. "How is Zach? He retired a few years ago, did he not?"

"He's fine." Alex's tone was clipped.

"I was older, of course." His voice turned reflective, like an ordinary old guy. "Knew Charlie better."

Nell stiffened. She suspected Alex did, too.

"Of course, we didn't run in the same circles. He played football. I...didn't."

He probably beat people up and sold drugs. A totally different "letter" jacket.

His chilly gaze traveled from Alex to Nell, then back again. "I liked Charlie."

Alex's face hadn't changed, but there was a rigidity to his shoulders that spoke of tight control.

"You have the look of Charlie," Aleksi added.

Family is everything.

Was that the message of this evening? Nell might not really be one of them, but she'd never be part of Alex's life because of Charlie?

Family is everything.

Alex's family was tight. She hadn't met many of his siblings, but she'd seen, she'd felt the connection, the love, the loyalty. She'd envied it. She'd...wanted it? In this big, cold room with a grand canyon between them, Nell realized two things.

That she might be more involved with Alex than she'd let herself realize.

And that even if her relations were pretending to like her, they wouldn't want Alex in her life simply because he was a cop. The son of cops.

Since she'd walked through the door, they'd been

dividing them, reminding Alex of who and what she came from. Reminding her of what she'd lost.

And what did they want for her? Guido had been tempting her with the allure of having family again, while the old man, well, it felt like he taunted her. Taunts were more his style.

She stared down at the food, her stomach roiling. Had there been more than pot stirring? Not just "remember Charlie," but don't be Charlie? Because you could disappear, too. Just walk away. That's all he had to do. His family ranks would close around him. He'd be safe.

How could she blame him? He hadn't known her that long. Spending time with her could put not just him, but his family at risk. Again. And she'd be...

Alone.

Her parents had each other when they'd disappeared all those years ago. She didn't know why these people wanted her alone, isolated from support. Maybe they got their kicks from it. It didn't matter why. They did. Would they run off Sarah, too? Or try to suck her into the slime?

Alone.

Her chest tight, she had a sense that someone was saying something, but she couldn't hear. It wasn't just the thunder. There was a roaring sound inside her head, inside her heart.

And that's when it finally happened.

A shot rang out.

❧

Alex heard the shot and saw the flash off to his left, where Nell sat. He dove for her, knocking her to the floor. The hard, unyielding floor. He felt her breath go out as they hit marble. He sure couldn't hear it over thunderclap.

And then he heard the sound of glass breaking...

...the thunder sounded louder with the windows gone...

...But it got swallowed up in sound of gunfire as some semi-autos opened up.

He tried to shield Nell, groped for his weapon, but it was not the right time to fire back. Not yet. His muzzle flash would give away their position.

Bullets chewed across the tabletop, spraying glassware and food in every direction.

More bullets slammed into wall above them. Near as he could tell, shooters were determined to write with bullets in both directions.

The air was thick with plaster dust and smoke.

Throw in thunder as background. Lightning. And the shooters.

A total Charlie Foxtrot.

Except...

Alex frowned. It didn't seem like anyone was shooting back. And the pattern of the shots seemed odd, though conditions were bad for an accurate assessment. But it seemed like some shots ought to be hitting marble and ricocheting around.

One shooter did take out a chandelier. It smashed into the tabletop with a crash.

And then it stopped.

The shooting, not the storm.

Through a couple of lightning flashes, Alex tensed, waiting for round two.

Rain splattered against the marble floor. Outside smells mingled with the smell of food and cordite.

Cautiously he lifted his head, then came to his knees beside Nell, his body between her and where the shooting had come from, but his head still below the table. He popped up for a quick look. Lightning flash confirmed shattering of food and dishes.

Oh well, he'd lost his appetite anyway.

And then he noted wide eyes peering over the edge of the table at nine, eleven, twelve, and one o'clocks, and another set over at three o'clock. He did a mental count. Then did it again. All that shooting and not a single casualty? Not even the old man? How was that possible—his heart jerked and his breathing stalled.

Nell.

As abruptly as they'd gone out, the lights flickered a couple of times, then stayed on. Nell lay where he'd left her, seemingly not moving.

The first shot.

He turned, panic clawing up his throat, but before he reached her, she moved. She shifted, flexed her legs and arms, groaned and then rolled over.

"Ow." She grimaced. Or maybe she tried to smile.

The hit to the marble had to have hurt.

"Are you all right?"

He crouched by her. Without being told, his hands moved up her legs, then her arms, wandered over her head, probing for injuries.

He wanted to keep going, wanted to check out the good stuff, but a look in her eyes stalled him. He helped her sit up, then get up, as other figures around the table rose like they were puppets on strings.

It would have been funny any other time. Any other place. He was aware that the two men moved to help the old man back into his wheelchair, but he didn't care that much. "Where does it hurt?"

His gaze raked over her without seeing. Like a blind man, his hands run up her arms again.

She tried to grin. "There are a few spots that don't hurt."

His fingers found the tear in the shoulder of her dress. That focused his attention. He probed it, but only the surface had been torn as the bullet passed by. That first shot had come from inside the room.

One of them had tried to kill her. His money was on one of the two women. The two men had been circling Nell. He didn't know for sure, but he had his suspicions. His gaze lifted, met her widened gaze as she studied the spot, then looked at him.

She managed a shaky, sort of smile. "Bruised but not broken."

He pulled her into a fierce hug. Too near, the miss. And not just the bullets.

Starkly, clearly he saw Nell in his life and Nell out of

his life. He swallowed dryly. Her gaze had been shadowed by more than the shots. And there'd been a question that hadn't been there when they arrived.

He wasn't—couldn't be—in love with her, but he was deep in like. Deep. Lots of like.

Over her shoulder, Alex saw the old man, saw the look in his eyes.

He wasn't happy. Neither were Guido Calvino and Dimitri Afoniki.

The moment they walked through the door, the dividing had begun. And it almost worked. Guido's smiles, the toast, mention of his Uncle Charlie—it all took on new meaning.

He knew they they wanted him gone. He was a cop. He didn't know why they wanted to isolate Nell, but it didn't matter. They were bad guys. It wouldn't be for her good.

And he'd almost let them. He'd almost helped them.

He sighed, tightening his hold on Nell. How much damage had been done? Their relationship—his insides flinched at the word, but he manned up—was so new. With some unseen bracing, Alex found her chin and looked into her eyes.

"Are you okay?" he asked, hoping she caught the double meaning to the question. Women were supposed to know these things but—

Her gaze searched his. It felt like it took a long time. Slowly, so slow it made his chest hurt, the edges of her mouth began to edge up, nudging the shadows and the question almost out.

It wasn't the smile that had started his fall into like. It was better than that. He held his breath and hoped.

"Yeah," she said. "I'm good."

His dad had always told him to pick his battles.

This was a good one. A battle worth the fight. They weren't running. There'd be no hiding. He wasn't Charlie. Nell wasn't Ellie.

If he quit being stupid she wouldn't give up on him. She wouldn't bend or break. He didn't know everything about her, but he knew this. Come mob or piles of kids, he sure as hell wasn't giving up on her.

Lesson learned.

As if she sensed this, her smile widened, and the vestiges of doubt, the lingering question faded like mist in the sun.

He adjusted the angle of her chin.

He shot the old man a hard bring-it-on look.

And then—in front of God and the mob—he kissed her.

Thank you for reading Family Treed! I hope you enjoyed it. Have you read the rest of the series? Check out *The Big Uneasy*!

To find out about all my releases, be sure to sign up for

my New Release eZine and get a free eBook by visiting my website.

If you enjoyed this book, I hope you'll consider leaving a review. It's not just because I'm needy (even though I try not to be!). Reviews help other readers decide which books to buy. :-)

ACKNOWLEDGMENTS

I'd like to thank my editors, Jessica and Richard Llanes, for their assistance in whipping this book into shape. They make a great team and I couldn't have done it without them.

I'd like to thank Elizabeth Vargas Greer for my amazing cover art. My books are never easy to capture in a single image and she knocked it out of the park.

Which brings me to my husband, Greg Jones. Thank you for letting me be the one who has permission to use your wonderful images and supporting my career for so long.

I'd also like to thank my copyeditor, Ana Baird. I would not want to clean up my mistakes, so I very much appreciate that she is willing do it. And another hearty thank you to Alexis Glynn Latner for coming in behind with insight and a keen eye to help with that final polish.

I would like to thank Heather Massey, Terry Cate, and Sharon McNulty for their friendship, help, encouragement and support.

I would be remiss if I did not also thank all the independent authors who have forged the path for those of us who follow and so graciously and willingly shared what they've learned.

The Spy Who Kissed Me

Perilously Fun Fiction Bundle (includes *The Spy Who Kissed Me* and *Do Wah Diddy Die*. Bonus: *Do Wah Diddy Delete Short Story Collection*)

Dangerous Dance

A Dangerous Duet - 2020

Science Fiction Romance/Paranormal

Project Universe Series:

The Key (book 1)

Girl Gone Nova (book 2)

Tangled in Time (book 3)

Steamrolled (book 4)

Kicking Ashe (book 5)

Found Girl (book 6)

Lost Valyr (book 7)

Maestra Rising (book 8)

Cosmic Boom (book 9)

Project Enterprise: The Short Stories

Time Trap: A Project Enterprise Series Short Story

Operation Ark: A Project Enterprise Story

Cyborg's Revenge: A Project Enterprise Series Short Story.

General's Holiday: A Project Enterprise Story

The Real Dragon

Nebula Nine (time travel adventure)

Open With Care (Christmas collection that includes, "Riding For Christmas" and "Up on the House Top"

Specters in the Storm: A paranormal/steampunk/science fiction romance novella

Out of Time (World War II Time Travel Romance)

Just in Time (An Out of Time Story)

An Uneasy Future

(A science fiction romance mystery series set in future New Orleans)

Core Punch (1.0)

Sucker Punch (2.0)

One Two Punch: An Uneasy Future Bundle

Short Story Collections

Project Enterprise: The Short Stories

Do Wah Diddy Delete

Let's Fall in Love

The Real Dragon and other short stories

ABOUT THE AUTHOR

Award-winning, *USA Today* Bestselling author, Pauline never liked reality, so she writes books. She likes to wander among the genres, rampaging like Godzilla, because she does love peril mixed in her romance.

To find out more about Pauline or her books:
http://paulinebjones.com
pauline@paulinebjones.com

www.ingramcontent.com/pod-product-compliance
Lightning Source LLC
Chambersburg PA
CBHW050034030726
47506CB00001B/272